Something strange was going on, and I didn't understand, but I had to figure it out—and fast!

If I didn't know better, I'd think I'd been thrown into some sort of sick *Invasion of the Body Snatchers* reboot. There was a word for the way the creatures all seemed to stop at the same time like they were controlled by a single brain, but I was too scared to think of it. So I just kept running. As far as I could tell, in all the darkness, I was headed away from home, but I couldn't be sure because all the houses, businesses, and every other town landmark had vanished into the night.

A noise came from somewhere behind me. I looked over my shoulder and saw several silhouettes limping along, their red eyes burning in the darkness. I think I moaned a little. Panting from exertion, my legs and lungs burning, I managed to speed up a little. But I wasn't going to last much longer. A runner, I'm not. Never had been. Probably never would be. But, hopefully, I'd last long enough to get away from the monsters that were chasing me.

Then, just as I thought I was going to get away, one of them came out of the darkness and grabbed me, knocking me to the ground. Before I could move, those things were on me. Snarling. Growling. Ripping my skin.

I struggled, trying to fight them off, but there were too many. I screamed at the intense burning as they flayed my flesh, shredding every last piece of meat off my bones.

Finally, as the life force drained quickly from my body, I closed my eyes and accepted my fate.

I was going to die.

James Manarro wakes up to a strange world in which nothing makes sense. As if it isn't bad enough that a werewolf has been stalking the town of Wolf Creek and James had to kill it, or that James is dealing with the fact that he is a werewolf too, now the whole world is silent, and everyone—his parents, neighbors, and friends—seems to have disappeared. Then he hears a voice…one he can't possibly hear because it belongs to his best friend, Riff, who has been dead for over three years, killed by the first werewolf to attack the town. But when James runs out to find Riff, he is plunged into a world of thick white fog filled with monsters determined to kill him once and for all…

KUDOS for *Moon Shadows*

In *Moon Shadows* by Lisanne Harrington, James Manarro is very confused because the world he has woken up to makes no sense. Everything is white and foggy, or dark and foggy, with monsters who seem to be trying to kill him. His cousin Beth, his best friend Riff who is dead, and a strange presence in his laptop appear to be the only ones who can see or hear him as everyone else has disappeared. James doesn't know what's going on, but he knows he needs to figure it out before it's too late—or he may be stuck in this strange new world forever. As usual. Harrington's character development is superb, her plot solid with plenty of surprises—an excellent addition/conclusion to the series. ~ *Taylor Jones, The Review Team of Taylor Jones & Regan Murphy*

Moon Shadows by Lisanne Harrington is the third book in her Wolf Creek Mystery series. This book is more complex than the other two, in that James doesn't just have to deal with a werewolf stalking the town, or the fact that he is one. Now the world inside his bedroom has gone white with a thick fog and the world outside the house is dark and also covered in a thick fog. On top of that, everyone in the world has disappeared. James feels like he is in the *Twilight Zone,* as he searches for some-one—anyone—in this strange new world. At first, he finds only monsters who come at him out of the dark, de-termined to kill him. But eventually, he makes contact with his cousin Beth, who is dealing with a *Twilight Zone* of her own, and together the two try to figure out what is going on—but will it be in time? Like the first two books, Harrington's characters are enchanting and fun, despite the horrors they are facing, the action fast paced, and the suspense enough to keep you turning pages from the very first page. If you liked the first two books, you have to read this one two. You'll love it. ~ *Regan Murphy, The Review Team of Taylor Jones & Regan Murphy*

ACKNOWLEDGMENTS

A lot of hard work and time goes into writing a book, and most of the time, it is a lonely business. We sit at our computers for weeks on end, ignoring everyone and every-ry thing. While I didn't miss any important events this time, I did miss daily life with my family. I hope they understand and know how much I love them and appreciate their patience and unwavering support.

Thanks as always to my team at Black Opal Books: Faith, my world class editor whose suggestions always make the story better; Jack, my wonderfully patient cover artist who put up with my bazillion ideas and gave me a fantastic cover; and as always, I'm indebted to Lauri for taking a chance on me in the first place.

You can contact me through my website, http://www.lisanneharrington.com, or shoot me an email at Lisanne@lisanneharrington.com. I would love to hear from you.

I hope you enjoy this third and final chapter in James's story.

Moon Shadows

BOOK 3 OF THE WOLF CREEK MYSTERIES

Lisanne Harrington

A Black Opal Books Publication

GENRE: YA/MYSTERY-DETECTIVE/PARANORMAL THRILLER

This is a work of fiction. Names, places, characters and incidents are either the product of the author's imagination or are used fictitiously, and any resemblance to any actual persons, living or dead, businesses, organizations, events or locales is entirely coincidental. All trademarks, service marks, registered trademarks, and registered service marks are the property of their respective owners and are used herein for identification purposes only. The publisher does not have any control over or assume any responsibility for author or third-party websites or their contents.

DEDICATION

For Karen
My bestie who has always been there for me.
Thanks for fifty years of fun and shenanigans!
I love you, sweetie.

Sunday, January 24, 2016
Day 1

Chapter 1

The boy walked quickly down the dirt trail that wound through the woods. Tree roots and tangled vines seemed to reach out and grab his feet. He took extra care not to trip and fall, for fear they would snatch him up and pull him into the dark shadows that threatened to devour him. Something moved just out of his line of sight. He shivered and hurried on.

What little moonlight was left barely penetrated the thick tree branches that hung over the trail, creating a tunnel where every sound was magnified. When a night bird screeched somewhere behind him, the boy turned and searched the dark sky but was unable to see where the bird hid. And he was sure it was hiding, along with the creature who was stalking him.

It was happening again. And, just like before, there was nothing he could do about it.

He continued on.

The dirt trail had narrowed almost to the point of disappearing, and the boy struggled to keep to it. A branch crackled to his right. He pulled out his Maglite and turned it on, pointing it into the brush. The beam flickered, and he banged it against his palm. He aimed it into the brush again, but it only reached a few feet.

Wishing he'd taken the time to grab some fresh batteries, he quickened his pace and squinted into the darkness that wrapped itself around him. The trail seemed to disappear into a thicket. After glancing over his shoulder again, he took a deep breath, wiped his dry lips on the back of his wrist, and plunged into the murky copse.

Wednesday, February 17, 2016
Day 24

Chapter 2

I woke up with a start. Sweat poured down my temples and pooled in the well made by my collarbone. *Damn.* It was nothing more than the nightmare. Again. I sat up and rubbed my face. Would it always haunt me, what happened last winter? More than all the people who had been killed, more than the look on Shaniqua's face as she realized what had happened and why, it was the betrayal that stayed with me.

I had to get over it.

My cell jangled and made me jump. I looked at my clock. Seven-forty-two. I'd overslept again. I seemed to be doing that more and more lately. After digging a piece of sleep out of the corner of my eye, I rolled over and grabbed the phone off my nightstand. A glance at the display showed a number I didn't recognize.

"Hello?" I scratched my cheek absently and frowned at the thickened stubble.

Static blasted through my head, and I yanked the phone away from my ear. *Dafuq?* I could still hear it crackling from six inches away. No way would I be able to hear whoever was on the other end.

"Bad connection," I shouted into the phone. "Call back."

I hung up and tossed it onto the bed beside me. Something about that weird static felt wrong. It raised goose bumps on my arms. I rubbed them absently. Even though it was really loud, it had sounded oddly remote and echoing, as if it was coming from the far side of an underground tunnel. Almost like it came from a distant and alien planet.

I shook my head and chuckled. Riff would have loved that. He was the best friend a dude could ever have, and I still missed him every day.

Just as I swung my feet off the bed, the phone rang again. Same unknown number. Same static, a little quieter this time.

"Hello?" The hair on my arms stood up, and there was a faint tightening of my bicep that I rubbed idly. I licked my lips then dried them with my hand. "Who's there?"

There was something faint coming from the phone, a voice or something. A girl's voice. And it sounded familiar. But I couldn't place it. I squinted and pressed the phone closer to my ear, as if that would help me hear better.

"James," the voice called. "James, I need to talk to you. James…"

In spite of my squinting, the voice sounded tinny and distant. I couldn't make out what she was saying, whoever she was. But she sounded desperate, like she was in some sort of trouble or something.

"I can't hear you," I yelled. "You're breaking up. Can you call back? Get better reception?"

Whoever it was, she was still talking. While I couldn't make out much more than that she needed to talk to me, and that I needed to do something, there was a sense of urgency about the voice that bordered on panic. But that was all I got because of that constant, oddly-loud-but-distant-at-the-same-time static. It was frustrating.

"Can't hear you." Maybe she couldn't hear me either, and that's why she kept talking. But if she couldn't hear me, why didn't she hang up and try again? It didn't make any sense.

The call dropped.

I pulled the phone away and glared at it. As if that would make her call back. Shaking my head, I looked at the display, but it had returned to the normal screen so I couldn't tell if she'd hung up or the connection had been lost.

I tossed it back on my nightstand and scratched my cheek. *You need a shave, dude.* I threw on a tee shirt and jeans, wondering who had called me and what she wanted. I'd been so close to recognizing the voice, but just couldn't figure it out.

Hopefully, she'd call back, and I'd find out who she was and what she wanted. But in the meantime, I'd better get my butt on to school, or Mom would kill me. I took a step toward the door then, on second thought, decided to grab my cell and jam it into my back pocket. Then I headed to the bathroom, which was down the hall from my room and next to my parents' bedroom.

Halfway there, I stopped. Something wasn't right. It was too quiet.

Aunt Judy and my cousin Beth had lived with us for a while, and the house had gotten really noisy but they were long gone, and things had pretty much gone back to normal. Which meant quiet. But Dad should have been in the kitchen slurping down his third cup of coffee while Mom flitted nearby, either swiping his toast crumbs off the table or putting on her make-up. Maybe even both at the same time. She was like that, my mom. Always doing something.

But there was absolutely no sound at all. Nothing. Nada. "Mom?" I looked into their bedroom. The bed was made, and everything was neat and tidy, like always, but otherwise, it was empty. "Dad?"

Shrugging, I went into the bathroom. It was late, so maybe Dad had already left for work and Mom had…what? Gone to the market for something? Run some errand or other, maybe?

Whatever. It didn't really matter. Time to get moving. Shaving as quick as I could without ripping my face to shreds, I concentrated on not thinking about the nightmare that had invaded my sleep these past few months, ever since that night in the meadow. I wondered if I would ever get over what happened.

At least I'd gotten over Mom throwing away my poster of the Kardashian sisters in their white bikinis. She'd claimed it was to make my room more "girl-friendly" when Beth and Aunt Judy moved in, and they'd given my room to my cousin, but I knew better. Mom always hated that poster. It had pissed me off, until the day she came home with Nicki Minaj's Pink Friday poster to replace it.

Was I ever surprised. Mom just shrugged it off like it was no big thing, but I could tell it was her way of apologizing, not only for the Kardashian poster, but for…everything.

I finished shaving and washed a couple of left-over spots of shaving cream off my face. A small spot of blood welled under my jawline. I ripped a tiny piece of toilet paper off the roll and pressed it against the cut. I'd have to remember to peel it off before I got to school.

After snagging my hoodie from my room and tossing it over my shoulder so I wouldn't forget to put it on before leaving for school, I hustled down the hall.

"Mom?" Usually, the smell of bacon or sausage wafted into the living room from the kitchen where she was busy making breakfast. She stood by the old adage that breakfast was the most important meal of the day and always cooked something, but I'd just as soon have a Pop-Tart and call it a day. While Mom cooked away, Dad could be heard commenting on some news story or other he'd read about. Normally, I could hear the sound of the ancient Mr. Coffee gurgling away. But this morning, everything was different. There was nothing. No sounds, no smells. Just silence.

What was going on?

I strode across the living room and burst into the kitchen. "Good morning!"

Empty. No dirty breakfast dishes. Mr. Coffee wasn't talking, either. *That's weird.* Where was everyone? Could they have left early for some reason, without telling me? It would explain why no one had bothered to wake me up. If I hadn't rolled out of bed on school days by about seven, Mom always squirted me with her water bottle to wake me up. I glanced at the vintage Felix the Cat clock Dad loved and would never let my mom donate to Goodwill. Eight-fifteen. I was already way late. I scratched my head. *What the—*

Something was definitely up. But what? Maybe I should check on the car, see if it was still in the driveway. Then at least I could go to school without worrying about what was happening. As I headed to the front door, there was a vague fluttering in my stomach. What if the car wasn't there? What would that mean?

I reached for the doorknob but didn't turn it right away. Instead, I closed my eyes and took a deep breath. *Please let the car be there. Please let the car be there.* Something told me it was going to be sitting in the driveway, where Dad always parked it. I opened my eyes, let my breath out slowly, and opened the door.

My Le Mans was there, but Dad's beat up Honda was gone. I rubbed the back of my neck. I had no idea what was going on, but it was starting to freak me out.

Wolf Creek, the Southern California town I lived in, was your average small town. Not counting the two serial killers who'd roamed the streets in the past. Oh, and the werewolf population, of course. It was hot and dry most of the time, but now heavy shadows crept along the street.

Between the silence and the darkness, the whole neighborhood felt empty.

Where the hell was everybody?

It was as if everyone had simply vanished. But that was crazy, wasn't it? As I stood there, something else occurred to me. Not only were my parents missing in action, but it was as quiet outside as it was in the house. Not a sound. No dogs barking. No birds chirping. It was morning. Birds liked morning. They couldn't have all gone to some birdie brunch or something, not all at the same time. And where was the traffic? A major highway was only a few blocks away. Usually, I didn't even hear the traffic unless I really concentrated. It just sort of faded into the background. But as much as I strained to hear it now, it just wasn't there. It wasn't that I couldn't hear it. It was…gone.

Vanished.

Like the birds.

And my parents.

And everybody else.

Dread skulked up my spine. My scalp crinkled, and I was nearly overcome with fear. It only lasted an instant, but it shot straight into my soul. No birds or angry dogs? No highway noise? No traffic on the street? Not even the faint sounds of the freight trains that passed by every hour? What was going on?

I walked onto the porch and peered into the darkness, which seemed to be getting thicker as it moved slowly down the street. There should be someone out here. Benny next door revving his Harley as he left for work. Miss Hastings walking her nasty little Yorkie around the neighborhood. Something. Anything.

I stepped off the porch and walked to the edge of the driveway. The three little Baker kids should have been playing in the front yard by now. Shelley Baker, their mom, once told my mom she couldn't wait for the triplets' birthday when they would be old enough to go to Kindergarten so she could have the mornings to herself. How come they weren't climbing the trees or pulling up the flowers lining their driveway, like every other day? They just weren't there. No one was there, as far as I could tell.

A sour taste rose in my mouth, and the back of my throat ached. Had something just moved out there, deep in the shadows? Something dark, and…what? It felt like I was being watched by something creeping through the swirling thickness, something that would jump out any second and devour me. I strained to hear something, anything, that would either tell me there was something out there, or that I was imagining things. No sound came, and I didn't see anything else move.

It had to be my imagination.

"Doofus." I shook my head and snorted. My mom would have giggled and called me a silly goose, and I guessed I was. As a writer, I was gifted with an overactive imagination, and this had to be a result of that.

But if so, if everything really was just in my mind, where was everyone? Why couldn't I just blink them all back or something?

"Oh, cut it out already," I chided myself as I headed back inside. "This isn't one of your short stories. Nothing paranormal happened. No alien abductions going on."

The fact of the matter was, I was running late, and everything that I normally saw on school days had already happened. Benny was already on his way to work, the nasty Yorkie's walk was over, and the triplets? Well, maybe they were sick or something, and they were staying inside today. Kids got sick all the time, right?

I left the door open when I went inside because I was just going to grab my backpack from the couch and get going. I wasn't looking forward to dealing with Miz Anderson, the Attendance Nazi at school. She would no doubt give me a stern lecture about being late without bringing a note from home. Geez, like she was never late before.

Wiping my feet on the mat without thinking about it, I thought I heard something deep inside the house. Cocking my head, I stopped in mid-wipe and listened intently.

It was a voice. At first, I thought Mom was talking to someone on the phone, but then I realized it was a male voice. Dad? No, it wasn't deep enough. This voice was younger and cracked every once in a while. It was also vaguely familiar. That feeling that overcame me outside, the one about something moving around just beyond my sight, hadn't left me completely, and that feeling combined with this voice was more than a little creepy. My heart fluttered a little. I swallowed the saliva that filled my mouth and started hesitantly down the hall toward where I thought the voice was coming from. It got a little louder and clearer the closer I got to it.

When I passed the kitchen, I glanced inside and realized that no one had been in there at all this morning. It looked just like it did every night after we cleaned it. The lights were off, the counter had been wiped down, all the dinner dishes were put away, and there was nothing to indicate breakfast had ever been made.

Nothing to indicate what happened to my parents.

The voice drew me on. While I couldn't tell what it was saying, I could hear the urgent tone. And it was coming from my bedroom.

Had someone snuck in while I wasn't looking? How was that even possible? I'd only been outside a minute or two and hadn't gone more than a few steps from the front door. When I'd gotten that weird feeling and thought I'd seen something moving out there, it had come from the street in front of me, not the house behind me.

I could just make out a few words. "You remember…" the voice said in a firm, even tone. "Well, you have to…"

I thought about just running the other way, but the voice drew me on.

"Dude, you gotta do this," the voice continued. "You hear me? It all starts here. There's no going back."

My mouth went completely dry, and my balls crawled up inside me. I didn't understand the words, but now that I could hear them clearly, I recognized the voice. I'd have known it anywhere. It was Riff, my best friend.

I licked my lips and tried to swallow, but the fear that grew inside me made it impossible.

Because Riff was dead.

He was killed almost three years ago, ripped to shreds by a werewolf.

Chapter 3

I had to be dreaming. There was no other way I could be hearing Riff. It just wasn't possible. Way back when, I hadn't had a smartphone or a camera, so I didn't even have any pictures of him, except the moronic school pictures we'd been forced to have taken every year. The last one he'd given me, when we were fourteen, showed him mugging to the camera, his eyes crossed and tongue lolling out the side of his mouth like the weird-looking dog from that World's Ugliest Dog contest. On the back, he'd written something about that year being our best yet. It still made me sad—and a little mad—to think it had been his last year on earth.

There wasn't anything to be afraid of. If the voice I'd heard coming from my room was Riff, then I had to be asleep. There was no reason to be afraid of a dream, no matter how scary it was. Dreams can't hurt you.

"Hey, Dude." Riff's voice was stronger and clearer now, hardly muffled at all. "You awake out there? You hear me?"

I nodded without thinking. Riff could be demanding like that. *Used to be demanding.* I reached for the door-knob. It felt like I was in some sort of trance, not fully in control of what I was doing. All I knew for sure was that

I had to open the door. Had to see Riff again. Had to find out what was going on.

But anything could be in there. Anything. One thing was for sure, it couldn't actually be Riff. It couldn't.

Could it?

The doorknob felt cold and hard when I grabbed it. Taking a deep breath, I turned the knob and pushed the door open a few inches, then hesitated. Anything could be on the other side. Riff. PJ, the diner-owner-turned-werewolf, overcome with Moonspell sickness, that I'd slain when I was fourteen. Mr. Hansen, my Literature teacher, who turned out to be her brother, another were-wolf, bent on my destruction. I'd been forced into a showdown with him last winter and was lucky to still be here. Yes, it could be anything in there.

But standing out here in the hall wasn't getting me anywhere. So I took another deep breath. Trying to ignore the heaviness in my chest that I figured was fear, I slowly let it out while I counted to three, opened the door all the way, and…

Chapter 4

I plunged into complete and total whiteness. It was like being inside a jar of that marshmallow fluff Mom used to make her special holiday fudge. A high-pitched, incessant ringing seemed to fill my brain. I covered my ears with my hands, but it did no good. I winced and looked around the room. It was harder to see in here than it had been outside. How could that be? What was this white stuff, anyway?

Lights flashed from what might be the direction of my laptop. Was that where Riff's voice had come from? It was impossible to tell. "Riff?" I whispered, looking over my shoulder. "Riff, are you here?"

If Riff was here, he was playing games, because the only response I got was more weird beeping that filled my head like a car alarm that had been accidentally set off. But if he wasn't, why had I heard him calling to me?

This is stupid. Time to quit farting around and find out what's going on. I fumbled my way through the whiteness and stood in the doorway. My chest itched all of a sudden, and I scratched it furiously. I staggered around my room, aiming for where I thought my desk was. The white stuff was so thick it was hard to walk through. It pushed against me, and it was sort of like swimming underwater. Hoping I'd be able to get reception on my cell, I pulled it out of my pocket and ran my thumb across the screen.

It stayed dark.

I scowled and ran my thumb over it again, harder this time.

Still dark.

"Dafuq?" My mouth went dry, and I swallowed, hard. "What's happening here?"

Maybe I was still asleep. You saw it all the time on TV and in movies. The hero has a nightmare and wakes up screaming. Then he wanders around and finds himself all alone. He feels like he's being watched, and before he knows it, the boogeyman gets him. And he wakes up screaming…

Except I had the feeling this wasn't a dream. It was all so…real. Everything in the house, in my *room*, was exactly where it should be, where it would be if I was awake. So, this was really happening, wasn't it? Whatever "this" was.

But what was going on with the phones? There were no dead zones in the area, and the weather normally wasn't a factor in reception, at least not in Wolf Creek, so why couldn't I make a call? I looked at my phone screen again and was shocked to see it all lit up. When it rang a split second later, I almost dropped it.

"Hello?"

"Jaime?" Mom's voice came through loud and clear, and I didn't even care that she used the nickname I despised.

"Mom? Mom, where are you?"

"Honey, are you there? Can you hear me?"

"I hear you fine, Mom." I gripped the phone a little tighter. "Where are you?"

"Oh, Jaime, please." She started to cry. "Please answer me."

By now, my hand was beginning to throb from the stranglehold I had on the phone. "I'm here, Mom," I shouted. "At home."

Her crying had turned into quiet sobs, and I knew it was useless. No way would she be able to hear me, wherever she was. She didn't cry easily. She wasn't one of those women who cried at those sappy Mother's Day card commercials.

In fact, the only other time I'd heard her actually sob was when Beth was in the hospital, all hooked up to machines and tubes and things. The day the rogue werewolf attacked the Ranger we were riding in, causing Beth's forehead to connect with the dashboard so hard it knocked her unconscious. Later that same night, with the help of the only adult in town who knew what was really going on, I'd killed that same werewolf.

And even that hadn't made Mom cry for very long. So the fact that she was crying now scared me. More than the nightmares, more than knowing werewolves existed, even more than knowing I was one.

"Oh, my sweet boy." Mom continued to sob. "You have to answer me, Jaime. Jaime! Oh, baby, where are you?"

I ran down the hall. I had to find her. Had to let her know I was okay. "Mom!" I screamed so hard the vein in my forehead felt close to bursting. "I'm coming. Just tell me where you are."

Silence.

When I got to the front door, I hesitated. "Mom?"

More silence.

I closed my eyes and held my breath. "Mom?" I whispered. She had to be there, wherever "there" was. She couldn't be gone. My heart seemed to stop for a beat or two. Shaking my head, I pulled the phone away from my ear and held it in front of me. Opening one eye halfway, I peeked at the screen. Black again.

I'd lost her.

And I couldn't call her back because the screen stayed dark no matter how many times I ran my thumb across it.

It was all so bizarre. First the weird daytime darkness outside, then the heavy white nothingness in my room. And now Mom's phone call. What was going on? For a second, I thought it might be the zombie apocalypse, but that was dumb. Even as heavy a sleeper as I am, I couldn't possibly have slept through something like that. And as far as I could tell, there were no zombies around. So was I a "left behind-er"? Or whatever they called the people stuck on earth after the rapture. My brain reeled as I tried to think if Father Michael had ever talked about it during one of his sermons, but nothing came to mind.

"There has to be some sort of logical explanation," I said. "There's gotta be."

But what? Whatever it was couldn't be good. Not if it made my mom cry like that. And where was Dad? Were they together? Or had he disappeared into the darkness, along with everyone else in town?

I didn't know what to do, standing there in the entryway, looking out the huge bay window Dad had surprised Mom with after my deadly encounter with the sick werewolf, who'd leaped through the living room window to get at me. The sheriff had covered the incident up and claimed the original window had been busted by the serial killer the media had dubbed the Wolf Creek Shredder. I always suspected Sheriff Brazelton of leaking that name. He wasn't bad, for a cop.

Too bad he'd been voted out when everyone thought he'd taken way too long to solve the murders.

But there were no rogue werewolves around this time. Everyone was gone. Mom had called me, so that meant there had to be people somewhere nearby. Didn't it?

Wait a minute. I frowned and squinted. *What was that?* Something outside, just beyond the window, had moved. Hadn't it? I took a step closer and leaned forward. The darkness had become so thick, it was like trying to look through one of Aunt Judy's burnt pancakes.

But something was definitely moving around out there.

Chapter 5

I flung the door open so hard, it gouged a hole in the stucco. Dad could kill me later. Right now, I had to see who—or what—was out there. I hesitated. What if it was a some*thing* instead of a some*one*? What then?

I ran my fingers through my hair. Too many questions. Time to get some answers.

Stepping out onto the porch, I left the door open and took a few steps. After scanning the area and finding nothing, I went a few more feet into the yard.

Still nothing. But the cold sweat dripping from my armpits and the churning in my stomach told me otherwise. There was something out there, all right. Hiding in the darkness. I could feel it.

Inching closer to my Le Mans, I scanned the yard again then took a quick look in the car. Nothing in the front seat. A glance over my shoulder, and another in the back seat, did nothing to ease my nerves.

Wait. Right there, at the end of the driveway. Was that…yes, it was! A dark figure lurked in the shadows.

"Hello?" I started toward it. But it turned slowly and walked away. "Wait! Don't go."

No way was I going to be left alone again. Maybe this person could tell me what was going on. I trotted down the driveway. As I got closer, I realized that the person's walk was familiar, and I was pretty sure I would recognize whoever it was if only I could catch up to them. Even though they were walking slowly—and by this point, I'd broken into a swift trot—I was having trouble catching them. The gloom was doing something to my sense of time and space, and it felt like I was moving in slow motion.

"Wait up," I called. "Please."

The figure was getting darker, and I was finally closing in. I reached out, and my fingers brushed against their shirt, but I couldn't grab hold. I was racing after them by this point and stumbled when I didn't connect. Righting myself, I lunged forward and managed to catch a big red bow at the person's waist. I suddenly realized who it was.

"Diane." I was panting heavily and struggled to catch my breath. The bow of my favorite diner server's apron came undone, and I nearly lost her again. Clutching it tightly, I spun her around. "Diane, what's going on? Why didn't you stop when I called to you?"

Diane cocked her head slowly and stared at me. Her eyes were as black as Christian Bale's clothes. I'd never seen anything so lifeless, so…dead, and I took a step back. "Diane? Are you okay?"

She sluggishly tilted her head the other way, a slow, hideous grin spreading across her face. It reminded me of some malformed Halloween jack-o-lantern. But when her eyes turned red, and her face began to flicker and wobble like a heat shimmer on the horizon, I was beyond scared.

Because I'd seen it before, enough times to last my entire life.

Hot saliva began to drip from her elongating muzzle. Her cheeks sprouted thick, wiry hair. Her fingernails grew as long as steak knives.

Werewolf! My mind raced. She'd taken me by surprise. Would I survive another attack?

When she lunged at me, I ducked, but it was too late. Searing hot pain sliced through my chest. My belly. My leg. I crumpled to the ground. Turned and tried to crawl away. Was this really how it was going to end?

"Mom!" I screamed as I reached out for something—anything—to save me…

Chapter 6

I was thrust back into the marshmallow fluff of my room.

What's happening to me? Whatever it was, it couldn't be good. I needed to get a grip. After shaking my head like a dog to clear it, I tried to walk over to my bedroom window but the air was so thick, it made my legs heavy, and I found myself pushing against it, struggling to go farther than a few feet. It reminded me of that water aerobics class I took once with my mom. The pressure of the water pressed against your body with every move and the resistance gave you a great workout.

When I finally reached the window, I opened up the curtains and looked outside. The weird darkness had not only grown thicker, it was starting to swirl. And it was changing color, no longer simply black. Shades of brown and gray twisted around and through it, along with an eerie yellow that seemed to reside deep within the shadows, almost as a living entity separate from yet part of the darkness.

And it was calling to me. "James? James."

The lump in my throat I was trying to swallow got caught half-way down, and I coughed.

"Can you hear me?" the voice continued. Where was

it coming from? Then I saw it. Something was moving around out there. I could barely make it out, but the longer I stared, the more it materialized, emerging from the shadows one piece at a time. But it was definitely there.

"Please, oh, please can you hear me?"

"I hear you." My voice trembled almost as much as my hands. "Who are you? What do you want?"

The shape moved a little, and a leg became visible. It was skinny and wore jeans. On its foot was a black flowery hi-top. I laughed and ran my fingers through my hair. Shaniqua. Of course. How could I not recognize her voice?

"Shaniqua, I'm right here." I tapped on the window with my index finger. "In my room."

The rest of her slowly became visible as she seemed to force her way out of the slowly whirling gloom. She was wearing the same skinny jeans, pink tank top thingy—*camisole*, I reminded myself—and green scarf that she wore the day we met. Had that only been seven months ago? Felt like we'd always been together.

She was standing there, in the yard, looking up at the house. I leaned over my desk and tapped on the window again. "Shaniqua? Hey!" Why couldn't she hear me? I pushed open the window. She must have heard that because she turned and looked directly at me. "Hey," I called to her. "I'm so glad to see you."

She was really smart, and maybe she'd figured out what was going on. But she just stuck her hands in her pockets and slowly rocked back and forth on the balls of her feet. There were deep purple smudges under her eyes, and she looked so sad. I couldn't help but wonder why.

I held up my finger. "Hang on. I'll be right there." I ran through the house and practically flew out the front door before coming to a stop so sudden I nearly lost my balance.

Shaniqua was gone.

Why had she left? I looked around, frantically searching the yard, trying to see beyond the ever-thickening night. The silence was so loud, I wanted to scream. It wasn't just quiet. There was an absence of sound altogether. Even my footsteps on the asphalt were silent, as if this was a movie, and someone had muted the TV. Only this was no movie. I didn't know what was going on, but I was pretty sure it wasn't a dream. This was really happening.

It was getting colder and clammier, and my arm tightened up again. The damp clung to me like plastic wrap. I shivered as I stood at the foot of the driveway and looked down the street. That feeling of being watched came over me again. I turned quickly and looked the other way. That same silhouette I'd seen earlier moved slowly away from me, fading back into the dark.

Something was terribly wrong. Not just with the night, and the silence, but with my girlfriend. The way she wouldn't answer me, didn't even seem to hear me. The look on her face. The slow, methodical way she moved, like she was an apparition, just floating above the pavement. It scared me.

"Shaniqua!" I rushed through the darkness after her. "Wait up. Don't leave."

It was important that I catch up with her. Maybe between the two of us, we could figure out what was going on. And if not, at least I wouldn't be alone.

I stumbled blindly along as fast as I dared with the darkness so total it was like being in a cave. Why couldn't I catch up to her? I was practically running, and she had been inching along. It was so weird. There was no sign of her. She had completely disappeared into the night, almost as if she'd been vaporized.

After a few blocks, I stopped to catch my breath and

look around, but there was nothing to see but darkness. It was so thick it seemed to erase every detail. I turned in a full circle, but all I could see was the pavement immediately beneath my feet. All I could hear was the pounding of my heart. Sweat trickled down my armpits.

How could she have vanished so quickly?

"Hello? Shaniqua?" I yelled. "Where are you? Are you there?"

At first, I was met with silence so complete it seemed to roar. But then, as I listened, I could hear a sort of shuffling sound. I peered into the dark, and for several seconds saw nothing, but then a figure slowly emerged, a shadow of a shadow that grew darker and more defined as it gradually materialized.

"There you are," I said. "Where did you go? Why did you run—" I narrowed my eyes and squinted into the darkness. The silhouette moving toward me wasn't Shaniqua. It was someone—*something*—else.

It shambled toward me, dragging one leg, its arms hanging limply by its sides. I took a step back. Hot, putrid air hit the back of my neck. I whirled around.

Shaniqua.

Her eyes burned a deep red. I gasped and took a step away from her. When her face began to shimmer like a heat wave on the horizon, I backed up another step. This couldn't be happening. Not Shaniqua. She was human, for God's sake.

Wasn't she?

I glanced over my shoulder and licked my chapped lips. Several pairs of red eyes glowed back at me. The silhouettes became figures, shuffling toward me relentlessly, each dragging a leg in a strange, wobbly gait.

I was surrounded.

"No!" I screamed.

The eyes moved closer. More and more of them appeared. I turned back to Shaniqua, who glared at me with her hideous werewolf smile, fangs dripping steaming hot, foul-smelling saliva. Her head was weirdly shaped, elongated like a piece of pulled taffy. Her face was distorted, fuzzy. Coarse hair covered her cheeks. Maggots crawled across her snout.

Fear churned inside me. Rooted me to the spot. It swirled up out of my core, as dark as the night that surrounded me, and seemed to swallow everything. I should have listened to my instincts and gotten the hell out of there. But I hadn't because I'd wanted to find out what was going on. All I knew for sure was that I had to move, to flee, to get away. Now. This second. But how? The creatures were everywhere. I turned in a tight circle as they closed in on me. How could I get away? Only one thing came to me: run.

"Shaniqua?" Maybe, just maybe, if she recognized me, if I could get through to her somehow, she would let me go. Convince the others that I wasn't worth the bother. "Shaniqua, it's me. James. Remember, Shaniqua?"

She hesitated for just a moment, but it was long enough for the others to stop as well. I saw my chance, and I took it. Racing past what used to be my girlfriend, I ran without thinking, in panic mode. Didn't even know where I was going. I just had to get out of there. Get somewhere safe, where I could have a chance to think, to try and figure out what was going on. To somewhere normal, out of this nightmare land, where things like common sense and logic counted for something. But it didn't feel like a nightmare. It seemed too…what? Real? But that was dumb. This wasn't real, it couldn't be.

If I didn't know better, I'd think I'd been thrown into some sort of sick *Invasion of the Body Snatchers* reboot. There was a word for the way the creatures all seemed to stop at the same time like they were controlled by a single brain, but I was too scared to think of it. So I just kept running. As far as I could tell, in all the darkness, I was headed away from home, but I couldn't be sure because all the houses, businesses, and every other town landmark had vanished into the night.

A noise came from somewhere behind me. I looked over my shoulder and saw several silhouettes limping along, their red eyes burning in the darkness. I think I moaned a little. Panting from exertion, my legs and lungs burning, I managed to speed up a little. But I wasn't going to last much longer. A runner, I'm not. Never had been. Probably never would be. But, hopefully, I'd last long enough to get away from the monsters that were chasing me.

Then, just as I thought I was going to get away, one of them came out of the darkness and grabbed me, knocking me to the ground. Before I could move, those things were on me. Snarling. Growling. Ripping my skin.

I struggled, trying to fight them off, but there were too many. I screamed at the intense burning as they flayed my flesh, shredding every last piece of meat off my bones.

Finally, as the life force drained quickly from my body, I closed my eyes and accepted my fate.

I was going to die.

Tuesday, August 11, 2015
4 Months, 1 Week,
4 Days Before

Chapter 7

BETH

At thirteen, it had been two years since Beth had lain unconscious in the hospital after being attacked by a werewolf.

And learning that she was one, too.

She hadn't started to transform yet, but she figured since her cousin James had first transformed right before he turned sixteen, it would be around then for her, too. She couldn't wait.

Lately, she let herself think about it a lot. Especially since Kimberlin, her friend and next-door neighbor, didn't seem to really like Beth much these days and hardly paid any attention to her any more. Beth struggled to understand why, but couldn't think of anything she'd said or done to turn Kimberlin away.

Kimberlin was seventeen and way cool. Beth had looked up to her former babysitter almost as much as she had resisted her mother's belief last summer that, at twelve, she'd even needed one. Beth and Kimberlin had always gotten along, had had a lot of fun times, and generally enjoyed being together, but there had been several times lately that Beth had gotten the feeling that Kimber-

lin's feelings had changed. Beth's mom had finally re-
lented and let Beth stay by herself this summer while her
mom worked, but Beth knew that her mom had secretly
asked Kimberlin to keep an eye on her. Beth resented it.
Maybe Kimberlin did, too.

But summer vacation was coming to a close and
Beth was bored and willing to put up with Kimberlin's
moodiness for a chance to get out of the house. So when
Kimberlin's friend Sarah showed up—as Beth pretended
to read on the front porch while she watched Kimberlin
playing Angry Birds on her phone—and wanted Kimberlin to go to the mall with her, Beth had practically begged
Kimberlin to let her tag along.

Now, Kimberlin and Sarah were chatting in the front
seat, completely ignoring Beth, when Kimberlin's
smartphone chirped. She pulled it out of her pocket and
swiped her thumb across its face to access the text mes-
sage.

"Who's it?" Sarah asked.

Kimberlin grinned like the Cheshire cat. "Guess."

"Baden? Are you kidding me?"

Kimberlin showed the text to Sarah. "See?"

Sarah read it and then looked back at Kimberlin.
"What are you gonna say?"

"Who's Baden?" Beth asked from the depths of the
back seat.

"Just a guy we know," Kimberlin told her.

She looked at Sarah, and they both giggled. Beth
looked out the window and sighed. There was no use
pressing her right now, but Beth sure was going to ask
her about this Baden dude when they got home. Kimberlin wasn't the type to get all giggly and girly over some
guy—Beth was pretty sure Kimberlin was gay—and Beth
wondered if it was an act she was putting on for Sarah's
sake.

"So, you gonna answer him?" Sarah asked.

"What do you think?"

They both giggled again.

"What are you going to tell him?"

"Watch."

Sarah leaned closer to Kimberlin. When Beth heard Kimberlin's nails clicking on the phone's keyboard, she frowned. *Since when does Kimberlin text while driving?* She was just about to say something about that when their car slammed into a light pole. She saw it the millisecond before they hit and didn't even have time to scream before the window shattered, spewing glass into her face. The door crumpled in on her as the car wrapped itself around the pole.

In that split second before impact, she felt her heartbeat thunder in her chest and was positive that the whole world could hear it. Enormous pain, worse than she'd ever felt before, engulfed her like a cocoon.

The world turned red as blood filled her eyes.

Her body shuddered, and dizziness overtook her. She tried to take a small breath, but her lungs fought against her—demanding air, even as they refused to work. It was too hard. She began to let go. Her lungs stilled, no longer fighting against her.

A deep coldness filled her.

Beth wished she was anywhere but here, anywhere but the backseat of Kimberlin's car. She should have stayed home. She felt herself falling softly away from her body, through the bottom of the car, past the asphalt of the street, to somewhere icy and silent.

And dark.

A long time went by where nothing happened.

And then she woke up.

Everything was wrong. The air was cold, and a gray mist kept her from seeing anything. Her whole body hurt.

She gently touched her forehead and grimaced at the stickiness there. When she looked at her fingers, they were full of blood. She blinked a few times and used the heel of her hand to wipe the blood out of her eye. But that didn't make things any easier to see.

The mist had a quality to it that gave her the creeps. It felt like it was almost…alive. But that was impossible.

Wasn't it?

Where am I?

She sat up slowly and looked around. Everything was colorless, including what little light penetrated the mist. The air tasted like an old penny. Chilled, she wrapped her arms gingerly around herself and shivered.

Out of the corner of her eye, she saw something move—something dark and shadowy. But when she turned her head to look, it vanished. Beth went to chew on her nail but remembered the blood and put her hands back on her lap instead.

She wanted to call out to the shape, but her ears rang violently, and she didn't think she could hear it anyway. Besides, who's to say it was something friendly? Maybe it was evil. She didn't want to call attention to herself if it was. Just in case.

Beth closed her eyes, in an attempt to ward off the sick feeling in her stomach, but opened them quickly, fearing that, whatever the dark shape was, it would take that opportunity to get her. The shadow stood just a few feet away, hidden in the mist. But she could feel its presence.

"Who's there?" she cried.

A little girl walked slowly toward her. "Just me," she said.

A baseball cap sat rakishly on her head. She looked like a skater. A little girl skater. She wore a striped tee shirt, jeans with holes in the knees, and tiny little sneakers with big soles that Beth was pretty sure lit up. What looked like wings decorated the sides. Skater rides, for sure. Beth wondered if she was trying to look like someone, an older brother, maybe. Everything was gray, including her skin. She reminded Beth of the pencil sketches Kimberlin used to draw of her, back when she actually liked Beth. Beth wondered where Kimberlin was right now.

"Who are you?"

"Timmy."

"Timmy?" Beth almost laughed. She even had a little boy name.

"Short for Timothea. Gross, huh?" Timmy wrinkled her nose in distaste.

"It's different, that's for sure."

"Yeah." Timmy snorted. "You can say that again." She cocked her head and looked at Beth with huge gray eyes. "You can really see me?"

"Uh huh. Why?" Beth asked. "Is that weird?"

"Well, yeah. No one ever sees us."

Beth looked around frantically. "Us?"

Timmy simply looked at her.

"Where are we?"

"Don't you know?"

Beth shook her head, still looking around, peering into the mist. Wherever they were, it didn't feel safe. She wrapped her arms around herself and tried not to shiver.

"You've crossed over."

Beth looked at Timmy and frowned. "Crossed over?"

"To the other side, silly." Timmy giggled.

"What are you saying? Are you telling me I—I'm dead?" Beth's panic was like a cobra under the spell of a snake charmer. It swayed back and forth, in her mind and her body. Her mind told her that this was impossible, while her body felt like the floor had dropped out from underneath her, just like that final instant in the car.

She didn't belong in this gray world, she was sure of it. Energy seemed to course through her, somehow warm, even while she and everything around her was so cold. She was too feisty, too vivacious to be here. Hadn't her father always told her how much he loved her high-spirited personality? She was too alive to be in this God-forsaken place. And certainly too young. She couldn't be dead. She couldn't be.

Timmy shook her head. "Don't know. You're kinda..."

"Kind of what?"

"Kinda...I don't know. Twinkly."

Beth had a quick vision of that Edward guy, the vampire who sparkled, and shook her head to get rid of the image. "Twinkly? What does that mean?"

"See, everyone here's just plain. But you—you twinkle. Kinda."

"Twinkle." Beth felt tears welling up in her eyes and blinked rapidly to try to keep them inside. "So I'm not dead?"

"Don't think so. The dead don't bleed, you know." Timmy held out a small gray cloth.

Beth took it and pressed it against her forehead. *The dead don't bleed.* That helped her calm down a little. She was definitely bleeding.

"And we don't feel pain. Do you?"

Beth touched her side and grimaced again. "I feel like I got run over by a truck or something."

Timmy covered her mouth with her hand and giggled.

"What?"

"Dude! You kinda did."

The memory of the car wrapping itself around the light pole, glass shattering all over her, flew through her mind and was gone. "So, how did I get here?" Beth looked around. "Wherever 'here' is."

"The only way the living can. You wished yourself here."

Beth shook her head. "What? No, I didn't. What are you talking about?"

"What was the last thing you remember thinking before you got here?" Timmy asked.

"I...I don't know." Beth looked around and tried to remember whatever brought her here. Her mind was a little foggy. *Kind of like this place.* She closed her eyes tightly then opened them quickly. It was too creepy to keep them closed for long. Something was hiding out there in the mist, something she couldn't quite see. But she could feel it.

"Beth."

Beth jerked a little. She turned back to Timmy. "What?"

"You need to remember what you were thinking." Timmy gestured to either side. "They need you to remember."

Shapes, unclear and indefinable, emerged from the mist and became first shadowy figures, then actual people. Dozens of them. Hundreds, maybe. And all walking slowly toward her, chanting something low.

"What's happening?" Beth exclaimed.

"Don't be afraid," Timmy told her. "This is Shadowland, where the dead walk. They need you to remember so you can help them cross over."

"Cross over?"

"Like this." Timmy knelt down and touched the ground. An inky darkness fanned out from her fingertips, covering the land like Nutella on white bread, rapidly spreading itself outward until it reached the crowd. Then it swelled up like a huge ocean wave, shimmered, and

split into more parts than Beth could count. Each part became a colorful animal—horses, dogs, foxes, owls, crows
and other birds, even a man with a jackal head that she
thought had something to do with Egyptian mythology.
There were also women warriors on horseback and a
skeleton in a hooded cape carrying some sort of farm
tool. The creatures looked real, not gray like the ghosts in
the mist. "It's your job to call the spirit guides so they can
take the dead the rest of the way."

The mist started to dissipate, and the world around
her blurred. Colors rippled through the grayness. The
ghosts flickered and disappeared as each spirit guide em-
braced them.

"What's going on?" Beth's heart beat so hard she felt
it in her head and her fingertips. She swallowed several
times and tried to quell the tidal wave in her stomach.
*What are those things and where are they taking every-
one?*

And would they come for her next?

Timmy tugged on Beth's tee shirt. "Don't be scared.
It's okay. That's what you're here for."

"It's *not* okay," Beth cried, pushing Timmy's hand
away. "It's not!"

"Beth, calm down. It's okay, really."

Beth whirled toward whoever was calling to her. A
shape slowly emerged from the gray mist. Squinting, she
peered into the gloom and tried to figure out who it was.
It seemed vaguely familiar, almost like someone she used
to know, a long, long time ago.

She took a step toward it and stared as the shape took
form. The more solid it became, the more her chest tin-
gled. It felt like the cold, lifeless fingers of something
long dead was squeezing the life force out of her. She
took a step back and cried out in fear when it called her
name again.

"Beth, don't be scared. It's me, Daddy."

Beth scowled and took a step toward him. "Daddy?"

Her father died two years ago when she was eleven. Plowed his car into the side of a mountain during a snowstorm.

The shape wavered a little before clearing enough for her to see who it was.

"Daddy!" She raced toward her father, arms outstretched. An icy electric jolt ran through her, and she stopped short. Her father was nowhere in sight. "Daddy?" she asked again, confused.

"Over here."

She turned around and there he was, smiling sadly at her. "Did I…"

He nodded.

"Are you…"

"A ghost? Well, sort of." He scratched his head. "But not really. Not here in Shadowland, anyway."

"What does that mean?" she asked impatiently.

"Oh, my irascible little Bethie. Nice to know some things never change."

"What are you talking about?" She'd forgotten how much her father sometimes bugged her, even though she loved him with all her heart.

"Here." He gestured toward a couch that hadn't been there before—she was sure of it. And not just any couch. The one they'd had back in Colorado before her father died. Before she and her mother'd had to pack up and leave their home and all their belongings and move in with James and his family. Before she thought her mother was a rabid werewolf serial killer. Before Beth started seeing ghosts. "Sit down."

"How…" She shook her head as she sat on the edge of the couch. "Never mind. Are you going to tell me what's going on?"

Daddy sat down next to her, being careful not to touch her. She crossed her arms and waited for him to answer her.

He sighed heavily. "I always meant to tell you about your heritage. About what we are. It just never seemed to be the right time."

"If you mean werewolves, I already know that. I—"

"No, honey, not that."

Now she was really confused. "Then what?"

"What do you know about genetics?"

"Not sure we learn that until ninth grade, Dad." He grinned and the tightness in her chest loosened its grip a little. She grinned back, shifting and turning a little toward Daddy. "All's I know is that the parents pass certain things on to the child through genes and DNA and stuff."

"Right. In this case, you're half werewolf."

"Half? What do you mean, half?"

"Have you ever heard of a psychopomp?"

"Psycho? Like that old movie?"

Daddy shook his head. "Not psycho. Psycho*pomp*."

"What's that?"

"It's a kind of a spirit guide. We help people cross over."

"Cross over?"

"When someone dies, their body stays on earth, but their spirit or soul travels to the afterlife. We psychopomps who have already crossed over escort the souls to wherever they need to go. Sometimes, when they refuse to leave because of some sort of baggage, a psychopomp who hasn't died yet can help them solve their issue so they can leave." He looked at Beth intently. "That's where you come in."

"Me?" she squeaked.

"Yeah, you."

"How? Why me? I'm not a psycho whatever. I'm a werewolf. Aren't I?"

"Remember I asked you about genetics?"

"Yeah."

"Well, you're only half werewolf. On your mother's side."

"Does that mean—"

"You're also half psychopomp. Like me." He tapped his chest with his thumb. "So you come by it naturally."

"Is that why I'm here? Why I can see ghosts now?" All of a sudden, she remembered the flashes of people she'd been seeing ever since the accident in Donna Glass's Ranger when the werewolf had attacked them. She hadn't seen all that many, and she'd always assumed she'd been dreaming when she did see them, but now she wondered if they'd all been ghosts.

"Yep."

"But why now?"

"Usually, the ability comes on in your mid-twenties or so. We can see the dead, talk to them, even. But sometimes, a traumatic event can bring on the gift much earlier than normal. In your case—" He reached out as if he was going to brush the hair out of her eyes, like he always used to, hesitated, then let his hand fall back to his side. "—the car accident seems to have been the catalyst."

Beth frowned. "Catalyst?"

Daddy chuckled. "Something that causes significant or sudden change."

"I know what it means, Dad." She scratched her cheek. This whole thing was so confusing. "What car accident? You mean the one with James? Or was I in one just now?" She could almost remember what happened. It was right there...but for some reason, she couldn't seem to retrieve the memory. "Is that why I'm in this weird place?"

Daddy whipped around and looked over his shoulder as if something startled him, but Beth didn't hear anything. He seemed to flicker. That gray mist wafted in from the sides again and bathed everything in a dull, leaden gloom. Was it hiding something? Was something getting ready to jump out and get them? She looked quickly from one side to the other, but the mist was too thick to see through. It disoriented her, and she got a little dizzy.

She turned back to Daddy, but he had disappeared. She was on her own in this freaky place. Chewing on her lower lip, it was all she could do to keep from screaming. Where had he gone? Why had he left her alone?

"Daddy?" she cried out. "Daddy, where are you?"

She wanted to run, but where? Instinct told her that running like crazy through this gray soup would be dangerous. She could run right into anything—or anyone. She jumped up and looked around frantically. As she tried to figure out what to do, the mist began to fade, and she was once again standing next to Timmy.

Without warning, her fear receded, and anger flooded through her. Images of the accident hit her all at once, and she remembered everything. The trip to the mall, the giggles of Kimberlin and Sarah over someone named Baden, and the text. The stupid text Kimberlin was writing while she drove. The one she was writing when she slammed into the light pole.

The smell of gasoline flooded her nostrils. Her mouth filled with the taste of blood. Her lungs were on fire, and she could hardly draw a breath. A black shape swooped past her head, something dark with wings, screeching loudly.

"What—what's hap—pening?" she sputtered.

"It's time to go back," Timmy whispered. "C'mon. Hurry up." She took Beth's hand and tugged until Beth took a step forward. Timmy's hand was icy cold, and darkness seemed to fill Beth's insides at her touch.

"But—" Her body was so cold and hurt so much she could barely speak. There was hardly an inch that wasn't screaming at her.

"You're not safe here," Timmy told her. "You have to go back. Now."

Beth's eyes rolled back in her head, and her knees buckled. She felt her body collapsing in on itself, coiling around and around like an enormous whirlpool, plummeting down through the grayness and into whatever lay beneath.

❦❦❦

The next thing Beth knew, the world had gone blindingly white. She seemed to be in some sort of cocoon, wrapped tightly like a chrysalis, and she struggled against the bindings. Narrowing her eyes against the glare, she was able to make out some vague shapes that slowly sharpened into some type of machines. Tubes and cords extended out in all directions, and she followed them with her eyes. Shock registered as she realized one of the tubes was attached to the back of her hand. Something that looked like a chip clip was attached to her index finger. Recognition dawned, and she realized she was in the hospital.

She tried to sit up, but a tsunami of nausea crashed into the walls of her stomach. She lay back down and groaned.

"Oh, crap." She covered her mouth with her hand and tried not to puke.

"Grown-ups always tell us not to swear, but they do it all the time, don't they?"

Beth looked up and saw a girl dressed all in black,

Emo bangs hiding one eye, standing in the doorway to her room. She looked to be about twelve or thirteen. She could have been one of Beth's classmates.

"Seriously," Beth agreed. "My name's Beth. What's yours?"

"Jasmine." The girl scrunched up her nose. "Sounds like a stupid Disney princess, don't it? The 'rents musta been high." She giggled. "My friends call me Jazz."

"Hi, Jazz." Beth liked this girl immediately. There was something about her, though, that felt a little…off. "Are you a patient here?"

Jazz shifted from one foot to the other, jammed her hands in her back pockets, and studied the floor in front of her.

"Jazz?"

"I was…before."

"Before? Before what?"

Jazz looked out the window and said nothing.

Confused, Beth frowned. "Jazz?"

"Before the bad man took me."

"Bad man? What bad man?"

Jazz kept looking out the window, not moving or speaking.

Goose bumps ran up Beth's arms and down her back. A cold sweat broke out on her forehead and under her arms. Outside her hospital room, the world seemed to slow down to a near stop. People glided ever so slowly past her door. The world was thrown into silent chaos, as if the beeps and chirps of equipment, the *squeak, squeak, squeak* of rubber-soled shoes, and whispered emergency room conversations had been sucked up by some creepy thing that lived in the mist and had a humongous appetite for noise and commotion.

And people.

Fear overtook her. Beth shut her eyes but quickly

opened them again, panic overtaking the terror. At least she'd be able to see anything that came at her.

Jazz was still there, her head cocked to one side, looking at her with a funny expression on her face. "You okay?"

Beth shook her head. "I'm not sure. I think…I think I died today."

"Naw," Jazz said. "If you did, you wouldn't twinkle."

"I twinkle?" Something stirred in her memory, but she couldn't quite grasp it. "What do you mean, I twinkle?"

Jazz shrugged. "I don't know. It's hard to explain. It's kinda like there's really sparkly glitter all over your body, and a bright light keeps shining on you."

"Oh. Well," Beth said. Jazz's voice sounded far away and tinny, as if it was coming from the far end of a tunnel. Beth sighed. "This whole thing has been super weird. I guess I'm a little tired."

"Oh, okay, guess I'll go, then." Jazz turned and walked to the door, then turned back and gave a little half-wave. "Bye."

"See you."

The monitor beside the bed beeped steadily. Beth closed her eyes and counted, taking a deep breath and letting it out slowly in between each number. When she reached ten, she opened her eyes. The world beyond her door had returned to normal. Men and women in scrubs scurried past, paying no attention to her while visitors in street clothes glanced into her room before hurrying on to wherever it was they were going.

Beth pulled the clip off her finger, wrestled the sheet wrapped around her until she was finally able to fling it off in frustration, slipped her legs over the side of the bed, and stood up. The nausea returned and brought its good friend dizziness, forcing her to lean against the mattress until it subsided. When it did, she took a few wobbly steps that ended with her crumpling to the floor. She hadn't realized how weak she was and wondered if it was because of the accident or her visits with Timmy and Jazz.

She was trying to figure it out when a gravelly voice spoke to her. "And just what do you think you're doing?"

There was no way she was ready for a third dead person to tell her she twinkled, so she closed her eyes and wished the voice away.

A hand clamped down on her upper arm, and she nearly screamed.

"Hey, are you okay?" the voice said. "Were you trying to get to the bathroom and got dizzy?"

She opened her eyes. An old lady smiled and grasped her wrist before looking at her watch. Beth guessed she was a nurse and relaxed.

"No, I—"

The nurse shushed her without looking up from her watch. After what seemed like forever, she turned to Beth. "Here, let's get you back to bed. Do you need to go to the bathroom first?"

Beth shook her head and let the nurse help her up.

"I'm Rosa," the nurse said and gripped Beth's elbow before taking her hand and walking her to the bed. "You better lie down."

Beth did as she was told and climbed into bed. "Where's my mom? Where's Kimberlin?"

Rosa pursed her lips. "I'm not sure where your mom went. Maybe she went to get something to eat."

"What about Kimberlin? Is she okay?"

Rosa pulled the sheet up over Beth. "I'm going to get the doctor."

Rosa was avoiding answering her questions. Her

mother might think that Beth was still a baby, but she was old enough to know when someone was hiding something. "What's going on?" she exclaimed. "Where's my mom?"

Rosa patted her arm. "Calm down, sweetie," she said. "It's going to be okay. Trust me."

Beth wanted to believe that, but something told her that nothing was ever going to okay again.

Turns out, she was right.

Chapter 8

Everyone kept telling Beth how lucky she was that she only had a minor concussion and lots of bruises, but lucky would have been to have stayed home that day. They kept her in the hospital overnight for observation. The doctors said she was okay, but they didn't know about the cold gray mist that encircled her heart. She couldn't seem to shake the numbness she felt, as if it had oozed up from the inky darkness Timmy's fingers had spread across the frozen Shadowland, grabbed her by the ankles, and wormed its way through her body to her very soul.

She couldn't explain the feeling and didn't even try. Besides, if she did tell someone, she'd also have to tell them what had happened, and she sure wasn't going to do that. The people in the white coats would come and take her away, where she'd live out her days in a rubber room taking little white pills that turned her into a zombie. No thank you.

She stayed silent on the matter, and whenever someone asked her what had happened, she just said she didn't remember. Safer that way.

Besides, who would believe her, anyway?

So when she was released and her mother took her

home from the hospital and asked her how she was, Beth simply said, "fine," and left it at that.

It was the only thing they said to each other the whole way home. Which was okay by Beth, since it gave her time to think about Timmy and some of the things she'd said. Beth had crossed over, from the world of the living to some sort of afterworld where the dead walked. Shadowland, Timmy had called it. It must be like some kind of way station where people went after they died but before they went to heaven. Or Hell. But if that was true, and all those animals had been spirit guides for the dead, like Timmy said, then what had she been doing there?

"We're home," her mother said as she unbuckled her seat belt.

"What?"

Her mother looked at her questioningly. "You okay?"

"Yeah, sorry." Beth shrugged. "Guess I was off in my own little world."

"Well, come on, then." Mom climbed out of the car and poked her head back inside. "You need to pick up your room."

Beth watched as her mother went inside. "Well," she muttered as she released her seat belt and got out of the car. "Good to see not everything's changed."

Sunday, January 10, 2016
14 Days Before

Chapter 9

BETH

Life for Beth was pretty much the same for the rest of the summer, which was exactly one week from the day she got home from the hospital.

Then school started and, as her mom was so fond of saying, things went to hell in a hand basket really quickly.

Eighth grade started out just like every other school year, and she settled in. She was comfortable, actually enjoyed school, and loved to learn new things. She liked her teachers well enough, and she'd gone to school last year with most of her classmates, so that was good. She felt at home there.

Until the day the mist people found her again. Or rather, Timmy, who seemed to be some sort of ambassador for them.

In between classes one day in January, Beth was washing her hands in the girl's bathroom when things slowly went gray. A familiar energy, dark and warm, seemed to run through her body, just like when she had ended up in that gray world after the accident. The light above her flickered, and she realized that the cold mist had returned and was filling the room. Darkness pushed in against her, and it felt as though it were alive.

An indistinct shape appeared in the mirror. Beth whirled around to face whatever was behind her.

Timmy gave a little wave as she materialized from the mist. "Hiya."

"Oh, it's you," Beth said. "You scared me."

Timmy giggled. "Sorry."

"What are you doing here?"

Timmy cocked her head at Beth, and annoyance flashed briefly. Beth remembered Timmy doing the same thing in that other place…Shadowland, was it called?…and wanted to smack her.

"What?" Beth asked.

"Don't you know?"

Beth sighed heavily and tossed the paper towel she'd dried her hands on into the trash can. "Look, I've got to get back to class."

"You need to remember, Beth."

"Remember what?"

But Timmy had already faded away. And taken the mist with her.

Wednesday, February 17, 2016
Day 24

Chapter 10

JAMES

I sat on my bed with my head in my hands. What was happening to me?

First, I woke up to an empty house with no sign of my parents, the neighbors, or the rest of the town, or even any indication of where they all went. Then it was so dark outside you could hardly see past your nose. My dead friend talked to me, my mom called me but couldn't hear me talking to her, and the best thing of all? Diane and Shaniqua showed up, acting weird, and then turned into monsters that tried to kill me. And every single time anything happened, I wound up back in my room, like nothing was wrong.

Just another day in paradise, right?

What were those zombie werewolf things? Where did they come from?

And why were they trying to kill me?

"Well." I slapped my hands on my knees and stood. "Sitting around here feeling sorry for yourself sure as hell won't give you any answers."

I looked out my window. The answers had to lay out there somewhere. But where?

That was the $64,000 question, wasn't it?

Without warning, my room flickered, and my whole field of vision was filled with stucco. I was so close, I couldn't tell what it was. I actually took a step back—it felt so real—and was surprised when the image shrank noticeably, and I could tell what it was.

Cinemopolis, the cut-rate theater where Beth and I had been going to the movies ever since we were little. Dad would drop us off with a stern warning to behave ourselves, which we mostly did—when we weren't theater-hopping or throwing popcorn at the screen when they showed old sci-fi movies on Saturday afternoons. Movies like *The Blob* and *I Was a Teenaged Werewolf*. I smiled at the thought. We always had so much fun together.

I didn't know why, but something was drawing me to the theater.

I didn't want to go.

I was afraid those things out there would get me. But I couldn't just sit around here and do nothing, either.

As the image faded and was replaced by the fluffy whiteness I'd come to expect in my room, I made up my mind.

"Move it, loser." I grabbed my cell and backpack and headed for the door.

〇〇〇

The yard seemed clear of those things, so I shifted my backpack a little, checked to make sure my cell was still in my pocket, and crept slowly into the darkness. It was so murky that, for a while, I was a little disoriented. I stood in the middle of the yard and scratched my head. Blackness surrounded me. Almost instantly, it had swallowed the house, obliterating any landmark I might have been able to use to orient myself again.

Town and the theater were only several blocks down the road, but which way?

Instinct guided me in, what I hoped was, the right direction, and I walked steadily down the sidewalk. Time seemed different here in the darkness, and it was hard to tell just how long I'd been walking when something appeared on the horizon. I stopped and peered into the darkness, in an attempt to get a clear image of whatever it was.

It seemed to be a light of some sort. Confused, I took a few hesitant steps toward it. The next thing I knew, the light split into two and barreled toward me. Everything shuddered, like in those true crime shows Beth liked to watch on TV when they wanted to speed up the time it took for a car to drive down the highway.

Was that what was happening here? Was that a car?

I blinked, and the image sharpened. It *was* a car. Excited, I ran toward it then skidded to a stop once I realized who it was.

Deputy Riggs, the one person I knew who wouldn't bother to pour water on me if I spontaneously combusted. Sure, I'd gotten into some trouble when I was eleven, had broken the window on his beloved Mustang, but I'd apologized and even done community service to make up for it. No matter what I'd said or done since then, he still held a grudge against me.

But there had to be some reason he was here now, wasn't there? It had to mean something.

The squad car rolled to a stop just short of where I was standing. I couldn't see into the car because the windshield seemed to have been darkened.

I slowly approached the cruiser. "Deputy Riggs?"

"Sheriff," Riggs growled.

I'd forgotten he'd been elected sheriff after Sheriff

Brazelton had been given the boot. "Sorry," I said. "Sheriff Riggs." I gestured vaguely. "Do you know what's happening here?"

There was no answer.

"Sheriff?" I took another step towards the car.

Still no answer.

I put my hand on the door and leaned over, hoping to see what was going on with Riggs, why he wasn't answering me. Was he hurt? Had those things gotten to him?

A hairy arm shot out and grabbed my wrist. Ragged claws dug into my flesh. As I tried to pull away, I looked at Riggs's face and screamed.

Two glowing red eyes glared maliciously back at me. Dagger-like fangs dripped burning hot saliva onto my arm.

Riggs was one of them.

Struggling to get away from him, I grabbed his fingers and was able to pry them back just enough to force him to let go. As soon as he released his grip, I stumbled back, tripped over the curb, and fell to the ground.

Riggs stepped out of the car and towered over me. Crab-walking backward, I barely managed to get far enough away to stand up and try to run when a swarm of those monsters surrounded me.

"Got you now, ass wipe," Riggs growled. "I told you I'd get you one day."

He reached out and tried to grab me by the throat, but I dropped to my hands and knees and scrambled through the legs of one of the other creatures. They were so slow-moving that it wasn't all that difficult.

Once out of the middle of the horde of zombie werewolves, I jumped up and sprinted down the street. When I thought I was far enough away from them, I glanced over my shoulder and was relieved to find that the road, as far as I could see, anyway, was clear.

I had escaped Riggs and his cohorts.

∽∾∽

And then I saw it. Or thought I did, anyway. The parking lot of the three-dollar theater. I hadn't been here since I took Beth to see *Bubba Ho-Tep* as a distraction after her father had died. Before things had gotten serious in town. If I could only make it inside, maybe I could get away from those things that were chasing me.

Just as I started to slow down, though, I saw several more of the monsters coming at me. They were traveling at an angle, and if I didn't do something quick, they'd cut me off from the entrance to the theater. And who knows what would happen then? They were a little ways away, though, so if I hurried, I just might make it. A quick look behind me showed three or four more back there, but they didn't seem to be gaining on me.

And thankfully, Riggs was nowhere to be seen.

Determined to get to safety, I turned forward again and nearly ran smack into one of them. It lunged at me, grabbing my sleeve and ripping it. As I twisted away, it growled deep in its throat. It wasn't a normal growl like that of a Mastiff or Neapolitan. It was angry, yes, but it also sounded almost…hungry.

It was a werewolf, after all. And that was how they sounded. And yet, something was off. Not right.

But I couldn't worry about that now. I had to get to safety.

Ragged claws swiped inches from my face. I cried out, stumbling and nearly falling to the pavement. As I scrambled up, the werewolf disappeared into the gloom. I was pretty sure it would return quickly, but I wasn't going to wait around to find out. I raced toward the doors of the theater, praying that they would be unlocked. At this time of day—or night, I reminded myself—they could very well be locked. The closer to the doors I got, though, the more I could feel the presence of the monsters and knew they were still after me.

Just a few more steps and I'd be at the door. Three, two…Skidding to a stop, I grabbed the door handle and pulled.

The door rattled but did not open. Locked. It was locked! I was screwed. I looked wildly over my shoulder, expecting one of the creatures to grab me at any second.

"Open up, dammit!" I jangled the handle, and when it didn't open, I moved to the next one. It was locked, too. I raced back the other way, past the first door, and tried the handle of the third and final entrance to the theater. When it didn't open either, I pounded on it in frustration. What was I going to do now? Turning around, I leaned against the glass and tried to see into the shadows. Where those creatures still coming for me? How soon would they get here?

"James?"

My heart stopped for a brief moment. It sounded like the voice was coming from behind me, but that would mean that one of the monsters was inside the theater. I closed my eyes tight and, just for a second, wished for it to all be over.

"James, what are you doing? Can you hear me?"

As realization struck, I smiled. I knew that voice. Of course, I did. I'd recognize it anywhere. It was as familiar to me as my own.

"James?"

With a crazy rush of relief, I threw myself at her. "Beth!"

Chapter 11

BETH

Something rapped on the glass front of the theater. Beth turned toward the sound, which seemed amplified here when she would have expected it to be muffled, what with the thickness of the shadows. The glass panes that made up the front wall of the lobby rattled again.

A dark figure shook the locked door as it looked over its shoulder at something she couldn't see.

She crept slowly toward the door and watched as whoever was out there ran from door to door, trying to get inside and away from whatever was chasing him. Finally, he pounded once, with both fists, on the last door before turning around and leaning against it.

"James?" Beth called out, cautiously walking toward him. "James, what are you doing? Can you hear me?"

Whoever it was didn't move, didn't seem to have heard her. She opened the door and poked her head out. "James?"

James turned, a goofy, lopsided grin on his face, his eyes wild. His hair, never particularly neat, was a tousled mess and his clothes were disheveled. She wondered what he had been going through, what terrors his mind was throwing at him.

He threw himself into her arms so hard it nearly knocked them both over. "Beth!" he shouted.

She'd never been so happy to see anyone in all her life.

"Come on, come on, get in here." Beth ushered James inside, leaned out and looked around before closing and locking the door. She took a last peek through the glass and then grabbed James by the hand and led him to the inside of the theater lobby, near the concession stand. She threw her arms around him and hugged him tight. "I'm so glad you're all right," she whispered.

James hugged her back, stroking her hair and whispering, "It's good to see you. What are you doing here?"

"Someone had to save your butt," she joked. "Who better than your favorite cousin?"

James pulled her gently away. "You're my only cousin."

"That's what I said." She hugged him again then let go and tucked a strand of hair behind her ear. "I thought you'd probably come here."

"Yeah, this was the first place I thought of." He scratched his cheek nervously. "It's weird."

"What?" She picked a tiny piece of toilet paper off his jaw and flicked it onto the floor. "Cut yourself shaving again?"

James ignored her. "It's like…like this was the only place I could find. Everything was so dark. All the way here, I never saw anything else. No buildings, nothing." He looked at her, his eyebrows furrowed. "Like I was supposed to come here."

"How could that be?" She shook her head. "It probably just seemed like it, 'cuz you were so scared."

"Yeah, maybe." James pointed toward the darkness. "Any idea what's going on out there?"

Beth shook her head. "Whatever it is, I think maybe we'd better stay here. At least till the sun comes out."

"If it ever does."

"What does that mean? You think it's going to be dark from now on?" She shuddered visibly. She wasn't afraid of the dark. At least, she never had been before. But with those things out there, she might have to rethink it. "That would suck."

"Yeah, it would." He sighed. "But I think we're safe in here. For now, anyway."

Beth wondered how true that was. It felt safe, but who really knew? She supposed they wouldn't really know for sure until they figured out just what those things out there were. And how to get rid of them, if they even could. "Maybe. Any idea what's happening?"

"Not a clue. You're the only other person I've seen since I woke up this morning." He scratched his head. "Well, talked to, anyway. Or maybe it was tonight. I'm not sure any more."

She stuck her hands in her hoodie pockets and turned to look outside. Those things, whatever they were, seemed to be patrolling the parking lot. It was so dark it was hard to make anything out. Except for their glowing red eyes. What were those things? Where did they come from?

"Beth."

She turned back to James. "What?"

"I said, do you think it's happening all over? Or just here, in Wolf Creek?"

She shrugged and wondered how much about what she did know she should share with him. Keeping secrets from him had never been easy for her, but this was different. "I don't have any idea. All I know for sure is that

Uncle Robbie called me and told me that I had to find you. That you were the only person who could fix this." She swallowed the lie, figuring that it was too soon to tell James what was really going on.

"Wait. Why would Dad call you?"

"Well, I could barely make out what he was saying because there was a lot of static on the line, but I guess Aunt Annette tried calling you and couldn't get through, so they called me instead. Mom couldn't take off work, but she sent me out here right away." Only a half-lie this time.

"Yeah, Mom called, but she couldn't hear me." He frowned again. "But you live in Colorado now. Why call you?"

"How the hell should I know?" She did know, actually, but that was one of the things she couldn't tell him. Not yet, anyway. "I'm hungry. You hungry?" Without waiting for an answer, she walked behind the concession counter and rummaged through the candy. Pulling out a bag of butter toffee peanuts, she ripped it open with her teeth and popped a few into her mouth. "Remember when we went to see *Bubba Ho-tep* that time—" She spat out the nuts and wiped her mouth with the back of her hand. "Ew, gross."

"What's the matter?"

She tossed the bag into the trash under the register. "They taste like sawdust." She plucked a bit of the toffee coating off her tongue and flicked it onto the floor.

"Do you…" His voice squeaked a little, and he cleared his throat. "Do you think we're…dead?"

"Why? Because of some yucky peanuts?"

"Try another bag."

"I don't want to."

"Why not?" He grinned that lopsided smile of his. "Chicken?"

"Gah!" She feigned annoyance. "Fine." Opening a second bag, she pulled out a single nut and tentatively took a bite. And promptly spit it out.

"Try something else."

"You try something else."

"Okay, hand me some moth balls."

She giggled. "Malted milk, you goofball." She handed him a box. "Not moth."

"Yeah, that's what I said." He ripped open the box and popped one into his mouth. And quickly spit it out. "What the hell? What's going on?"

Beth looked out the doors. She certainly couldn't look James in the eye. "I'm not sure."

He walked across the lobby to stand in front of the glass. "I had this weird thought earlier."

She went to stand next to him. A heavy feeling had come over her, making her more tired than she'd ever felt. She stared out at the parking lot but didn't really see anything. "What was that?"

"I was thinking that it almost felt like…" He shook his head. "No, forget it."

"Tell me."

He sighed heavily and looked at her like he was trying to decide if he could trust her. Or maybe she was just feeling guilty and projecting that onto her cousin.

"It sort of felt like a movie or something, you know? Like when the hero wakes up from a nightmare to find strange creatures trying to eat him. Only it happens so much that you start to think none of it is real. Like it's a nightmare within a nightmare, you know?"

She did.

"Or better yet, the main character realizes he's gone crazy, or someone slipped him a roofie, and he's having a massive hallucination. Or maybe he's even dead." He turned to her. "You think maybe that's what's going on?

One of us is crazy, and we're in some sort of hallucination?" He paused to lick his chapped lips. "Or," he whispered. "Do you think we're…dead?" He grimaced. "You never answered me before."

She couldn't go on letting him think he might be dead. It wasn't fair. Especially since he might actually die if this whole thing didn't work out. Shaking her head, she put her hand on his arm and looked him in the eye. No lie, this time at least.

"I'm pretty sure we're not dead." She gave him her best smile. "But I've always thought you were just a little bit cuckoo." Her smile faded when she realized he didn't get the joke. Or was ignoring it.

"But if we're not dead, and this isn't a dream or hallucination, then what? There has to be some kind of logical explanation. Doesn't there?"

"Come and sit down with me." She took his hand and led him to one of the cute little café tables on the other side of the lobby. "Now listen." She sat in one of the cane-backed chairs and motioned for him to do the same. "I'm going to tell you something, and you need to listen to me. This isn't like when I told you I thought my mom was a werewolf. This isn't something I think. This is what I know, and it's the absolute truth."

He cocked his head and frowned at her as she took hold of his hands. They were cold, and she realized that time was running out.

They had to hurry, before it was too late.

Chapter 12

JAMES

You remember what happened in the meadow that day?"

Of course, I remembered. How could I forget? My teacher, the one who had helped me learn how to control the Wolf, the one I thought was my friend, had lured me to a meadow in Cailleach Canyon and tried to kill me.

The canyon had been named for a Scottish goddess who ruled the dark half of the year, brought winter and destruction with her, rode a speeding wolf, and carried a hammer made out of human flesh. Everyone who grew up in Wolf Creek knew the legend. They taught it in school. "How could I forget? But what does that have to do with anything?"

"Uncle Robbie said you have to go there, that that's where everything started, and the only way to end this is for you to go there and find the answers. You need to go now. If you can get there, you can make all this stop. You're the only one who can."

Beth gestured vaguely, and I couldn't tell if she meant this, as in those things out there, or this, as in the darkness. Or maybe she meant something else. I couldn't be sure. But whatever she meant, it was craziness.

"What do you mean, I'm the only one who can?"

She shrugged.

I couldn't help but stare at her. She just stared back. When it became obvious that not only would she win the staring contest but she wasn't going to answer my question, I got up and walked angrily away. When I got to the back of the ticket booth, I leaned my forehead on the wooden door and closed my eyes. Why was I the only one who could stop this? What did it mean?

"I don't want to go out there, Beth," I said without opening my eyes. "I'm scared." It was hard to admit it, but it is what it is. And it is scary.

"I know, James. I'm scared too. But it's the only way."

"Why? Why is it the only way?" I had a feeling she wasn't being completely honest with me, that she was hiding something. Turning to look at her, with her arms crossed tightly over her chest and her face pale, freckles standing out like spots on a Dalmatian, I could tell she was as scared as I was. All of a sudden, she looked like a little girl again. I had forgotten she's only thirteen. Even though I'm not huggy by nature, she was, so I wrapped my arms around her and squeezed.

She mumbled something into my hoodie, and I pushed her gently away. "What?"

"Nothing." After wiping her nose with the back of her finger, she sat down again, this time on top of the table, and dangled her legs in tight circles. "Look, all your dad said was that it had to be you. And you have to do it now."

I did not want to go out there with those things, especially by myself. "I don't want to go out there, Beth. I—"

My cell phone rang and startled me so badly a rush

of adrenaline flooded through me and my body heated up in an instant, as if I had a high fever. The Wolf in me wanted out, and I struggled to keep him under control. When I pulled my cell out of my pocket, Beth slapped it out of my hand, and it went crashing to the floor.

"What'd you do that for?" I stooped to pick it up and she grabbed my wrist.

"Don't answer that!"

I yanked my hand away. "What's your problem? What if it's my mom again? Or my dad?"

"It's not, James. Trust me. It's not them. Just go. You've got to get to the meadow as soon as possible so you can stop this. Seriously."

Picking up the phone, I stood and swiped my thumb across the screen to answer it, but it stayed black. There was a small crack in the corner. "Oh, that's just great." I threw my hands up in the air. "Thanks a lot. You broke it."

I thought I caught a tiny smile flashing across her face before she turned and walked away. I swiped the screen again, harder, and this time the display came on. "Ha, ha. Still works."

She shook her head at me but said nothing. Just sighed loudly and chewed on her thumbnail.

Restricted number. If it was my parents, they weren't calling from their own phones, but that was okay so long as the connection was good and they could hear me this time. "Hello? Mom?"

That same alien static blasted in my ear again, although it wasn't as loud or echoey as before. Goosebumps rose all over my body this time, not just on my arms, and I shivered.

"You okay?" I hadn't even noticed Beth walking toward me. Weird. I nodded.

Just as I pressed the phone closer to my ear, Mom's

voice came on the line. It was faint, but it was her. Thank God. "Jaime, can you hear me this time? I really need to talk to you."

Gripping the phone tightly, I practically shouted into it. "Mom! I can't hear you. Your voice…it's all fuzzy."

"Please listen to me. Please."

"What is it, Mom? What do you need?"

The static was getting louder as her voice faded. "Sweetie, I need to talk to you. Can you…?"

"Can I what?" I was screaming by now. Why couldn't she hear me?

"Jaime…"

"Mom? Mom!"

She was gone. The static lasted another second or two, then it was gone, too. I looked at my phone, discouraged to see the screen had gone black again. "Damn." I tossed it on the nearest table and sat down heavily in one of the chairs. Beth sat across from me.

"James, listen."

"That's the second time she's called, and the second time she couldn't hear me. What's up with the phone lines? Did the darkness do something to the networks? I just…"

"Dammit, James," Beth practically shouted at me. "Will you just shut up and listen to me for a change?"

"What? What is it, Beth?"

"You have to go. Now." Looked at her watch, the Jack Skellington one my parents had given her last Christmas. "Before it's too late."

"Okay," I said, standing up so hard the chair toppled over behind me. "I've had just about enough of this. You know something, and you're going to tell me right now what it is. Or else—" I shook my fist at her.

"Seriously, 'cuz, I don't know anything but what I've already told you."

Cocking my head, I narrowed my eyes and searched her face. "Why are you lying to me?"

"I'm not!" Her voice wavered just enough so that I knew I was right. But why would she lie? Especially to me.

I grunted. "Whatever."

"James, look—"

She was cut off by another voice. This one was loud and clear and seemed to come from inside one of the internal theater rooms. I recognized it instantly, and I think she did, too.

"Dude, think of *The Purge,*" Riff said. "Remember that movie?"

How could I forget? It was the last movie we ever watched together, the day he was slaughtered. How he loved that movie.

It reminded me of him so much that I still couldn't bring myself to watch it again. It did occur to me that the voice that had spoken to me earlier, the one that had talked about the night that saved the country, had been Riff quoting a line from the movie.

I headed down the hall toward the theater that blasted Riff's voice. Beth ran after me and grabbed my arm. "Wait," she cried. "Don't go down there."

"Why not? It's Riff. He tried to Skype me before. At the house."

"Are you crazy? Riff's dead. You know that."

"I know, but still…" I continued down the hall.

"James, listen." I was walking so fast, she had to trot to keep up with me. "You can't go in there."

"Sure I can. Watch me."

"Gawd," she exclaimed. "You really are as dumb as a box of bricks, you know that?"

Gritting my teeth so as not to say something I might regret later, I quickened my pace. Now she was running.

"Stop," she pleaded. "Will you just stop for a second?"

I realized she was crying. That stopped me.

"What? Dammit, Beth, what is it?" Tired of all the unanswered questions, I took my frustration out on her. Her lower lip trembled, but I couldn't stop myself. I had to know. "Why don't you want me to go in there? What is it you don't want me to see?"

"All I know for sure is that you have to go to the meadow. You just have to. You can't let anything stop you. You can't!"

The waterworks were in full force. She knew how much I hated to see her cry, and I wondered briefly if she was putting on an act. But the tears looked real, so I smiled and punched her lightly on the arm. I didn't know what else to do.

"When you get there—" She sniffed and wiped her nose on her sleeve. "—you'll figure it out. I know you will."

"If you say so." I was just about to relent and go back to the lobby when Riff spoke again.

"Remember *The Purge*, James," he told me. "Remember Zoey."

Zoey was the one who ended up saving the day in that movie. So was Riff telling me it was up to me to save the town from this…whatever it was?

Frustration and something else, something I couldn't identify, flashed in Beth's eyes. Her lips were pulled back from her teeth, contorting her mouth in a bizarre and menacing way, and I felt bad. I really did. But it didn't matter. I had to see for myself, if only to find out if Riff's voice was real or just a figment of my imagination. "Sorry, Beth. I've just got to go check it out. It'll be okay. Be right back." I hurried away before she could try and stop me.

Riff called to me again. "James. You've got to do it."

When I reached the door to the theater, I grasped the handle and looked over my shoulder at Beth.

"Don't go in there, James. Please."

"I'll just be a sec." I pulled the door open and dashed into the cool darkness of the theater. After waiting until my eyes adjusted, I took a few hesitant steps toward the front. Light and dark flashed across my eyes as indistinct images played out on the screen.

"Riff?" I took a few more steps until I was almost to the stairs that led up to the top of the stadium seating. "Riff, where are you?"

"Remember Zoey."

"I will. But what does that have to do with what's going on now?"

There was a single step down to the seats where Beth and I had sometimes sat so we could throw popcorn at the screen. When I stepped down, I stumbled a little and reached out to steady myself on one of the seats.

As I stood, a sharp pain hit me in the chest like a brick in the face. I struggled to take several deep breaths. When the pain finally subsided, I opened my eyes and found myself right back in that fluffy white marshmallowness that had become my room.

Chapter 13

BETH

Tears streamed down Beth's cheeks, and she angrily brushed them away. It just wasn't fair, what was happening. Or that she couldn't be totally honest with James. That was the worst thing. She'd never lied to him before, not successfully, anyway.

But this was different. She had her reasons, and she just had to keep certain things to herself until the time was right.

Even if it did suck.

She followed James to the theater that he'd gone in to, but when she got to the door, she hesitated before pulling it open a crack. She listened to see if she could hear who he was talking to or what they were saying, but there was nothing but silence. Frowning, she looked over her shoulder before pulling the door all the way open and stepping cautiously into the darkness.

She ran her hand along the wall as she inched forward. When she came around the corner, she blinked at the sudden light coming from the huge movie screen.

"James?"

She took a few more steps into the theater and called

to her cousin again. "James, are you here?"

But she could tell that he was already gone by the total and complete silence that swallowed up her voice. Where did he go? What happened to him? Maybe Riff could tell her where he went.

"Riff?" Even though she didn't really like James's best friend, if he could help James figure things out, then that was okay with her. She dreaded being the one to tell James what was really going on. "Riff, are you here?"

There was no answer, and she wondered if his calling out to James had just been wishful thinking. But on who's part? She sure as heck didn't conjure him up. So it must have been James.

Considering everything that was going on lately, Beth guessed that anything was possible.

Even bringing Riff back from the dead.

Monday, February 29, 2016
Day 36

Chapter 14

JAMES

You've got to be kidding me. My stomach was as hard as one of Aunt Judy's hamburger patties. I wanted to hit something but settled for hammering my fist against my thigh. How had I gotten here? One second I'm in the movie theater, listening to Riff trying to tell me something important about how to figure things out while Beth's waiting in the lobby, convinced that…what? Something bad would happen? What could be worse than the disappearance of all humanity? Than being chased by zombie werewolves?

The next second, I'm back in my room at home. At least, I thought it was my room. But I remembered that old show from the 1990s, *Quantum Leap*, where the scientist dude leaped from one person to the next "putting right what once went wrong." The real person, the one inside the body he leaped into, was transported into some kind of cosmic waiting room. An all-white waiting room. Was that what was going on here? But if so, then where was the dude to question me and find out things to help his buddy stop someone from being killed?

Wait…was that what Riff was doing?

I shook my head. That couldn't be it. It didn't make any sense. But then again, nothing about what was happening made sense. The hijacked daylight. Riff talking to me. The strange phone calls. Beth's mysterious words and my feeling that she was hiding something. What did it all mean?

Too many questions. I needed answers. Walking out into the hall, determined to find them, I hesitated when I got to the living room. A heavy sense of déjà vu weighed me down, and I shivered a little. My mom would have said that someone had just walked over my grave, but Dad would have explained it away by telling me that the scientific explanation was that my body had released adrenaline due to my fear or stress. Ordinarily, I would have believed him, but today I had to wonder if Mom's explanation was more accurate.

That was when I realized that something was off, just like it had been before. Only this time, it wasn't the strange silence, even though it was still there. Something was off about the living room, some little something that was out of place, or gone. Different. I looked around, trying to figure it out, but I couldn't quite place it. The ugly brown couch was there. It even had the same hole that Beth had dug in it the day she told me her mother was a werewolf.

The TV was where it always was, the coffee table with several books, an empty soda can I'd forgotten to put in the recycle bin last night and the napkin I'd used as a plate for my late-night ham sandwich was in the same spot directly in front of the couch, a strip of mustard and several bread crumbs sitting mutely on top. Even the fake Tiffany floor lamp was standing sentry in its corner.

Everything was the same, but not. It was familiar, but something, some little something, wasn't quite right, as if someone had created a movie set from a picture and forgotten to add some small but important knick-knack.

It was enough to drive me crazy.

But I couldn't worry about it now. My stomach growled, and I headed to the kitchen to find something to eat, since I'd been too late for breakfast. It wasn't until I looked in the fridge that I remembered the candy at the theater had tasted like sawdust. Was that just the candy there, or was it all food? I grabbed the last of the ham from Sunday's dinner and tentatively took a bite. And spit it into my hand.

That answers that question.

After tossing out my ham bite, I turned back to the living room and froze. It finally hit me what was different. The light, or rather the lack of it, coming in through the bay window. It gave the place an eerie, grayish cast. The blackness outside seemed to press in against the glass. I wiped my suddenly dry lips with an index finger and backed into the kitchen. As long as I was inside somewhere, either the theater or my house, I'd felt safe. But the darker it got outside, the quicker that feeling of protection fled. The darkness devoured everything, from the yard to the driveway, my car, everything.

The darkness threatened to get inside. If it did, would it bring those creatures with it? As scared as I was—and I was scared shitless by this time—I had to find out so I could try and protect myself. How, I wasn't sure. Steeling myself for what I was beginning to think might be the inevitable, I crept through the living room to the window and peered out into the thick, impenetrable darkness.

It was like standing mere inches away from a solid black canvas.

But there was nothing.

Relieved, I blew out the breath I hadn't realized I'd been holding and leaned my forehead against the cool glass. *Butt munch.* That's what Riff would have called me, and I smiled at the thought. For all of his faults, that dude always knew what to say to make me laugh at myself whenever I got too serious.

Then something moved out there, somewhere deep inside the blackness. I jolted back from the window. Tendrils of fear curled around my spine. Forcing myself to examine the darkness again, I searched the yard, and things seemed to lighten just a bit. Shadows appeared again where the night had been almost solid.

Out of the corner of my eye, I could have sworn I saw movement again, but of course, when I turned to look at it full on, there was nothing. I scratched my side as I plopped down on the couch. I was getting really tired of this. Maybe Beth was right. Maybe I needed to get to the meadow as soon as I could.

Something banged against the window, and I sprang up to check it out. Two glowing red eyes stared back at me.

I was screwed.

And to prove it, the window exploded, propelling splintered shards of glass at me as the zombie werewolf lurched through it, bared teeth snapping and snarling inches from my face.

Chapter 15

BETH

Something important was happening, something with James. Beth could feel it.

Chapter 16

JAMES

I stumbled away from the creature as fast as I could. Beyond freaked out, I covered my ears as the thing let out a horrifying screech louder than a jet engine. When the back of my knee slammed into the corner of the coffee table, I let out a yelp and went down, hard, which gave the zombie thing ample opportunity to clamber through the window. As I scrambled to get out of its reach, ragged, razor-sharp claws swiped at me, and I turned away. It missed my face but caught me in the chest. At first, I felt nothing, but within seconds, burning pain seared through me as I watched the front of my hoodie quickly fill with blood. My blood.

"Oh, my God." I gingerly touched my chest. Could this really be happening? Was I going to die without ever finding out what was going on?

"Jaime, honey, can you hear me?"

I whirled around expectantly. "Mom?"

"Oh, Jaime." Faint sobs came from somewhere deep inside the house.

"Mom, where are you?"

Only her sobs answered me.

Behind me, the creature screamed as it leaped off the windowsill, climbed across the couch and rushed toward me. Shards of glass and huge wooden splinters pierced its arms and chest where it had dragged itself across the broken window frame. I couldn't worry about Mom right now. I had to get away from the monster. Looking around for some way to protect myself, I wished I'd thought about grabbing Donna's pistol, which I kept loaded with silver bullets, when I'd gotten up this morning. But it was safely locked away in a small gun box in Dad's closet. I didn't even have the key. Besides, how was I to know I'd need it? So for now, the only thing available to me was Mom's marble-topped table. A family heirloom, I hesitated a fraction of a second before grabbing it and swinging it at the thing that was trying to kill me. It connected, slamming into its shoulder. The werewolf staggered, a shocked look on its face, and I hit him a second time, this time catching the side of his head. The force sent him tumbling backward over the couch and out the window.

"Yes!" A fist pump later, I shook my head as I took in the ruined table. Hopefully, Mom would forgive me for smashing it.

The darkness seeped in through the hole in the living room wall, creeping along like thick fog. Hoping it was unconscious—or dead—I looked outside, but that thing had disappeared like Michael Myers. I figured it would only be a matter of time before it, or one of its friends, came after me again.

Suddenly, I felt a little woozy. My knees nearly buckled. Touching the hole in my chest, I grimaced when I pulled my hand away. Expecting to see blood, it was all I could do to keep from fainting at the sight of the black goo that drenched my hand.

"Dafuq?" I whispered. But that was as far as I got because the patio slider in the back of the house exploded. A half dozen of those things shuffled in, their eyes glowing, fangs dripping. Their growls sounded like a chorus of angry lawnmowers. Darkness crept in behind them like smoke from that out-of-control, thirty-thousand acre Freeway Complex fire years ago. Over twenty-two thousand people had been evacuated, including me and my family, and it was something I'll never forget. I was only seven or eight, and it had freaked me out. But if I thought I'd been scared then, it was nothing compared to what I felt now. The terror was nearly crippling and rooted me in place. But then there was a loud thundering boom and the front door splintered open. Another one of the creatures had crashed through and was ripping the door apart in its effort to get inside the house.

To get me.

How was I going to get away? And where was my mom?

"Mom?" I screamed. "Mom, where are you?"

But there was no answer.

Taking the time to search for her now was dangerous, and the only thing I could think to do was run to the bathroom. It was the only room in the house with a lock on the door. But it wouldn't keep me safe for very long, and the only way out would be through a small window above the toilet. And that meant I'd have to go outside. How many more of those things were out there, waiting for me?

I'd have to worry about that later. Out of options, I limped quickly down the hall, just out of reach of the werewolves who'd broken in through the slider. I could feel their hot breath on my face as I brushed past them, flattening myself against the wall as far away from their reach as I could get. It wasn't far enough, though, and one of them managed to rake its ragged claws across my cheek. My flesh burned and I cried out as a numbing darkness flooded my mind. What little strength I had left quickly drained away, and I nearly crumpled to the floor. Stumbling along, I finally reached the bathroom and lunged inside, scrambled to get the door shut, and locked it.

The creatures were right behind me. Their claws clanked against the door, softly at first, then with more force. They tried the doorknob, rattling it back and forth. They must have realized it was locked because they began pounding furiously on it, and I wondered how long it would be before they broke through. Sinking to the floor, I looked around for something to defend myself with. Nothing. There was nothing in here that would save me.

Would it really be so bad, letting them take me? I was so tired, exhausted beyond ever before. Nausea roiled my stomach, and I thought I might puke. "At least, if they kill you," I mumbled as I lay down on the cold linoleum, "this whole messed up day will end. Maybe you'll even find the answers to what's going on."

I snorted. "Yeah. Right."

I lay there, listening to those things scratching on the bathroom door, and felt myself fade away. Just couldn't fight the darkness that filled me with some sort of black poison any longer. My eyes must have rolled back in my head because my sight was nearly gone as I started to lose consciousness. This was it. I was going to die.

"Dude, pull yourself together."

Startled, I looked around as the bathroom came into focus again. "What? Who's that?"

"It hasn't been that long, has it? You've already forgotten me?"

I shook my head and pulled myself up to lean back on my elbows. "Riff? That you?"

"You were expecting Freddy Krueger, maybe?"

"Where are you?" I looked around but except for me,

the bathroom was empty. I glanced nervously at the door, which actually shuddered as the creatures continued their pounding.

"Up here."

"Where?" The pounding stopped, and for a moment, I thought it was over. Until the scratching started. They were trying to dig their way through. It wouldn't be long now. Wood slivers dotted the linoleum in front of the door where their hammering had weakened it.

"Here. Geez, do I have to do everything for you?"

I looked up and saw Riff glaring at me from the mirrored door of the medicine cabinet. Sitting up more, I leaned against the wall. "What are you doing in there?" Every time the zombie werewolves scratched on the door, the wall vibrated. I glanced at the door and licked my lips before turning back to Riff.

"No time for that now. You have to fight it, James. Don't give in to the darkness."

The creatures were snarling now, growling and shrieking as their digging grew more insistent.

"But I'm so tired. I—I don't think I can fight any more."

"What are you, a girl? Or just chicken shit?"

"Give me a break, Riff. You don't know what it's like."

"Don't you get it? There's no time for your self-pity." Riff's voice rose until he was practically screaming. "Now get up off your ass and *fight it*."

My blood heated up like it did when I transformed, and I smiled as strength surged though me. I scrambled to my feet, swayed a little, then stood straight. I flexed my fists, feeling stronger than ever.

I could do this.

"That's right. It has to be you. You have to do it," Riff encouraged me. "Remember Zoey. Remember…"

His voice faded away. When I looked in the mirror, his face was gone as well.

Several ragged claws plowed through the door and back again, and were immediately replaced by the head of one of the creatures in a Jack Nicholson "Here's Johnny" moment. I grabbed Mom's heavy make-up mirror off the vanity and slammed it into the face glowering at me. The creature screeched in pain and rage but backed out of the door. Another one appeared seconds later.

There was nothing else to do but try to make it out the window. It wasn't very big, and while I was pretty sure Beth could make it through no problem, I wasn't so sure I could. But I had to try. It was the only way.

Using my foot to close the lid, I climbed up on the toilet seat. But when I tried to open the window, it was stuck. Behind me, the creatures had torn more of the door apart and they would be through it any second. Sweat poured down my temples and into my eyes. I wiped it away as best I could. Kneeling on the top of the tank, I pushed at the window with all my might. At first, nothing, but then it opened so suddenly that I nearly fell through it. After catching myself, I removed the screen and tossed it out into the darkness, threw one leg out the window and looked back just as the first zombie werewolf broke all the way through. Wood shards went everywhere. I swung back and hurled myself out the window, but unfortunately, I wasn't fast enough.

One of those damn things grabbed me around the knee, raking its claws down my leg before taking hold in a vicious death grip and pulling me out of the window. I tumbled backward, hitting my head on the toilet seat and nearly knocking myself out. It was all over. There was nothing else I could do to keep myself out of the putrid mouth of death.

Chapter 17

I found myself not in the jaws of death, but back in my solid white room again, surrounded by that infuriating marshmallowy thickness. I rubbed my head and looked around. Everything appeared normal, or as normal as it could be inside a Mallomar. Books were piled high on my desk, papers scattered all around, bed unmade. Just as I'd left things…was it only this morning? It seemed like forever ago. Even my laptop was where I'd left it, open and on.

But wasn't that always how things appeared in *The Twilight Zone*? Because that's where it felt like I was. "Not complaining." I sat on the edge of my bed. "At least those things didn't follow me."

Not sure exactly what I should do, I just sat there. Maybe I should try to call my folks again. I reached into my pocket, but my cell was gone. Checking each pocket, I frowned when I realized that I must have left it on the table at the theater. Damn.

My ankle itched, so I pulled up the leg of my jeans and scratched it. There was a slight red mark, more like the very beginning of a bruise than a scratch, but other than that, there was no sign that the zombie werewolf's claws had shredded my skin. One more tic on the *Twi-*

light Zone tally. Not that I minded. Those claws had burned, and the pain was intense. I was glad it was gone.

Maybe I could try to Skype someone. When was the last time I charged the battery on my laptop? I couldn't remember. All I could do was try to make a call and hope there was enough juice for it to go through, since there didn't seem to be any power. But who to call? My parents? Beth? Shaniqua? The way Beth had acted at the theater kept nagging at me. She was hiding something from me. I knew it. I could totally tell. But what? What could she possibly know about what was going on?

I shrugged. It was worth a try. Pulling my laptop onto the bed next to me, I pushed the button to take it out of hibernation. It took so long I was worried the battery had died, but it finally popped on.

"Oh, good. There." Now if I could just remember Beth's phone number. She was number four on my speed dial so I never actually dialed her number, and it had been months since I'd input it into my contacts, but after a little bit, I was able to recall it. I was just about to log on to Skype when the screen went black.

"Oh, that's just great." I blew out a huge breath. My battery had died after all. Angrily pushing my laptop away, I got up and paced. When I got to the closet, I kicked it, hard, turned around and walked to the other side of the room. Kicked the wall. A flash of a memory made me smile, in spite of everything. Donna Glass in the lobby of the hospital where Beth lay unconscious after the werewolf attacked us the first time. But the smile quickly dissolved from the seriousness of this situation. I sighed. "Now what do I do?"

"I'll tell you what you do."

Whirling around so fast I almost lost my balance, I looked for the source of the voice. It was vaguely familiar, but I couldn't quite place it, and I was getting really tired of all these voices chatting me up. "Who said that?"

"I did. Over here."

"Where?"

"Here. In your computer." The black screen of my laptop had been replaced with a flickering whiteness. It was just as bright and clean as the weird whiteness of my room, and I wondered if whoever was speaking was also responsible for it. But at this point, I was just happy someone else could hear me, even if I couldn't tell who it was. It made me feel a little less alone.

I sat down on the bed and started to pull the laptop to me but at the last second, I sprang up without touching it. Warning bells went off in my brain. "Who are you?"

The screen flickered a final time and settled into a solid white. There was a very faint spot in the lower right corner that grew larger as I watched. "You can call me…D. R."

"D. R.?"

"That's right."

"What does that stand for?" The spot wavered and fluttered, as if it were in water, growing and diminishing like that stuff in the Lava Lamps from the seventies.

"Just D. R. Now, look, kid, you need to listen to me."

"Why?" I crossed my arms over my chest. The hole the first creature had dug there was gone, and I wondered again how any of this was possible. "Why should I trust you?"

"Don't worry, I'm your friend." The voice was calm, and in spite of my initial mistrust, I was somewhat reassured. "Everything's going to be okay, if you just do what I say."

A faint rustling came from somewhere outside my room, and I glanced at the door.

"Don't worry, James. The monstrosities are gone."

"Is that what those things are called? Monstrosities?"

"For all intents and purposes, yes."

"What exactly are they?"

"Worry about that later. There's no time for it now." The shape-shifting spot on the screen seemed to be taking on the form of a silhouette of some kind. It was mesmerizing, and I couldn't seem to take my eyes off it.

"James."

"Hmm?" Try as hard as I might, I couldn't stop staring at the screen.

"James!" The voice became insistent, and I blinked and shook my head to clear it. "I'm your friend. I'm here to help you."

"Help me? How?"

"Those things out there? The monstrosities?"

I nodded.

"They're gone because of me, you know." The image on the screen, the almost-silhouette, wavered before coming into focus. Its darkness appeared in sharp relief against the white of the screen. There was something about the shape of the face…

"They are? How'd you do it?"

"Suffice it to say I did. If you don't believe me, go ahead and check. I'll wait." The image dimmed and became a blurry blob again. Hesitantly, I walked to the door and put my ear against it, listening for any sound on the other side. Nothing. I glanced at the screen, where the blob danced slowly back and forth. I grasped the doorknob but couldn't bring myself to open the door.

"Go on, James," the blob said. "Trust me. They're gone."

Get a grip. I rubbed the corner of my eye, took a deep breath, and turned the knob, but before I opened the door, I looked over my shoulder again. The blob bounced slowly around the screen. My stomach felt heavy and empty at the same time, as if there was a flock of hummingbirds flying around in there. *Why would he lie?* I didn't know, but this whole thing made me uneasy.

Taking a deep breath, I cracked open the door and peeked out. Nothing moved. The hall appeared empty. At least as far as I could tell. The darkness had crept in like a ninja, and it was hard to see further than about ten feet. It wouldn't be long before it would be everywhere.

"See?" D. R. said. "Told you, you could trust me."

"Yeah." I rubbed the back of my neck. "I guess so." Not only did I not see anything, there was no sound, either. It was like the darkness had swallowed it. I pulled my head back inside and glanced at my laptop. The blob had coalesced into a humanistic form. At least the head and shoulders of one. Squinting, I tried to get a clearer look but as soon as D. R. realized I was looking at him, the figure broke apart into several globules that bounced around the screen. For some reason, a shiver ran through me that was hard to ignore. "It seems like they're gone." I poked my head out the door again to check. "I don't see or hear them anymore." Even if things didn't feel right.

"That's right, you don't, because I sent them away."

"How are you able to control those things?"

"I just can. But not forever. They'll be back soon."

I had to make a decision. While I didn't trust him completely, I knew I couldn't afford to distrust him entirely. I needed help, and he was the only one who seemed to be able to do that. At least, that's what he claimed. So I sucked it up and tried my best to ignore my gut instinct.

"Yeah, but how? How did you make them go away?" I took another look down the hall before closing the door.

"That's not important right now."

"But it is! It's important to me."

"I know it is. But we don't always get the answers we want."

"Well, if you won't tell me that, then can you at least tell me what they want? Or how they got here in the first place?"

"Answers are very important to you, aren't they? But sometimes, we just don't get them. Why did Riff have to die? Or Donna? Why didn't Shaniqua's parents understand what she was going through and support her instead of shipping her off to Wolf Creek? Life is full of mysteries, kid, and most of the time, we never solve them." The shapes on the screen continued their slow boogie from side to side and top to bottom.

I forced myself to look away. My eyes wandered around the room, finally lighting on the picture Shaniqua had insisted on having taken at MORP. Dressed in one of my dad's Hawaiian shirts, I remembered feeling like a dork, but I had to admit, Shaniqua looked awesome in her brightly-colored wrap-around thing, and I was glad we'd had a professional picture made. It sure beat the slightly out-of-focus selfies we'd taken.

I turned back to the dude on the laptop, and couldn't help but wonder if he was trying to confuse me. I had enough questions buzzing through my brain without him adding more. "What does any of that have to do with me? Or with what's going on now?"

"If you want to figure all this out, then you have to do what Beth told you to do."

"What Beth...what do you mean, what she told me to do?"

"You know what I mean."

"She said I had to go to the meadow, that I would be able to end this...this whatever it is...if I went there. Is that what you mean?"

"Yes."

"But what am I supposed to do once I get there?"

D. R. didn't answer me. This whole thing was so

confusing. My mind raced through the possibilities: thrown back in time, I would lose the battle with Mr. Hansen and die, but the world would be saved; Mr. Hansen didn't actually die, but had somehow survived and become one of those things, leading the others to my home with the intention of killing me; Shaniqua followed me to the meadow but was killed somehow—even though I couldn't figure out how that would cause these zombie werewolves to appear; or, the one I thought most likely, Mr. Hansen went to hell after I killed his werewolf form and somehow summoned the monstrosities to do his bidding. It seemed a little extreme and far-fetched, but then, this whole thing was hardly normal.

The silence was pissing me off. "Are you going to help me or not?"

"James, you'll have to find the answers yourself. In the meadow."

"But *how*?"

"By facing your fears. I'm not going to lie to you, it won't be easy. It never is. No one can tell you certain truths. You have to discover them, and grasp them, yourself. In your mind. Then once you do that, you have to take those truths into your heart and accept them. Make them your own. Only then will you find the answers you crave. Do you understand what I'm telling you?"

It made sense, so I nodded. "Yeah, I guess so." I snuck a peek at the screen and saw that same almost-familiar figure and looked quickly away. The dude seriously creeped me out, and the truth was, I didn't want to get a good look at D. R., whoever he was. "So what do you want me to do? And will I have to fight more of those things?"

"Go to the meadow. You'll find the Le Mans outside where you parked her. But you have to hurry. I can't keep those things at bay much longer."

"Can you at least tell me one more thing?"

D. R. didn't answer, so I continued. "My mom and dad. Are they safe? Are they okay?"

"You'll find all your answers at the meadow. But you have to hurry."

I licked my lips and dried them on the back of my hand. Cracked open the door again and took a last look. All clear. At least it seemed like it. Turning back to D. R. without actually looking at the laptop, I asked, "If I go out there, I'll be safe? They're really gone? Not hiding in the living room or kitchen just waiting for me? I'll be able to get to the Le Mans and then drive to the meadow with no problem?"

"They're gone, James. Trust me. You'll be safe as long as you don't take any detours."

I still didn't trust him, but what choice did I have?

"Go now, James. Time is running out. For all of us."

There was something wrong with what he was telling me. He was just a little too urgent, a little too pushy. Why wouldn't he tell me who he really was? How was he able to control the monstrosities? And most importantly, why did he scare me?

But I couldn't fight the monstrosities off forever. Not by myself.

And he was basically telling me the same thing Beth did, that I had to go to the meadow. Even though I still felt she was hiding something, she wouldn't be in cahoots with D. R. She couldn't be.

So that pretty much made up my mind for me. I would go outside, hop in the Le Mans, and drive to the meadow as quickly as I could. I rested my hand on the doorknob and took a deep breath.

"That's right," the voice said. "Go. Quickly now. You wouldn't want to disappoint your family, would you?"

That seemed like an odd thing to say, and it made me even more uneasy, but there was nothing I could do about it now. I turned the knob and stepped out into the hall.

 espes

Shadows filled the darkened hall, but otherwise, it was empty. Or so it seemed. I hesitated at the door, glancing back into my room. Maybe for reassurance, I don't know. The blob on the screen floated along, silently urging me forward. I inhaled deeply and took a step toward the living room, then stood and listened to the silence. When I felt safely alone, I put my apprehension aside and walked swiftly down the hall.

I almost made it to the living room when I caught a glimpse of two fiery red spots glowing deep in the shadows. Then two more appeared, and two more. Before I knew it, the entire room was filled with the blazing eyes of those vile monstrosities, all hungry for my flesh.

LIAR! My mind whirled as I realized that the voice in the computer had surely lured me to my death. He'd lied to me after all. I looked frantically around, but those creatures were everywhere, their jaws filled with razor-sharp incisors chomping and snapping at me, trying to rip my face off. There was no escape.

I supposed I'd known all along, somewhere in the deepest recesses of my mind, that the voice in the computer had been lying to me. It's just that I so wanted to believe him, that he was there to help me, and that everything would turn out okay. But it wasn't okay.

This time, I was going to die.

The zombie werewolves rushed me, slicing their jagged claws across my chest, my arms, my legs. I fought them off as best as I could, but it was hopeless. Maybe it was for the best, if it meant I didn't have to save the world by myself or live in a world full of these things. Maybe I'd even get to see Riff again, for real this time, and not on a movie screen or in a bathroom mirror.

I was overrun by the monstrosities as they swarmed me, teeth ripping chunks of my flesh from my body, their claws shredding the flesh that remained.

"Mom! Mom," I screamed. I was really going to miss her.

The last thing I remember was hearing laughter.

Chapter 18

BETH

She didn't really think she could bring Riff, or any-one else, back from the dead. But maybe she could call on her dead friends to help out.

In the time since Timmy had appeared to her in the school bathroom, Beth had thought a lot about what she'd meant when she'd told Beth she needed to remember. Could it have been something that Daddy had told her? Or something Jazz said?

She felt sure that it had something to do with what was going on now, something that could help James. It was right there, if she could just grab it out of her memory.

Beth was so deep in thought that she didn't notice when a shadow fell over her as she slumped onto a chair at one of the theater's café tables.

"I can help you, if you want."

Startled, Beth jumped at the voice. She looked up at Timmy. "I wish you'd stop doing that. You scared me."

Timmy giggled. "Sorry. But I can, you know."

"Can what?"

"Help you, silly." Timmy tried to act all nonchalant,

polishing her fingernails on her shirt and then inspecting them, but all she really managed to do was look like she was playing grown-up. Which Beth figured she was.

"Help me what?"

"Help you help your cousin. That's what you wanna do, isn't it?"

"Sure!" Beth jumped up from her chair. "How?"

"Well, first you have to make him go to the meadow." Timmy looked at her for so long that it made Beth ill at ease. "I mean *really* make him. It's important."

"But why?" Beth somehow already knew that, but Timmy's urgings made her uncomfortable. Did the little ghost girl know something about James, about what really happened to him? If so, why was she being so mysterious about it? "Why is it so important to you?"

Timmy shrugged, running the toe of her sneaker along the floor. "Just is." She took a deep breath and looked up at Beth. "So do you want me to help you or not?"

"Of course." Whatever Timmy was hiding, Beth couldn't worry about it now. The most important thing right now was helping James.

"Okay, then." Timmy pulled a chair over next to Beth. "Do you have your tablet with you?"

"Yeah." Beth dug into her tote bag and pulled it out. "Here."

Timmy nodded. "Nice." She waved her hand at Beth. "Just put it on the table." Timmy sat on her knees and leaned over the table. "Okay, here we go. Watch."

Beth watched, amazed, as her ghost friend wiggled her fingers over the tablet. Images seemed to appear out of nowhere, flitting across the tablet's screen almost faster than she could see them.

In just a few moments, Timmy sat back and grinned at her. "Done."

The next thing Beth knew, she was standing outside James's house, near the end of the driveway. James was chasing after one of those zombie werewolf things. She thought he was calling her Shaniqua. Wasn't that his girl-friend's name?

Weird.

Saturday, March 5, 2016
Day 41

Chapter 19

JAMES

I didn't know which was worse, the pain or the fear. But when I opened my eyes, I was back in my bedroom again.

"Son of a bitch." I shook my head in disbelief. Would this nightmare ever end? But at least those things were gone. For now, anyway. How much longer was I going to be subjected to the creature-filled darkness, only to be thrown back into the relatively safe but just as confusing nearly blinding whiteness that had become my room? I felt like I was on some sort of bizarre teeter-totter. Up, I'm in my room. Down, thrown into the shadowy darkness. And back up again. Safe and sound? I wondered.

"Well, at least I can rest up a bit." I climbed onto my bed and curled up. I just wanted to sleep for a while. Like a week. I was so tired, and my chest hurt. I pulled up my shirt and wasn't really surprised to see that I was in one piece. The monstrosities had shredded me, flayed my flesh, and pulled it off my body, but that was in the darkness. Here in the light, I was whole again. But that didn't explain why my chest throbbed.

As I drifted off, a feeling of peace settled over me like a blanket. Was this the end? If so, it was okay with me. I could just float away. If I was lucky, maybe I'd be with Riff again. Even Uncle Fred. Donna. If not, I might just end up with Boy-o, one of the dudes that Mr. Hansen had killed in his lame attempt to frame me. And if I was really unlucky, I'd spend eternity with Logan, my tormentor since third grade.

And there went my mood. Serenity was replaced by confusion and a touch of anxiety. A faint noise in the background slowly filled my senses. Steady. Slightly shrill. As it became a little more distinct, I realized it was some sort of beeping.

It sounded almost like…*my phone*. Whatever it had started out as, it had become my cell phone's ringtone. Apparently, I hadn't left it at the theater, after all. I rolled over onto my back and sighed. How I had wanted to go to sleep, to dream about something nice, like flying kites with Riff, or chowing down on one of PJ's awesome pastrami sandwiches. Or Shaniqua's kisses.

If I answered it, would I be plunged right back into the darkness? And would those things be waiting for me? The one thing I knew for sure was that whoever it was that had spoken to me from my laptop had lied to me. I couldn't tell if he could control those things or not, because he might have made them wait in the living room for me, but he had assured me that I would be safe out there. So whether or not he could control the zombie werewolves didn't really matter, did it?

My phone continued to ring. I broke into a cold sweat, and my stomach threatened to spew. This whole thing was so bizarre. I just wanted to be left alone, and it was a pretty sure thing that if I answered the phone, it would never happen.

But then I thought about all the people I loved: Mom,

Dad, Beth. Shaniqua. Even Aunt Judy. What had happened to them? Beth had appeared briefly, but that time in the theater was beginning to seem more like a dream that was already fading into a haze. But what about my parents? Where were they? If I answered the phone, would whoever was on the other end be able to give me the answers I needed?

So many questions and no answers. It made me want to pull the covers over my head like I did when I was five and just hide from everything. Let someone else be the hero.

I shook my head vigorously. No, I couldn't risk it. I had to find out what was going on.

Sighing heavily, I grabbed my phone off the nightstand. Not surprisingly, the display showed what seemed like the same unknown number that I'd gotten that very first call from, the one that had launched this whole nightmare. Without even answering it, I knew what I'd hear—that strange static from before, the one that sounded like spiked-golf-shoe-wearing aliens were shuffling across rough granite. Summoning all my willpower to keep from hurling my cell against the wall, I slid my thumb across the screen to activate it and put the phone up to my ear.

"Hello?" This time, the screeching static wasn't quite so loud, but it still echoed. Underneath it, there was the faint sound of a voice. "Hello? Are you there?"

"James, you have to..." The familiar voice trailed off.

"I have to what?" It's funny how you end up yelling when you can't hear the other person. I stood and ran my fingers through my hair, ignoring the tangles. "What?"

"I'll be waiting," the voice continued just barely loud enough for me to hear.

"Where? Where are you? *Who* are you?"

"Hurry, James…" The static stopped abruptly.

I checked the screen. *Call dropped.* Now, what was I supposed to do? Whoever it was, was apparently waiting for me. But where? And who? Was it someone I could trust, or just another liar set on tricking me into leaving the relative safety of my room and being mauled by the monstrosities again? I didn't want to go outside, but I couldn't stay here forever. At some point, I'd need food. Water. I'd need to go to the bathroom.

"No time like the present, right Dad?" At least, that's what he always said. Says. Because he wasn't gone. He couldn't be. He was just…missing. Like everyone else in the world. Crossing to my desk, I grabbed my backpack, which I thought I'd left in the living room earlier when I first got up. Maybe since I kept being zapped back to my room, everything reset, like in that old Bill Murray movie *Groundhog's Day.* That movie always cracked me up. Only now, it didn't seem so funny. I dumped everything out of my pack and replaced them with a spiral notebook and pen, my flashlight, some fresh batteries and an old granola bar I found in the back of my desk drawer. Probably tasted like sawdust, like everything else, but just in case it didn't, I figured it couldn't hurt. After grabbing my car keys on the off chance my car would be parked in the driveway, which would definitely make life a little easier, I started for the door, then turned and on impulse, picked up the MORP picture and added it before zipping my backpack up and slinging it over my shoulder.

Pausing only briefly, I turned the knob and stuck my head cautiously out the door. Looked up and down. The darkness seemed lighter somehow, with fewer shadows and dark spots. I could see all the way to the bay window in the living room. It seemed strange, but at least the way was clear.

For now, anyway.

I crept down the hall, my back flat against the wall, nervously trying to watch both ends as I headed toward the living room. I didn't know where I was going, only that I needed to get there as soon as I could. Should I head to the meadow, like Beth said? She might not have been completely honest with me, but she would never knowingly send me somewhere where I could be hurt. That much I knew for sure.

When I got to the living room, I wasn't really surprised to see that the window was whole again. There were no glass shards littering the floor or wooden splinters hanging from the window frame. Mom's marble-topped table was in one piece. Like I said, the world seemed to have reset.

I sidled up to the window and peeked outside. It no longer had that sinister appearance. It seemed like a normal night. No deep shadows, no glowing red eyes, no drooling, snarling jaws.

I could see the front yard, the end of the driveway with Dad's Honda and my Le Mans sitting quietly side by side, even the Baker's mailbox across the street.

While appearances could be deceiving—the man in my laptop had *seemed* to want to help me—it looked safe. Since I really didn't have much choice, I sucked it up, went outside, and walked slowly down the driveway.

That's when I saw the first shadow, way down the street. No big surprise, but I knew it meant I didn't have much time.

The darkness would move in quickly and bring with it those zombie werewolf things.

I had to hurry. But where? Pulling my keys out of my pocket, I jogged over to my car and promptly dropped them. I bent over to pick them up and, as I reached for them, a shadow darkened the air around me. I froze.

"Oh, shit," I mumbled then forced my trembling

hand to snatch the keys and clutch them as tightly as possible in my fist.

I turned my head slowly and looked up, expecting to see those horrible red eyes. Instead, the most unusual green eyes were looking at me from a face surrounded by a tangle of reddish-brown curls that framed it like a nimbus.

"Shaniqua!" I stood and grabbed her hands, which were cold. "What…how…"

"James." Her voice was eerily quiet, without emotion. A spark of memory raced through my mind. What was it? "James." She pulled her hands away and turned around, walking so slowly down the driveway that she seemed to be floating, like some sort of ghost.

"Shaniqua, wait!" I ran after her, but as slowly as she was moving, she disappeared into the darkness before I could catch up. As soon as I realized that the darkness had advanced and was now almost to the driveway, I stopped, uncertain what to do next.

"Never mind her, doofus." I whirled around at the voice behind me. "We have work to do if you're going to figure this whole thing out."

"Beth! Where'd you come from?" I threw my arms around her and hugged her tight. "Never mind, I'm just glad to see you."

"Yeah, yeah, all right." She pushed me roughly away but not before I saw the grin on her face. It really was good to see her. Maybe now, between the two of us, we could figure out what was going on and fix it.

"Come on." I looked over my shoulder, half expecting a nasty horde to be crashing toward us. "Let's get inside." At least we could pretend we were safe there. For a little while, anyway. When she threw her arm over my shoulder, I realized how much she'd grown in the past two years. She'd gone from a little girl with Wendy's

Hamburger Girl braids to a bit of a hottie, with long golden chestnut hair and even longer legs. She still had the little girl connect-the-dot freckles smattered across her nose, though, and that made me smile for the first time in a long while as I wrapped my arm around her waist and steered her inside.

Before closing the door, I paused long enough to glance around the yard. The shadows were thickening, and that heavy darkness, the one that was almost alive, was creeping up the driveway. Something lurked deep inside it, lingering until it reached the house. To do what, I didn't want to wait around to find out.

Whatever it was, it wouldn't be long now.

I shut the door a little harder than I meant to and followed Beth down the hall and into the kitchen, where we sat at the table. We each dropped our school bags onto the floor beside us.

"Remember all the tea the 'rents drank, sitting here like everything was normal when they knew it wasn't?" Beth curled the edge of the placemat in front of her between her fingers. She sounded angry.

"Yeah, when my mom made it, it was blueberry, but when your mom did, it was that nasty Earl Grey stuff. Blech." I studied her face, which seemed devoid of emotion. At the very least, it didn't match the tone of her voice. I cocked my head. "What's going on, Beth?"

"How come you didn't go to the meadow?" She looked at me, her eyes shining with something I couldn't identify. "I told you to go to the meadow."

I reached across the table and put my hand on hers. She tried to pull away, but I tightened my grip. "Why, Beth? What do you know about what's going on here?"

She looked up, and her eyes burned into me. "I want you to think, hard, before you answer me. What's the last thing you remember? Before all this, I mean."

I did as she said, and thought back to this morning. Had it really been this morning? It seemed so long ago that I'd woken up late and rushed to get ready for school, only to find everything was wonky with the world. But what happened before that? I struggled to remember, searching my memory for something, anything that would tell me.

"I…I'm not sure. It's all fuzzy."

"Think," she urged. "Hard."

I narrowed my eyes and tapped my thumb on the edge of the table. "I am."

"I know." She flashed a weak smile. "I'm sorry."

"It's okay." I rubbed my face vigorously with both hands. "I remember getting ready for school and walking in here expecting Mom to be making breakfast and Dad to be drinking his coffee. But the house was empty, and it looked like it was nighttime outside."

"Okay, good. Now, what about before that?"

I shook my head. "Nothing. I just can't seem to…Wait!" I stood up so quickly, my chair toppled over. I ignored it and started to pace. "The last thing I remember is being in the meadow. With Mr. Hansen. But how can that be?" I leaned against the counter, crossed my ankles, and scratched my cheek. "I feel like that was months ago."

Beth shook her head slightly. "It was."

"What?" I charged across the room and leaned on the table across from her. "What do you mean?"

Chapter 20

Beth didn't know how to tell James what had happened that night in the meadow. He obviously had no idea. It was going to be harder for him to hear than when his parents told him about their heritage—that they were, in fact, werewolves.

"Settle down." He was leaning so far over the table that his face was mere inches from hers. "I'll tell you what you need to know as long as you stop spitting on me." She wiped her face and grinned at him, hoping to lighten the mood, but he wasn't having any of it.

"Fine." He picked up his overturned chair, sat down with a thump, and crossed his arms tightly across his chest. "Spill it, little girlie."

She pretended to be angry by flaring her nostrils and frowning deeply at him. "Girlie? Really?"

His mouth twitched on one side, and she could tell he was trying not to laugh. "You heard me."

She smiled back at him. His shoulders loosened a little, and his jaw unclenched. He almost seemed like the old James again. Hopefully, what she was about to tell him wouldn't change that.

She took a deep breath and dove right in. "I suppose I should start at the beginning."

"You think?"

"Okay. Here goes. The last thing you remember before waking up late for school this morning is being in the meadow, right?"

James nodded.

"Do you remember what happened there?"

"Yeah." James leaned his elbows on the table and shrugged. "Mr. Hansen lured me there. Put a note in my locker, told me to meet him. Then he transformed into the biggest werewolf I've ever seen and attacked me." He sat back in the chair and slung an arm over the top, trying to be nonchalant but not really succeeding. She knew her cousin and knew that having to kill anyone—especially someone he liked and respected as much as Mr. Hansen—upset him much more than he would ever let on.

"Well, not exactly."

"What do you mean, not exactly?"

"Everything you remember from the meadow? That all really happened."

"Okay, fine. So?"

Beth took a deep breath. "So there's something else you need to remember about what happened that night. You know what that is?"

"Dammit, Beth." James got up and started to pace again. "I don't get it. What are you talking about?"

This was the part she dreaded most. Telling him what he had forgotten. How would he take it? He was strong, sure, but was he strong enough to go on, to save their world, once he knew the truth?

"I know you don't." She reached into her school tote, the one with her latest obsession, Fall Out Boy, plastered all over the front, and pulled out her tablet. Gesturing at

James, she switched it on and navigated to a video. "Stop pacing and come here. I want to show you something."

Chapter 21

Beth was my favorite cousin—actually, she was my *only* cousin, although she would have been my favorite, even if I'd had a hundred others— but she could drive me crazy. She always tried to be so mysterious, so grown up, but frankly, I was losing my patience.

"I don't have time for this." I snatched my backpack off the floor and headed out of the kitchen, intending to jump in my car and drive to the meadow, which seemed to be where everybody wanted me to go.

She grabbed my wrist and yanked me hard enough to pull me off-balance. I stumbled into her chair. She sighed. "Just look, will you?"

Searching her eyes, I could see that it was important to her that I watch the video, that whatever it was she wanted to show me was important to her. She was dead serious about it.

"Fine."

I leaned my hands on the table and bent over her, waiting for the video to load onto her tablet. Our internet connection was normally slow, and I wondered if it would even work in this strange world, since cell phone coverage was spotty at best, the electricity had gone out, and the computer only seemed to work when that shadow man wanted it to. I glanced toward my room and wondered where he was and what he was up to.

Then the video started.

Doctors and nurses, crowded around a gurney that was being pushed down a hall, raced toward the emergency room. Someone ran alongside carrying a plastic bag that was attached by a long tube to the arm of the person on the gurney. I guessed it was full of saline, or glucose or something. They were met by a tall, thin man in black scrubs. A paper cap was tied on his head, and he snapped on a pair of latex gloves. "What do we have?"

"Two gunshot wounds. One to the arm, one in the upper torso, doctor."

"Okay, let's have a look. Clear Trauma Four."

"Yes, Doctor."

Someone opened the curtain to the trauma room and the gurney was rushed inside.

"We're losing him!" someone shouted.

"On the table, count of three."

Several nurses grabbed the patient's arms and legs and waited for the count.

"One, two, three." When the doctor calmly reached three, the person on the gurney was transferred to the operating table. I could feel my pulse start to race as I watched. My gorge rose, burning my throat on the way up. Afraid of what I might see—what I *knew* I would see—I closed my eyes tightly.

"Hey!"

Beth jammed her elbow into my side, and I reluctantly opened my eyes. She was glaring at me from her spot at the kitchen table. I'd almost forgotten she was there.

"Sorry."

She paused the video and patted my shoulder. "I know this is difficult, but you've just got to watch it if you want to understand what all's happening."

"I know. Go on."

She started the video again, and I watched as the nurses scattered to prepare for their roles in the surgery, then I groaned when I saw the pallid, sweat-drenched, filthy face of the person with the huge, bloody hole in his chest. It was me. I was lying there, unconscious and probably dying, from the look of all the blood. A nurse wearing purple scrubs cut off my shirt, and another one worked on cleaning the wound. Someone else jammed a tube down my throat, I guess to help me breathe, and I gagged.

Beth looked up at me. "You okay?"

"I think I better sit down." On wobbly legs, I pulled out the chair next to her and dropped into it. "Give me a sec."

"You want some water?"

"Naw, I'm okay." I rubbed my eyes with the heels of my palms and smiled thinly. "Go on."

"You sure?" A look of real concern flashed across her face and made me realize that, if I had to go through whatever this was, I was glad she was here with me.

"Yeah." I nodded. "Go on."

She unpaused the video, and we were thrown back into the middle of things. The doctor sliced into my flesh, drawing the sharp blade of the scalpel across my chest. Blood, thick and red, spurted out of the incision. Watching this, I was so lightheaded I was afraid I was going to pass out.

Was this really happening to me? I clutched my chest, as red-hot pain seared though me, and hung my head, tried to slow my breathing. I could actually feel the knife ripping through my flesh, tearing it apart, digging into it to get to the bullet wedged inside. Had it nicked my heart? Was that why my chest kept hurting, here in the present?

The world swayed and shifted, going in and out of focus. My mind seemed to fade in and out right along with it as I struggled to stay conscious. It wasn't going to get the best of me, not if I had anything to say about it, so I took a great big breath, blew it out slowly, rolled my shoulders, and continued to watch through eyes so narrow they were hardly more than slits. That way, I figured, maybe things wouldn't seem so real, so *personal*, and I could stomach it a little better. Maybe not hurl. Whatever I had to do to figure out what had happened to me, how this zombie werewolf apocalypse thing had been jumpstarted, and why.

Glancing at Beth, I saw that she was studying me. Probably trying to decide if I was going to make it through the entire video. How long was it, anyway? Five minutes? Ten? An hour? However long it took, I was in it for the long haul. I would watch it to the end.

"It's okay." She rubbed my shoulder again. "The worst is over."

We turned back to the tablet. Gone was the operating room, replaced by a blindingly white hospital room. Machines beeped and blipped. The lighting was subdued. Someone lay in a hospital bed attached to tubes that snaked out from his mouth, his arm, and some unknown place under the blanket. I winced when I realized that person was me, hooked up to a respirator that noisily pumped air into my lungs. I watched, fascinated, as my chest rose and fell in rhythm with the machine. When I realized that the tube whose end was hidden under the sheet was a catheter, I shuddered violently. A blood pressure cuff was wrapped around one arm. A large bandage bound my other bicep, and an IV with that same saline stuff dripped down one of the tubes into my hand.

I wasn't moving. Probably not dead, or the machines wouldn't be making noise and keeping my lungs going. So the operation had worked. I was still alive. That answered that question.

Whoever had filmed this panned the camera back, showing the rest of the room. Slightly wilted flowers sat in a plastic pitcher that now doubled as a makeshift vase. Get well cards, the edges slightly curled, had been taped to the wall behind me. A curtain divided the room in half, so there might have been someone else in another bed. *At least I got the bed by the window*. Small comfort.

Two chairs had been pulled up next to the bed. A woman sat in one, her forehead lying on the bed in front of her. She was rubbing my arm. Mom.

The chair beside her was empty. *Where's Dad?*

I looked at Beth. She shrugged and motioned for me to keep watching. When I turned back, I could hear my mom moaning quietly. My heart went out to her. I'd never seen her so grief stricken. If only I could reach out and touch her. *Wake up!* My mind cried out, trying to get the unconscious me to hear the conscious me. But it was hopeless.

Dad came in, carrying a cup of tea. He put his hand on Mom's back, and she looked up into his eyes, then down at the tea.

"Here, honey," he said. "Drink this."

She smiled half-heartedly. He gently took her hands and placed the cup into them, then brought them up to her lips. She took a small sip. "Thanks."

Dad sat down next to her. "How's he doing?"

She put the cup down on the medical table next to her and picked up one of my hands and held it in both of hers. "Same."

"He's going to be okay, Annette."

She turned on him, her eyes flashing with a mixture of anger and fear. "You don't know that. You can't know that." Her face crumpled as a single tear trickled down her cheek. "He hasn't even turned since…"

"That doesn't mean anything." Dad was trying to reassure her, but, when he ran his hand through his hair, I could tell he wasn't so sure.

She looked at my father, fresh tears streaming down her cheeks again. "Why did this have to happen?"

Dad shook his head. "I don't know, honey. But James is strong." He patted Mom's shoulder. "He's strong enough to pull through." He turned away, his face crumpling in anguish. "He's just got to," he whispered. I didn't think my mom heard him.

As I kept watching, I felt so helpless, as helpless as the me in the bed. If the me in the bed was the real me, then who was I, the me in this weird reality of darkness and marshmallow fluff? And how was I supposed to be able to fix things, to get back to the real world?

Mom began to rock, my hand pressed to her lips. Dad was now sitting with his forehead on my leg. Faint sobs escaped him, and hearing that was even worse than watching Mom.

"Mr. and Mrs. Manarro?" A tall, thin, balding man entered the room and crossed directly to them. The doctor who operated on me. Dad immediately stood and extended his hand. The doctor shook it, nodding at my mom at the same time. She sprang up as soon as she realized who he was.

My throat went dry, and I couldn't swallow when I saw Mom's drawn face, so full of fear and panic. And a tiny bit of hope. She searched his face for answers, but must not have seen what she was looking for because the hope drained quickly away.

"How is he, Doctor?" Dad asked. "Is he going to be all right?"

"He's going to die, isn't he?" Mom sank slowly into the chair and buried her face in her hands.

I looked at Beth. "Is that what this is all about? Am I dead?"

"No. I told you already you weren't. Remember? At the theater."

"I know. But maybe you're wrong. Maybe you don't know everything."

"You're right, I don't know everything. But I do know that you are alive. Unconscious, but alive."

"So, am I dying, then? Is that what this is all about?"

"Shh." She put her finger to her lips. "Just watch."

I reluctantly turned back to the video.

"As you know, he lost a lot of blood," the doctor said. "So much that he's fallen into a coma."

Dad glanced at me. "But he'll come out of it." He fixed the doctor with a hard stare. "Right?"

"There's no way of knowing for sure. We're not even really sure why he became comatose. Please." He gestured toward the empty chair. "Sit down."

Dad, in typical Dad fashion, crossed his arms and shook his head. "I'll stand, thank you."

The doctor sighed. "Right." He leaned against the wall, his hands behind his back. "James was seriously wounded and is in critical condition."

Mom's head popped up. "What does that mean, exactly? Critical condition?"

"It means that his vital signs are unstable and not within normal limits. We got both of the bullets, but the one in his chest barely missed his heart."

Mom gasped.

"It punctured one of his lungs and chipped a tiny piece off one of his vertebrae."

"Oh, my God," Dad groaned. "Does that mean he can't walk?"

"We think he'll have full use of his extremities, once he comes out of the coma."

"Don't you mean 'if'? If he comes out of his coma?"

The doctor studied the floor for a moment before answering. "Yes. If he comes out."

"How long before we know?"

"The next twenty-four to forty-eight hours are critical. After that…"

"So you think he'll wake up by then?" Mom asked hopefully.

"We really can't say for sure when—or if—he'll wake up. The forty-eight hours refers to whether he will live or not. I'm sorry."

Mom broke down and sobbed. Dad looked like he wanted to hit something, which was so not like him. He was one of the most mellow people I knew. The doctor looked like he wanted to run away.

Instead, he pushed off the wall and moved to Mom's side. "You mustn't give up hope, Mrs. Manarro. James is young and strong. If anyone can survive what happened, it's him." He patted her back stiffly. "We can't promise anything, of course, but with a little luck and some time…"

Mom seemed to tune him out and went back to rubbing my arm.

The doctor sighed and turned to Dad. "If you have any questions, don't hesitate to have me paged." He shook Dad's hand again, patting him on the shoulder, and left. Lots of patting and rubbing going on. It was enough to drive you crazy.

The video ended with Dad sitting down beside Mom and staring off into space. It was more than I could bear. Their pain was gut-wrenching, and I vowed right then and there to do whatever was necessary to ease it. If that meant I had to go back to the meadow to find the answers I needed to end this whole thing, then that's exactly what I would do.

At least I finally knew the truth about what happened. Or most of it, anyway.

Chapter 22

Beth turned off her tablet and stuck it in her tote before turning back to me. I had to wonder, was she some sort of guide, some kind of dream walker, or something? If the real me was lying unconscious in a hospital somewhere, and the me that was here was actually some kind of manifestation of my subconscious mind, then what was she? And how did she get here? What was her role in all this?

I glanced into the living room and wasn't surprised to see that the darkness had grown thicker, deeper. Shadows seemed to fill the yard beyond the window. It wouldn't be long before the monstrosities would be back.

"So, do you get it now?" Beth asked.

"Yeah, I was shot." I sniffed and rubbed my chest absently. "But by who?"

Beth shrugged. Her face was pale again, her freckles standing out as if they'd been drawn on with a Sharpie. "That's the thing. We don't know. No one does. The police are trying to figure it out, but so far, they haven't found any clues. They think whoever shot you also killed Mr. Hansen."

"Well, that's not true. At least I remember that much."

She cocked her head and crinkled her nose. "What exactly do you remember?"

It was hard for me to sit still, so I got up and paced some more. "Like I told you, Mr. Hansen left a note in my locker to meet him in the meadow. When I went there, he was waiting for me. We fought, and, at first, I thought he was going to kill me. He was so strong! I tried to reason with him, once he told me who he was and what he wanted." I stopped in front of Beth. "Did you know he was PJ's brother?"

She shook her head, her eyes momentarily going wide before they blinked rapidly.

"Yeah, me neither." I paced some more. "Anyway, when he attacked me, and I knew he wanted me dead, I transformed. It took forever, but I finally got him by the throat." I swiped the hair out of my eyes impatiently. "And the last thing I remember, he was laying there on the ground. Next thing I knew, I was waking up for school this morning. Or at least, it seemed like this morning. Even if I have relived it over and over."

"Relived it?"

"Yeah, whenever those zombie werewolf things got me, or almost got me, I always wound up back in my room. Which looks like the inside of the Pillsbury Dough Boy, by the way."

"Probably because your hospital room is all white."

That made me stop and sit down again. I had been shot. In critical condition, maybe dying. At best, in a coma. And yet, sitting here, in my kitchen, talking to my cousin about what happened. So which was the "real" me? Comatose James, or confused James?

"So the police really don't have any leads on who shot me?"

"No, sorry."

"Figures, especially if Riggs is heading up the investigation."

Beth nodded, a small smirk on her face. "Seriously."

"It had to have been someone who was pissed at me, though, right?"

"I would think so."

"But why? The only people I knew hated me were all killed by Mr. Hansen, I guess."

"Those kids that were killed last Christmas?"

"Yeah. I think he was trying to frame me, but it didn't really work. Even Riggs didn't buy it. He knew I could never kill all those people in cold blood, and he despises me."

"Well, if it wasn't Mr. Hansen, then who else could it have been?"

I shrugged and blew a big breath out of the corner of my mouth. "No clue. Dammit!" I pounded my fist onto my leg. "I should remember it. Why can't I remember what happened?"

"Because you're hurt."

"That's no excuse."

She crinkled her nose, and it reminded me of when we were little. Before the shit hit the fan. "Sure it is, silly."

"No. It's not."

"What do you expect, James? You're unconscious in the hospital. In a coma. No one knows when you're going to wake up." Her eyes filled with tears. "Or if."

"Hey." Reaching across the table, I gently placed my hand on hers and rubbed it with my thumb. "Oh, hey, now."

She looked up at me, the tears now overflowing. "Everyone's so scared, James. It's the not knowing that's the worst."

"I'm sorry. I'm so, so sorry."

"I know." She pulled her hand out from under mine and rubbed her eyes with the back of it. "Not your fault."

I looked around the kitchen, as desperate for a topic change as I was for answers. "So all this, it's happening…in my *mind*?"

She nodded. "I think so, yeah."

"Mom always told me my writer's imagination was something fierce. But this—" I gestured with both hands. "—this is really something, isn't it?"

Beth cocked her head and narrowed her eyes. Her expression was unreadable, and I couldn't help but wonder once again what she was hiding from me.

She sighed. "You know, just because all this is going on in your imagination doesn't necessarily mean it's not really happening."

I frowned. "What does that mean?"

"Don't think of your imagination as some sort of playground. It's more like…" She looked up at the ceiling for a couple of seconds while she seemed to sort through what she wanted to say. "…a movie that your mind plays for you that shows things you can't or don't want to see when you're awake. They may be different from what you see in real life, but that doesn't make them any less real."

"So what's happening here, this weird darkness and those things out there, they're in my imagination but also real?"

"Yep."

"Does whatever happens in here effect what happens out there?"

"I think so."

"And what happens out there…"

We finished together. "…effects what happens in here."

"Hmm." I thought about that for a minute. Then

something occurred to me. "So what about you?"

"What about me?"

"Are you really here? Or am I imagining you because I'm…"

"Afraid?"

Scratching my chest, I nodded and grinned sheepishly. "Kind of."

"It's okay to be scared, James."

"You don't think any less of me?"

A huge grin spread across her face, and she giggled. "I couldn't think any less of you."

"Ha, ha, very funny." But I was laughing too.

"But seriously, James. This place is like a major war zone. You're fighting for your life. What happens here will definitely effect what happens out there. In the real world."

"So the shadows in the darkness and the monstrosities, when they attack me in here…"

"It means something bad is happening out there. Or maybe it works the other way around. I'm not really sure. But one thing's certain. You don't have much time. You've got to go."

"I know. I will. But just one more thing."

"What's that?"

Wanting to move away from the anxiety etched into Beth's face, I peered again through the living room and out the window, where I wasn't surprised to see that the darkness had deepened considerably. The monstrosities would be here soon, if they weren't already lurking out there in the shadows.

I turned back to Beth. "You never answered my question."

When she furrowed her forehead, it sent me back to when she was eleven, and her eyebrows were so thick that when she did that, they merged into a unibrow. Now, she was thirteen and had plucked eyebrows. I missed the bushiness. "What question?"

"Are you really real? Are you really here?"

"I am, and I'm not."

I blew out an exaggerated sigh. "What does that mean?"

"It means I'm here, in your imagination but I'm also sitting by your bed in the hospital. I'm holding your hand and talking to you. Well, whispering, actually." She glanced over her shoulder like she thought someone had walked up behind her and lowered her voice to just above a whisper. "Don't want anyone to hear us." Her voice returned to normal. "The doctors told all of us that we should talk to you, that you might be able to hear us, that it could help you find your way back."

"That must be why I could hear my mom calling me before."

"She never leaves you, except when Uncle Robbie makes her get something to eat. Then she runs to the cafeteria and is back in about ten or fifteen minutes. So we don't have much time left."

"Well, but, how are you able to be here with me but Mom can't?"

She slapped her hands on the table so hard it made me flinch. "There's no time for that now. But you have to know—"

"What?" She pursed her lips and avoided looking at me. "Beth?"

"Those times you were attacked and then found yourself back in your room?"

"What about them?"

"Your heart had stopped, and they had to resuscitate you. But if it happens again…"

"What?" Acid churned in my stomach like they say molten lava does in the center of the Earth. "Will I die?"

"They don't really know, but I heard the doctor tell your dad that there was a seventy-thirty chance."

"Seventy-thirty chance of what?"

Still unable to meet my gaze, she turned her back to me. From the way her voice quivered, I could tell she was about to cry again. "That they won't be able to bring you back. They don't think you're strong enough to make it back again." She whirled around to face me, tears streaming so hard they flew out of her eyes and spattered the floor. "You'll die!" She launched herself at me, bolting around the table and hugging me so tight around my shoulders that she nearly pulled me out of the chair.

My head was spinning. I patted her arm in a lame attempt to comfort her. "Seventy-thirty. So I probably only have one more chance to figure things out, and if those zombie werewolves get me again, I'm toast."

"Don't say that!" she sobbed into my neck.

"Wow, that really sucks. I'm only seventeen. Well, in a couple of months, I will be. I don't want to die. What if I just go back into my room, climb into my bed, and go to sleep? What will happen then?"

Beth raised her head a little, and her sobs slowed down a bit. "Well, you'll probably live, but I bet you never wake up. You'll stay in a coma forever." She let go of my neck, grabbed my chin, and turned my head so I had to look at her. Her eyes burned. "Is that what you want?"

"No, of course not." I put my head in my hands. "It's just all so overwhelming. I'm not ready to die, but I don't know if I can do this."

"Sure you can." She rubbed between my shoulder blades, then brushed the hair away from my face. "I have faith in you, 'cuz."

I smiled up at her. Her eyes were red and her face still too pale, but when she crinkled her nose and batted her eyes at me in that way she had, I couldn't help but chuckle. It was important to both of us for me to be strong. After all, I was the older cousin. It had always been my job to protect her, one that I just couldn't abandon simply because I was in a coma.

"I guess seventy-thirty is better than nothing, right?"

She wiped her eyes again. "Sure."

"So I'll go for it. Only…"

"What?"

"What do I do? How do I get out of here and away from the creatures out there? And then get to the meadow? And once I find the answers, how do I get back? How do I wake up?"

"You want to know what I think?"

"Duh."

"I think something's keeping you here, some deep part of your mind that doesn't want you to wake up. Maybe it even wants you to die."

"You saying I have a death wish?"

She shook her head vigorously. "Uh, un. I think it's your fear that's keeping you here. And I think the key is hidden inside your brain somewhere. It's something you know but can't get to for some reason."

"Something I've forgotten?"

"Or that you're blocking. If you find out what happened in the meadow, who shot you and why, then I'll bet you could figure it out."

"And if I do, I wake up? But if I don't…"

"But you will." She punched me on the arm. "You have to."

"Hope you're right." I pushed the chair away and stood. Even though I was still plenty scared, I also felt ready to go. If I didn't leave soon, it would be impossible to get through the darkness to my car, and even if I did, I wouldn't survive another round with the monstrosities. That much I knew for sure.

Beth backed away from me. When she got to her tote bag, she picked it up, slung it over her shoulder, and continued to back away. She seemed to be dissipating, flickering like a light bulb about to go out. A fresh wave of dread rolled though me. "Wait! Beth, don't leave. Not yet."

"I have to, James. Your parents are coming back. They're almost here." She smiled slightly as her image faded. "I wish I could do this with you, but I can't. You have to do it on your own. But remember, you're not alone. I'm here with you." She pulled something out of her pocket and tossed it to me. I caught it in my left hand. When I looked down, I saw a small square of blue and green swirly fabric and smiled. It was the piece of Aunt Judy's dress that Beth had wrapped around a hunk of coarse hair and then used to try and convince me that her mother was a werewolf. I remember how I had laughed at the impossibility of it all. But it turned out to be true.

That was the main reason why I knew what she'd just told me was all true. But when I looked back at her to reassure her, she was gone.

Chapter 23

BETH

Beth? Honey?"

Beth moaned softly. After flipping back from James's subconscious, her stomach felt funny, like when you want to puke but know you can't, and her head throbbed dully. Maybe she'd stayed too long there, maybe that was why she didn't feel so good. But even so, she knew that she'd do it as many times as she had to. She'd *make* him understand what had happened, no matter what. She just hoped he'd figure it out soon, before his heart gave out on him again.

"Beth." Someone was shaking her, and when she lifted her head to see who it was, a wave of dizziness hit her, and she moaned again.

"Stop," she said weakly, rubbing her forehead. "Please stop shaking me." She blinked several times and shook her head to clear it.

"You okay, Beth?" Uncle Robbie towered over her and had a funny look on his face. "You were draped over James like you were trying to protect him from something. That, or you were asleep." He cocked his head and looked at her in such a way that she wondered if he knew what she'd really been doing.

She dug the heel of her hand into her eye, hoping he'd think she'd been crying. Not that she wasn't upset about her cousin or hadn't had her share of tears, but she didn't want anyone to know about her trip into his subconscious. Not yet, anyway. Not until it was all over.

"Yeah, I'm okay." She smiled at him. "I think I fell asleep. How's Auntie?"

He shrugged and gave her a lame smile back. "Oh, you know…"

"Yeah."

He slumped into a chair at the end of James's bed, and they sat there, together, waiting. Waiting for Aunt Annette to come back from the cafeteria, where she'd finally agreed to sit and drink yet another cup of tea as long as Uncle Robbie agreed to stay with James until she came back.

Until James came back from wherever he was, they would all wait.

No matter how long it took.

Sunday, March 13, 2016
Day 49

Chapter 24

BETH

Uncle Robbie had finally convinced Aunt Annette that sitting around James's bedside, just waiting for him to wake up, wasn't doing anyone any good, least of all James. He'd finally been able to drag her home after she made him promise to bring her back first thing in the morning.

When they got home, Beth jumped in the shower, the first one she'd had in nearly three days. Back in James's bedroom drying off, she turned his clock radio on, grimacing at the *Paramore* song playing, and walked around looking at his things. A framed picture of the two of them, arms wrapped around each other with huge grins on their faces, sat on his desk and she picked it up. They'd been swimming at the community center, back when they were still oblivious to who—and *what*—they were. It had been such a fun day, that day. She smiled as she put the picture down and pulled on her favorite sweats and one of James's tee shirts. She didn't think he'd mind.

A knock at the door startled her. "Come in."

The door stayed closed.

"Come in," Beth repeated, a little louder.

The door didn't open, and Beth scowled as she walked across the room. As she reached for the door knob, the door rattled like it sometimes did when a big truck drove by, and a little girl with the blondest hair she'd ever seen appeared. She looked vaguely familiar in her red corduroy overalls and gingham shirt, her pigtails tied up with matching ribbon. A dirty teddy bear was clutched in her right hand. The fingers of her left hand curled over her nose as she sucked on her thumb.

"Oh, hey," was all Beth could think to say.

The little girl wriggled her fingers at her but didn't take her thumb out of her mouth.

"Who are you? What are you doing here?"

The little girl's eyes were huge as she continued to look at Beth without blinking.

Beth knelt on one knee and smiled. "My name's Beth. What's your name?"

She pulled her thumb out of her mouth with a pop. "Emma."

Beth gasped. "Emma? Emma Ridgewick?"

Emma nodded.

Beth sat back on her haunches. At the hospital, they'd kept the television on low nearly all the time, and one of the news stories that had played over and over had been about a little girl named Emma who'd been murdered right here in Wolf Creek just a few days before James had been shot. Her little girl panties, decorated with a dancing Elmo, and one shoe had been found in the dry river bed a few miles from the meadow where they'd found Mr. Hansen. The police had assumed James had found out that he'd killed the little girl and that's why Mr. Hansen had lured him to the meadow and shot him.

She knew that part, at least, wasn't true. Werewolves didn't need guns to kill someone, that's for sure.

Her fingertips began to tingle and that energy inside her heated up again, getting stronger. "Wait a minute. Are you…"

Emma nodded again.

"Wow. It must suck to be dead."

"It does. Ghosts are really scary." Emma stuck her thumb in her mouth again, laying her fingers on the bridge of her nose and rubbing it gently.

"Yeah, I'll bet. You know I'm not one, right?"

Emma giggled around her thumb. "Of course, silly. I know that."

"But how do you know?"

"At first, I thought you might be, but you kind of twinkle, you know? So that's how come I could tell you weren't."

Beth was about to ask Emma what she knew about the whole psychopomp thing when Emma looked quickly over her shoulder, as if she'd heard a noise or something. "Oh, no! He's here."

"Who's here?" Beth asked.

"I have to go." Emma turned to leave.

"No, wait. Don't leave yet. Tell me what's happening."

Emma wriggled her fingers, still wrapped around her nose, and vanished.

Who was Emma talking about? She'd been scared, that was for sure. Was it her killer? But how could that be, if he was alive and Emma was dead?

Beth plopped down on the bed. Why did Emma come to her now, when Beth needed to concentrate on helping James? Were the little ghost girls somehow connected to James?

Or was it just bad timing?

ೊೀ

When Emma left, Beth pulled a kitchen chair out into the backyard and sat with James's laptop on her knees. She needed to find out more about Shadowland. Was it heaven? Hell? And could going there help her help James?

She'd have to google it and see what she could find out about it, and about psychopomps, too. She searched for over an hour until she found a website that talked about all the different kind of psychopomps there were: spirit guides, shamans, Valkyries, even angels, and demons. Everything but the psychopomps her father had told her about.

But her father wouldn't have lied to her, would he?

"Did he ever lie to you before?"

Timmy sat cross-legged on the grass. She looked odd, out there in the daylight. It wasn't just her skater duds, which were so nineties. It was the way the sun shone on her. It took a minute for Beth to figure it out. Timmy didn't have a shadow. Not just the one that should have been on the ground underneath her, but all the little shadows that should have been in and around the wrinkles in her clothes, under her chin. It was like she was smooth all over, with no bumps or ridges to her.

Beth shook her head. "No."

"So why would you think he'd be lying to you now?"

"He wouldn't, I guess." She closed the laptop. "What are you doing here?"

"I need to show you something."

"What?"

"Not here. On the other side."

"The other side?"

"Don't tell me you've forgotten about it already?"

"No—o—o." Beth drew the word out hesitantly. Her trip into Shadowland, the one that had happened after the accident that killed Kimberlin, seemed fuzzy and unreal to her now. It had seemed so vivid, so *real*, when it first happened, but now, it felt more like a barely remembered dream.

"Then what?" Beth looked over her shoulder into the house. Her aunt had gone back to the hospital, of course, unable or unwilling to be away from James long enough to even take a decent nap, but her uncle was roaming around somewhere inside. "I'm not sure how to get there. To Shadowland."

"Don't be such a geek. Sheesh. Just call it the other side."

"Okay, fine. The other side. Whatever. Anyway, I'm not sure how to get there."

"But…you're a psychopomp, aren't you? They're just supposed to know, aren't they?

Beth shrugged, not entirely sure how she'd been able to go into James's subconscious. She figured being a psychopomp must have something to do with it. Some kind of natural ability she was just now learning about. Or maybe it had something to do with Timmy. She just wasn't sure. "I guess. But all my dad told me was that it was our heritage. He didn't really explain it very much."

Timmy sighed. "Guess I'll have to help you, then." She stretched out her arm. "Take my hand."

"What if someone sees me?"

"Don't worry, they won't."

Beth stood and put the laptop on the chair. Hesitantly, she took Timmy's hand. A faint tingle immediately flowed from the little girl's hand into hers and traveled up her arm. The air around them seemed to flatten out, and her mouth filled with the metallic taste of a penny. Everything went still, silent. Beth tried to let go of Timmy's hand, but the little girl held fast, squeezing tighter and tighter until the tingle was replaced by a throbbing ache.

Beth closed her eyes as a coldness welled up and wrapped itself around her insides, pouring into her brain. Everything seemed larger and smaller at the same time. Plus, it was all she could do not to throw up.

When she opened her eyes, she was only a little surprised to find that the world had gone completely gray, almost like all the color had been sucked out of it. It frightened her a little, and she realized she was breathing hard. There was a faint pounding in her ears.

It was weird. She'd expected to see her cousin's backyard, where they'd spent so much time hanging out over the summer, all gray and flat and misty, especially since that's where they'd started from. Instead, she was standing on a sidewalk somewhere, facing a two-story house across the street, with no idea where she was. She carefully took a couple of small steps and grimaced. That pins-and-needles feeling you got when your feet fell asleep stabbed her legs up to her calves. Her hands burned, too.

That hadn't happened before, and she wondered why it was happening now. She dropped Timmy's hand, and Beth's feet and hands stopped prickling. It must have something to do with Timmy being a ghost, or something.

"This is so weird," she said, turning back to the house.

Movement behind the curtains of the house across the street caught her eye. Someone was standing there, and she wondered if they were watching her. It made her stomach roll, and she began to sweat. The hair on her arms stood up.

She looked frantically around, trying to find somewhere to hide, even though she didn't know why she should be so afraid of whoever was in there.

"It's okay, Beth." Timmy patted her arm awkwardly. "He can't see you."

"Are you sure?" Beth had her doubts, but as she watched, she realized that a man was washing dishes at the kitchen sink. He was gray, like Timmy and the others, but not the same gray as everything else. He had different shades to him. There was a shadow under his chin.

"Positive. He's not a ghost."

"He's alive?"

"Yeah."

"How come he doesn't twinkle, like me?"

"Because he's not like you. He's just a man." She licked her lips and looked at the house. "A very *bad* man."

"What do you mean, bad?"

A door slammed, and the man strode across the yard, right toward them. He was wearing a big cowboy hat— Beth thought it was called a Stetson—that hid his face, but that didn't keep her heart from racing.

"We gotta get out of here," Timmy cried. She reached for Beth's hand. "Come on, let's go! Run!"

"What do you mean, run? You said he couldn't see me."

Beth shivered as the world around them flooded with sunlight that instantly burned through the gray mist. Her knees went weak, and her hold on the gray world around her seemed to slip a bit. Colors were too bright, too strong, and she closed her eyes against the intense glare.

A burning tingle seemed to singe her flesh when Timmy grabbed her hand and pulled her along at a dead run. Holding her breath, Beth let herself be dragged along, and the next thing she knew, they were back in James's back yard. A hummingbird whizzed by her head as she opened her eyes, blinking against the brightness of the normal, ordinary sunshine. That copper penny taste left her mouth, and she gulped in sweet, fresh air. "Whew." She wiped the sweat off her forehead with the palm of her hand. "That was close, wasn't it, Timmy?"

When Timmy didn't answer, Beth turned around and looked for her friend. "Timmy?"

The yard was empty. It hit Beth that if she ever got into trouble on the other side, Timmy probably wouldn't stick around to help out. Beth couldn't really blame her. After all, she was basically just a little kid.

"Beth?"

Beth whirled around, half expecting to see yet another ghost. Instead, her uncle stood there with an odd look on his face.

"Uncle Robbie?" She didn't like how pale he was, how the ugly purple smudges under his eyes stood out against his normally olive complexion. "Uncle Robbie, what is it?"

"We have to go." Were those tears that threatened to fall in his eyes? She'd never seen him cry before, not even when they'd first seen James, all bloody with that hole in his chest.

"Go? Go where?"

"To the hospital. There's been…a development."

Chapter 25

I sat down heavily and put my head in my hands. Everything Beth told me swirled around and around in my head. I was in the hospital? In a *coma*? But I was also here. How was that possible? I needed a minute. It was all too much to process.

Shaking my head, I slammed my hands down on the kitchen table and stood. I couldn't worry about that now. I had to get to the meadow. It was all too much, but so was someone shooting me. As I sank back into my chair, I couldn't help but wonder who would have done that. Who *could* have? Who besides Mr. Hansen hated me that much? If I was going to have any hope of waking up, of getting back to normal, I would have to figure that out. I had been shot in the chest, so I must have seen whoever it was. How could I not?

I rubbed my chest, which had begun to itch. Being in a coma must mean that there were things I couldn't remember, ideas and memories I couldn't access. Was my imagination different from my memories? From what I could remember from Psychology class, memories live in the subconscious while imagination was centered somewhere else. Ironically, I couldn't remember where. But I did remember that it flowed in the opposite direction from reality. Whatever that meant. To me, here, now, it meant that I must be living in my imagination. Reality was me in the hospital bed.

It all seemed to center around being shot. That was where I needed to begin. Beth was right. I had to go back to the meadow.

But that's also where D. R. told me to go. He had lied about the monstrosities, so was he also lying about going to the meadow? Was everything he said a lie, or just the part about controlling those things?

I didn't really want to do anything D. R. told me to do, not after what happened earlier. But even though I thought Beth was hiding something from me, I still trusted her. If she said I had to go there, then I probably should. After all, I didn't know what else to do. It was as good a place to start as any.

Right?

"Okay," I told myself. "Just get on with it already." I stood, slung my backpack over my shoulder again, and walked into the living room. Fingering the scrap of fabric Beth had given me, I sidled up to the window and peeked out. The darkness was so thick you could cut it into bricks and build a wall with it, like Irish peat. The front yard had vanished. All I could see now was what little bit the porch light shined on. Before too much longer, even that little bit would be gone. If I was going to do this, I had to leave now.

I could only hope the Le Mans was still out there, parked in the driveway.

Sensing rather than actually seeing zombie were-wolves lurking in the shadows, I checked the flashlight I'd stowed in my pack, aiming the beam out the window. It barely penetrated four feet before being swallowed by the dark. Not great, but it would have to do.

Filling my lungs with as much air as I could, I held my breath a few seconds, blew all the air out in a loud *whoosh*, threw open the door and rushed out into the malevolent darkness.

Chapter 26

BETH

They rushed to the hospital to find Aunt Annette nearly hysterical, yelling at the nurses who were taking care of James. When Uncle Robbie saw her, he ran over and threw his arm protectively across his wife's shoulders.

"Hey, now." He held his free hand palm up, waving it at the nurses. "What's going on here?"

Aunt Annette looked up at him, her eyes brimming with tears. "He opened his eyes and talked to me, Robbie."

"Now, Mrs. Manarro," one of the nurses said. "You know that's impossible. Your son's—"

Aunt Annette wriggled out from under Uncle Robbie's arm and looked at him pleadingly. "He did, Robbie! He did." She went over to James's bed and took hold of his hand. "He spoke to me."

Beth stood in the doorway and watched. She debated telling her aunt and uncle what was really going on with James, but decided now wasn't the time. Maybe it never would be. She didn't know.

But could her cousin have woken up for a split second, in spite of what the doctors said?

"Are you sure you weren't just imagining it, Annette?" Uncle Robbie placed his hand gently around her wrist and tried to pull her away from James.

Aunt Annette yanked her arm away. "I know what I saw, Robbie. And what I heard."

"What did he say, Auntie?" Beth was curious. Had James been trying to give them a clue about how to help him?

Both her aunt and uncle turned to look at her with their mouths hung open, like they'd forgotten she was even there.

"What?" Uncle Robbie was frowning at her, as if he was pissed Beth was encouraging her aunt's fantasy.

"I asked what he said." Beth turned to her aunt. "What did he say, Auntie? Did you get to talk to him?"

Aunt Annette shook her head. "No, I'm not really sure what he said. It was like he was screaming it, but quietly, you know?" She pursed her lips and turned back to James, stroking his hand.

"But what do you think he said?"

"That's enough, Beth." Uncle Robbie was definitely mad at her. But she couldn't help it. She had to know.

"Leave her alone, Robbie." Aunt Annette smiled tiredly at her. "It sounded like he said something about them or they." She knitted her brow in thought. "They lie, maybe?"

"Okay, I think everyone should leave now." The same nurse who'd acted like Aunt Annette was crazy tried to shoo Beth out the door.

Beth dodged her pushing and turned back to her aunt. "They? They who?"

Aunt Annette shrugged. "Don't know."

Could James be trying to tell her that the doctors

were lying, that he was going to come out of his coma soon? Or was he referring to someone—or some*thing*—else?

If that was the case, she'd have to make sure she followed her gut and did not let anyone trick her into anything.

Even if it meant putting James at risk.

⌘

Uncle Robbie sent her home after Aunt Annette flipped out, and, at first, Beth tried to figure out what James had been trying to tell them, but she was so uptight, she just couldn't focus on anything important. Sighing heavily, she decided to take a break and try to relax. She turned on the TV and settled on the couch. After a few minutes of channel surfing, she landed on *The Lego Movie*. Her favorite part was just starting, and she sang softly, her head bobbing from side to side, about everything being awesome and cool when you were part of a team and living out a dream.

Or flipping into someone's subconscious. She and James were a team, and together they would overcome this coma thing, no matter what warning he'd been trying to send her.

And he would recover. She was sure of it.

Her eyes fluttered shut, and she dozed off. With all the stress in her life these days, it was no wonder. But just as she was beginning to dream, a scream filled her head, and she bolted awake.

Unsure what just happened, she muted the TV and listened to the silence. Had she dreamed that scream, or had she really heard it?

When nothing else happened, she decided she'd been having a nightmare and sank back into the couch cushions. Her eyelids felt so heavy, and she slowly closed her eyes.

Monstrosities.

The word rang in her head like church bells on Sunday. Without knowing how, she knew it meant that James was in real trouble. She had to get out of here and back into her cousin's mind. And fast.

It was surprisingly easy to flip this time, and she was glad to see that the thick darkness had started to dissipate, making it a little easier to get through. Looking around her, she realized that she was in the middle of Wolf Creek Road, the main street into town, and she began walking.

Before long, she thought she heard something behind her, but when she looked, there was nothing there. Without her realizing it, the darkness had become so dense it was practically impenetrable. She peered into it and thought she could see a pinprick of light at the very far end of the street.

A low hum drifted in on a slight breeze that did nothing to slice through the darkness. As it slowly became louder, the pinprick of light split and became two.

It was a car. And not just any car. James's Le Mans. She'd know it anywhere.

But something was wrong. He was driving erratically, zig-zagging from one side of the street to the other. About a block and a half down from where she stood in the middle of the street, the car came to a sudden stop.

More confused than ever, Beth raced down the street, calling his name. "James! James, are you okay? What's wrong?"

Just then, several monsters with glowing red eyes; weirdly shaped heads; tons of hair everywhere, including on their faces; and razor-sharp fangs that dripped nasty hot slobber appeared from out of nowhere, shuffling along at a slow jog, and surrounded the Le Mans, pounding on it so hard she was afraid they would break the windshield and attack James. He must have put the car in gear because it lurched forward just as one of those things climbed onto the trunk. The car swerved across the street with the rest of the monsters—who seemed like a cross between a werewolf and a zombie and looked just like those things that had chased James to the theater—lumbering after him.

Monstrosities, he had called them.

The one monstrosity that managed to hold on had climbed onto the roof and was trying to dig his way inside. No matter how many times James swerved the car, he couldn't seem to knock it off. Even a block away, Beth could clearly hear its growls, and she ran as fast as she could to try and help her cousin.

She was about three houses down from him when James slammed on the brakes, sending the monstrosity flying, where it crashed with a thud onto the street.

Beth stopped short. The monstrosity looked like road kill. One leg was bent at an awkward angle, and blood was streaming out of its mouth and nose.

"Ew, gross," she said as she started toward it, curiosity winning out over fear. She wanted to see what it looked like up close. And see if James was okay.

Before she got close enough to really see anything, though, the tires of the Le Mans screeched and smoked, filling the air with the smell of burnt rubber. She wrinkled her nose and watched, wide-eyed, as the car lurched forward and ran over the monstrosity. The top half of its body flew up under the pressure of the tires and then dropped back down on the street, its head hitting with a loud crunch.

If it looked like road kill before, now it looked like raw hamburger.

The sound of James whooping and hollering made

her giggle. Maybe things were going to work out, after all. She turned to congratulate him, but she was alone.

James and the Le Mans had vanished.

Wednesday, April 20, 2016
Day 87

Chapter 27

Anxiety was her constant companion over the next few weeks. When he'd first disappeared, she'd worried that his heart had stopped again. But when she flipped back to the hospital, there was no change. James was fine. Or as fine as he could be, seeing as how he was in a coma.

While she was relieved, it did nothing to ease her general concern and anxiety. There was just so much going on right now. She was anxious about James, yes, but also about Timmy. Or rather, Timmy's "bad man." Beth couldn't seem to get him out of her mind. Thoughts of the strange sounds she'd heard but hadn't been able to see the source of through that swirling gray mist, of her father glancing nervously over his shoulder at some perceived threat that first time she went to Shadowland. But mostly, thoughts of the monster who had killed Timmy. Had he also killed Jazzy? And Emma?

Did Wolf Creek have yet another serial killer in its midst?

If so, what was she supposed to do about it? James was the only one who would believe her, and he was trapped in his own mind. He needed to concentrate on getting to the meadow, on figuring out how to break out of his coma. No way could she tell him about Timmy.

There was something Beth just had to know, though. As she walked slowly into the hospital cafeteria, it occurred to her that she'd heard about her somewhere, long before she'd appeared to Beth. She was almost positive. It was hidden away, deep in her memory. If only she could remember…

"I knew it wouldn't take you very long to figure it out," Timmy said.

"You…" Beth turned to her. "You were that little girl, the one who got…" Her eyes went wide. Timmy must have been the little girl who was stolen out of her bedroom one night and found three days later in a dumpster, her throat slit. Blue eye shadow that looked like it'd been applied with a gardening trowel had coated her eye lids, her lips smeared with bright red lipstick. Her clothes had been thrown carelessly on top of her.

"Killed." Timmy nodded. "By the bad man." She shuddered. Beth went to hug her, but her arm just went through the little girl instead. "He was mean to me."

"I'm so sorry, Timmy. But you know that he can't hurt you any more, right?"

She shrugged. "I guess." She still looked so sad that Beth actually ached for her. It must have been terrible, being murdered like that. "But sometimes, I wonder."

"Oh, I'm sure he can't." *As long as he's still alive, that is.* Who knew what he could do if he were dead like Timmy. "Well, I'd better get back. I'm supposed to be getting coffee for my aunt and uncle." Gesturing toward the big square coffee pot, she sighed heavily. What she wouldn't give for a Starbucks right now.

"Do you really have to go?"

"I'm sorry. I really do."

"Can't you stay for just a little while longer?" Timmy reached out her hand, and without thinking, Beth took it. That electric tingling filled her hand, not as strong as before but enough to give her a little jolt. She tasted that copper penny on her tongue.

"What are you doing?" Beth looked hastily around. "I can't cross over now. Not here."

"Please? Just for a minute or two?"

The cafeteria was fairly empty. There were two nurses eating at a table in the corner, and a cafeteria worker was lazily wiping down the salad bar, but other than that, the place was empty. No one was paying any attention to them. "Okay. But just for a minute."

The world went gray, and that eerie mist filled the air around them. Beth's stomach rolled a little, but, fortunately, the nausea didn't come.

"Yay!" Timmy threw herself at Beth and held her in a bear hug so tight she thought she might bust a rib.

"Hey, not so hard! I can't breathe."

Curiously, Timmy could touch her whenever she wanted to, but Beth couldn't always touch Timmy.

The little girl loosened her grip but kept her arms locked around Beth. Beth could feel her shaking, and wondered that the kid's fear hadn't diminished any. You'd think nothing could scare her, now that she was dead. What could happen that would be worse than death?

"It's okay, Timmy." Beth tried to soothe her by stroking her head. The cap Timmy wore slid down over one eye when she did, and it made the little girl giggle. Beth smiled as she gently pushed Timmy away. "You know that you're safe now, right? That the bad man can't hurt you anymore?"

"We—Well..." Timmy pushed her cap back up on her head and searched Beth's eyes with her own.

"What?"

"What about…when he dies? Will he be able to get me then? He'll be a ghost, just like me." Tears filled her eyes.

Beth pulled her tightly to her. "Don't worry. I won't let him hurt you."

"Honest?"

"Honest."

Timmy backed away from Beth. "Promise?"

"Yes. I promise." A strange dread filled Beth's core, and she hoped it was a promise she could keep.

"Hey," Timmy said cheerfully, "how about I teach you how to walk through walls?"

"Really? You can do that?"

"Sure."

"That's so cool."

"Okay." Timmy grabbed Beth's hand. "Here we go."

Nausea rolled briefly through Beth as her mouth filled with that familiar metallic taste.

The next thing she knew, they were no longer in the hospital cafeteria. Instead, they were outside, across the street from the hospital, standing in a vacant lot that used to be where the old hospital had been located before they'd found black mold growing in all the walls. It stood abandoned for several years before eventually being torn down.

Now, the silent building loomed before them. Here on the other side, though, it appeared as yet another gray structure shrouded in heavy mist. The roof and part of the top floor seemed solid, just like a regular building in what she was beginning to think of as the real world, while she could see through the rest. Faint images of bushes and flowers poked through the grayness. Graffiti adorned the bottom eight feet or so of all the walls. A rusted out fence topped with barbed wire listed precariously around the building, keeping out all but the heartiest taggers, who had filled every reachable space—and some that made Beth wonder how on earth a person could possibly have managed to climb into them. A wooden sign proclaimed the building *CONDEMNED*.

"Okay." Beth rubbed her hands together. "Let's do this."

Timmy cast her a sideways glance. "I don't know. This place is scary."

"Come on, Timmy. You said you could teach me. I have to learn some time, right?" Beth shrugged. "Might as well be now."

"Okay. Here goes." Taking a deep breath, Timmy closed her eyes and raced across the parking lot. Beth watched as she got closer and closer to the building without slowing down then gasped as she disappeared through the cinder block wall.

Seconds later, she reappeared. "See? Easy peasey."

"Yeah, for you, maybe." Beth looked at the wall Timmy had disappeared into. "So all I have to do is close my eyes and run at a wall to pass through it?"

Timmy giggled. "I just did that for funsies." She took Beth's hand again. "Here. I'll help you this one time."

The tingling started again, traveling up her arm. But there was something else this time. Something she didn't recognize. Reluctance? Dread, maybe? Whatever it was, she shook it off. There was no turning back. She had to push forward, had to figure out why this was happening to her, why now and not when she was older, like Daddy said it usually did. It had to have something to do with what was going on with James. It just had to.

And she'd do anything to help him, to get him back.

To keep him from dying.

Chapter 28

Beth reached out and gently touched the side of the building. It was rough and scratched her fingertips. She pushed a little, and her hand immediately sank into the wall and disappeared out of sight. She drew it back in a rush, shaking it and flexing her fingers.

"Whoa."

"I know. Weird, huh?"

"Yeah. Weird." Beth looked at Timmy and grinned. "Here goes nothing." Closing her eyes, she rushed headlong into the wall. The stucco scraped against her arms, momentarily holding her back, but she pushed ahead, stumbled, and came out the other side. "That wasn't so bad."

Timmy held tightly to her hand and looked nervously around.

"What is it?" Beth asked. "Are there other ghosts in here?"

"Don't know. Maybe."

"You don't have to stay with me if you don't want to."

The air felt heavy and pressed in around her. Everything inside the old hospital was gray, just like outside, but the mist was gone and Beth guessed it was that way inside all ghost buildings.

"No, that's okay," Timmy said quietly. "Just don't leave me, 'kay?"

"I won't." Beth took a few steps, and things around her seemed to get a little more solid, less ghostly. The moon shone in through a window, and she realized that she could actually see a few light shadows under some of the debris that littered the hallway where they stood. She turned toward Timmy. "Hey, do you see—"

Timmy was visibly shaking, and pale even for a ghost. She was mumbling something that Beth couldn't make out.

"What is it? What's wrong?"

"So—something bad happened here. Something really bad."

"What do you mean, something bad?"

"Can't you feel it?"

"Well, now that you mention it…"

The air felt thicker, like that nasty split pea soup her mom always made, and shapes were becoming harder to make out. The shadows seemed to be growing slowly. Getting darker.

A silhouette grew out of the shadow in the corner, slowly taking form, although she could still see through what appeared to be a little girl in red corduroy overalls over a red and white checked shirt. One of the overall straps was dangling down her back, the clip banging silently against her thigh. Her shirt was unbuttoned, and one side was shredded and stiff. Blood stained the bib of her overalls, and there was a huge gash across her throat. Her blonde pigtails were matted and filthy. Her fingers curled over her nose as she sucked on her thumb.

"Oh, my God," Beth cried. "Emma?"

Emma limped slowly past, apparently without seeing

them. They watched as she disappeared down the hall into the darkness.

"Told ya," Timmy whined. "I told you something bad happened here. Can we go now? Please?"

Beth stared after Emma. "You see that?"

"Of course I did. She's a ghost, ain't she?"

A faint voice, warm and soothing, whispered from some dark corner. "*Be—th*," it sing-songed.

A chill ran through Beth's core. Goosebumps prickled her arms. She whirled toward the sound. "You hear that?"

Trembling, Timmy looked at her, ghostly tears flowing in rivulets down her cheeks, spilling onto her tee shirt and staining it. "I wanna go now. Can we please go?" She grasped Beth's hand and squeezed it so tightly, Beth grimaced.

"Ow." Beth pushed at Timmy's hand, but the little girl wouldn't loosen her grip. "Not so hard, okay?" Little zaps of energy thwacked against Beth's palm.

Timmy pointed down the same hall that Emma disappeared into. Her lower lip quivered, and she moaned low in her throat.

Beth frowned. The shadows down there seemed darker, thicker somehow. And were they…*moving?* Growing larger? How was that even possible? The moon was hidden behind the dense grayness that enveloped the world outside the abandoned hospital, but the lack of light couldn't account for the darkness inside.

The singsong voice called out from the depths of the shadows.

"Beth, come and see me. I want to talk to you."

"No way," Beth retorted. "No way in hell am I going down there."

"I'll tell you what you want to know."

What she wanted to know? Could the voice really

help her? She needed to figure out her place, both in the real world and here, on the other side.

The problem was, she just didn't know how. She did need help.

But would the strange voice really be able to help her?

❧❧❧

Beth was tempted to follow Emma down the hall, but Timmy's insistent tugging wouldn't let her. That, and the shadows that were flowing stealthily across the floor. Thick, oozing, oily blackness rolled toward them, blocking out the grayness of the tiled floor beneath it. It seemed almost…alive…as it slithered along.

"That's it. We're out of here. I'm not waiting any longer." Timmy ran as fast as she could toward the place where they'd first entered the building, yanking Beth along with her.

Beth just had time to close her eyes and take a deep breath before they hit the wall. The cinder blocks scratched her arms and legs, and she brushed against something soft that clung to her cheek like a spider web. Her heart galloped faster than a racehorse, and she struggled to make it through. For a second, she was afraid she was going to get stuck there forever, her body half entombed in the wall. Then the building released its hold on her with a pop, and she burst through, stumbling down the steps that led to the sidewalk and freedom. When something grabbed her ankle, she tripped and fell, skinning both knees and the palm of her left hand. Screaming, she kicked out at it and scrambled to get away.

The world was suddenly full of color again. She sat up gingerly and waited for her pulse to slow. To help it along, she took big breaths in through her nose and let them out slowly through her mouth. Four or five of those and she felt a little better. Except that the throbbing in her knees kept time with her heartbeat, and her palm burned like crazy. But at least she was back in the real world, where she belonged. For now, anyway.

She looked around. The abandoned hospital was just a vacant lot again. The bushes and flowers that had surrounded the ghost hospital had been replaced by dirt and weeds, some nearly as tall as Timmy.

Whatever had seized her leg was gone. The thick, menacing darkness that had called to her was gone, replaced by ordinary shadows cast by the full moon, no longer hiding behind the grayness.

There was nothing there. Whatever that voice had belonged to was gone.

So was Timmy.

Chapter 29

Fear blazed inside me, burning my gut like acid, but I kept my flashlight aimed in front of me and hurried as quickly as I dared toward the driveway. I figured I would be relatively safe once inside the Le Mans, if only I could make it that far unscathed. The darkness moved stealthily forward like a dark, heavy fog. The monstrosities were still hidden, but I could hear them moving around me, whispering and chittering like crazed animals, which I suppose they were. Getting closer and closer. Soon, they would be on me.

"I hope you know what you're doing, Beth," I whispered. "Hope this isn't going to get me killed, coming out here like this."

I felt it more than heard it, that angry swipe of ragged claws that missed me by less than half an inch. They were on me!

"Oh, God."

I ran full out, praying that I wouldn't trip and fall, that I would make it to the car in time. A second monstrosity reached out to grab me. And a third. They were on me, more than I could count. Tearing at my clothes. I wrestled away from their grip, reached into my pocket and tried to pull out my keys. When they caught on the lining, I almost dropped them but finally managed to pull them free, jam them into the lock, and open the door. As I crawled inside, one of those things grabbed my ankle, its razor claws raking my skin. I kicked as hard as I could, but it held fast and tried to climb inside the car after me. I crab-walked across the console, pretty sure it was the end of me. Kicking with all my might—and screaming, too— I couldn't help but laugh hysterically when I heard the satisfying crunch as I connected with its nose. It screamed as well, and I kicked it again, this time knocking it out the door. I scrambled over, pulled the door shut and locked it, then lunged for the passenger door as another one reached for the handle. I hit the lock a millisecond before it connected.

"Ha ha!" I chortled with glee and reached for the ignition. But the keys weren't there. *Oh, no, did you drop them somewhere? Are they outside?* If so, I was screwed. I fumbled around on the floorboards, frantically searching for them, first under my seat, then under the passenger seat. I was just about to give up when my fingers hit them, and I latched onto the ring. After starting the engine, I revved it, glared at the monstrosities swarming the car, and shot backward out of the driveway.

The darkness seemed to fold in around me as I shoved the gear into first and punched the gas pedal. The car lurched forward, and I tried to even things out without slowing down, but it was so dark, I was afraid to go very fast. When I switched on the headlights, I wasn't surprised to see that the beams couldn't cut through it much farther than the flashlight had. There was only about ten feet of visibility, and going more than fifteen or twenty mph was dangerous. Fear urged me to go faster, but instinct held me back.

I leaned so far forward to look out the windshield that I was hunched over the steering wheel like some little old lady who only drove to church on Sundays, ten miles under the speed limit, her turn signal blinking happily as she puttered along. My heart thumped angrily in my chest, which was rising and falling in a staccato rhythm all on its own because I was breathing so hard. My eyes darted left and right before returning to center again, checking to see if I had company. With any luck, I wouldn't see any more of those things. If I did, I figured at least I could run them over before they could get to me.

A dark figure materialized about three feet down the road. Without even thinking about it, I pulled the wheel sharply to the left. The corner of the Le Mans hit the creature, who screamed with rage before disappearing back into the shadows.

After I'd driven another mile or so without seeing any others, I pulled over and rested my head on the steering wheel, waiting for my heart to slow down and my breathing to return to normal. That was just a little too close for comfort. When I could breathe again without fear of passing out, I leaned back against the seat, closed my eyes, and wiped my sweaty palms on my jeans.

"You and your stupid writer's mentality," I chided myself. "If you were into accounting, or science, or something boring like that, this wouldn't be happening." Then again, if I didn't have such a vivid imagination, would there be any hope for me at all?

After a few minutes, when my breathing was back to normal and I felt a little better about myself, I thought I heard someone—Beth?—calling my name. But how could that be?

"Please," I whispered, squeezing my eyes shut as tight as I could. "Please don't let her be one of those things. Please."

I opened my eyes just in time to see a flash of orangey red. I wasn't sure what it was, but I sat bolt upright and squinted out the windshield. Resisting the urge to floor it, fighting panic and terror, the rational side of my mind advocated easing along slowly. I didn't want to drive head-on into a brick wall or something equally deadly.

Several creatures swarmed the car, pounding on the hood and quarter panels as I drove off. One of them managed to climb onto the trunk, holding on tight as I swerved left and right in an attempt to dump him off. His buddies shuffled alongside as best they could, but they didn't seem to be able to move faster than a quick lumber, and within half a block, I left them behind with only the one hanging on to deal with. His nails click-click-clicked as he scrambled across the roof. He grabbed on to the door handle with one hand and the windshield wiper with the other. His hideously distorted face, eyes blazing red fire, hung down in front of me, blocking my view. I could hear his snarls and growls through the window. The wiper arm creaked as it bent under his touch.

There was only one thing I could think of to do to get rid of it. I took a deep breath, held it, and slammed on the brakes. The monstrosity's eyes went wide as its body was hurled off the end of the hood. I floored the Le Mans, and it lurched forward. My teeth clicked together so hard I was afraid I'd broken a tooth as the car ran over the creature, and again as the back wheels connected with it too.

Even though I wanted to check to make sure it was dead, I forced myself to just drive on. I had to get to the meadow. It was about a mile and a half east of Cailleach Canyon, which was about ten miles out of town. Normally a ten or fifteen minute ride, but at the rate I was going, it would take me almost an hour to get there. As thick as the darkness was, I was afraid to go much faster. It was tempting, though, because the street was flooded with the monstrosities. Half a dozen or more shuffled toward me from all around the car while two or three stood on the sidewalk and glared at me as I drove past, their crimson eyes glowing in the darkness.

"Don't look at them," I cautioned myself. "Just keep moving, slow and steady. Don't let them get to you."

I focused on driving slowly, keeping my eyes straight ahead, and felt myself begin to relax a little bit. But just as I rolled my shoulders and released the breath I'd been holding, static blasted from my cell, and I jumped so hard I hit my head on the top of the car.

"What the—" Rubbing my head, I took my eyes off the road long enough to grab my backpack off the floorboard and dump it on the passenger seat. I reached inside and fumbled around for my phone as I turned back to the road—and slammed on my brakes. The tires locked, screeched, and sent the Le Mans into a fishtail that seemed to go on forever until finally skidding to a stop. My backpack went flying, strewing the contents all over the floor. The static from my phone got louder.

A shadowy figure appeared at the edge of the headlights.

I think I screamed.

Chase Kennedy stood in the road directly in front of the car. I'd missed running him over by mere inches. He'd been part of Logan's crew but had started to fall away by the beginning of our senior year. It was a long story, but he was afraid of me, and at the party where so many of my classmates had been slaughtered by Mr. Hansen, Chase had left when he'd first seen me there. He'd been avoiding me ever since.

And now, here he was. He looked…normal. His eyes didn't glow, he wasn't snarling, and his color was the same as always. So if he wasn't a monstrosity, if he was, in fact, human, why was he here? Was he actually here to help me?

I put the car in Park but left the motor running. After looking carefully around to make sure he was alone, I opened the door and stepped cautiously out.

"Chase?" I kept the door open and took a step toward him. His eyes were wide and unblinking, filled with terror. Blood was smeared across his cheek and up into his hairline. "Chase?" I repeated. "What are you doing here? Are you all right?"

"They lie."

Confused, I tilted my head and frowned. "They? They who?"

Before he could respond, several sets of claws appeared and snatched him back into the darkness. His shrieks of terror and panic pierced my eardrums like they were made of tissue paper as the monstrosities' claws shredded his flesh. The last I saw of him was as he disappeared, his mouth stretched wide in horror. The gibbering of the creatures nearly drowned out Chase's screams.

The whole thing took mere seconds, but it took much longer for me to process it. What had Chase meant? Who was he talking about?

A chill passed through me, and I looked all around, suddenly aware of where I was. The middle of the street, and outside my car. Those things could be anywhere, watching me, and I knew there wasn't much time left for me to get to the meadow.

A chittering came from somewhere nearby, and I whirled around, peering into the darkness. Vague shadows hid within it.

I jumped into the Le Mans and slammed the door just as the monstrosities surrounded the car.

They were everywhere.

Chapter 30

BETH

Beth dabbed some ointment on her knees and covered the scrapes with a couple of Band-Aids she'd found in the medicine chest. She chuckled at the little figure grinning up at her from the back of the plastic strip—Sully, the hairy monster from Monsters Inc. Her aunt's attempt at werewolf humor, she supposed. Especially since everyone was too old for characters on their bandages anymore.

Beth had walked home from the vacant lot where the ghost building had sat. It wasn't very far—Wolf Creek was a small town, after all—and now that she was a psychopomp, the dark didn't scare her much. Not counting the darkness inside the ghost hospital.

Psychopomp. It was such a stuck-up word. Reminded her of pompous. There had to be some other word for it. Spirit guide? So far, there didn't seem to be much guiding going on. Reaper? That was too grim. She giggled at her pun. Maybe soul walker. That might work.

She called Uncle Robbie and told him where she was, not wanting him to worry about her. Lucky for her he was too distracted to really care. He'd even forgotten she'd originally said she would bring them some coffee. No great surprise there.

More research on various legends surrounding soul walkers was entertaining but didn't give her the answers she was looking for. She was beginning to think she'd never discover her place in all this.

A thought occurred to her: back when she and James had been battling the first werewolf and Donna had crashed the truck, Beth had lain in the hospital, unconscious. She'd had some really weird dreams, and now she wondered if that was when this whole soul walker thing had actually started. Didn't Daddy say that it was often brought on by some kind of trauma? Few things were more traumatic than being knocked unconscious by a werewolf. And ever since then, she'd had a lot of déjà vu, and even a few premonitions.

At first, she'd just assumed her abilities had started when Kimberlin crashed her car, but now she thought maybe, just maybe, they'd actually started way back when she was eleven and she was only just now beginning to recognize them.

She sat on James's bed and leaned back against the headboard, her hand resting lightly on the laptop. It was too much to process all at once. Her eyes drifted shut and she dozed.

"Beth, are you there? Beth?"

Beth stirred but didn't wake.

"I know you're there. It's time to wake up now."

"Huh?" Beth murmured. "What?"

"Don't you want to know what's going on? How to help that cousin of yours?"

At this, Beth woke up, rubbed her eyes, and moved the laptop off her lap.

"Oh, you don't want to do that." It was the voice from the ghost hospital.

"Huh? Do what?" She looked around the room, a little flustered. "Who are you? *Where* are you?"

"You can call me..." The voice paused, and Beth couldn't help but wonder why. What was he hiding? "Marty. And I'm right here."

She frowned. "Right where?"

The screen on the laptop flickered. "Here."

She pulled the laptop back onto her lap and stared at it. Something on the screen seemed to be moving, some shape a shade darker than the background it bounced around on. It was mesmerizing, and it felt like she was falling into it. Shifting around a little, she blinked and shook her head to clear it.

"Tell me what you want."

"I only want to help you."

"Help me what?"

The voice snickered. "What do you think?"

"You said before that you could tell me what I want to know."

"That's right."

"Okay, so tell me."

The voice snickered again. "Not so fast, little one."

She cocked her head, trying to figure out what he wanted. It was nearly impossible, since she didn't even know who he was or why he chose now to appear to her. Or how he was able to speak to her from inside a computer.

"What do you want?"

"Only to help you."

"Yeah, I know. You said that. Twice already. But what do you want from me before you'll help me and James?"

"A promise."

"What kind of promise?" A tiny trickle of fear inched its way through her, and the breath of a whisper caressed the back of her neck. She shuddered and rubbed her neck vigorously.

"Just a tiny little thing, actually."

The blob on the screen accelerated, bouncing merrily from one side to the other. As she watched, it turned from nearly transparent to yellow to orange to bright red before it settled back into a yellow-gray mass that moved sluggishly around the screen. That put her senses on high alert, and she wondered if that was how to tell the voice was lying to her.

"How tiny?"

"It's nothing, really."

"Okay."

"Just a little something."

"O-kay." This whole thing was getting tiresome. Would he ever spit it out, this "tiny little thing" he wanted from her?

"You won't have a problem with it. Probably…"

"Just get on with it already. Geez."

"When this thing is all over and done with…"

"Yeah?"

"I want you to come and be with me."

"Be with you? What do you mean, be with you?"

"You know. Be with me. In my house."

That trickle of fear had grown to a tidal wave that washed over her, and she couldn't shake the resulting chill. She wrapped her arms tightly around her body and shuddered.

"With you? You mean, *with you*, with you?"

The blob on the screen flashed crimson again. This time, it stayed that way.

"With me. Forever. Just like the others."

Chapter 31

Others? Other what? Soul walkers? Girls? Just what exactly did he mean, others?

"So," she said slowly, still trying to think things through. "Let me see if I got this right. You want me to promise to be your friend for the rest of my life. And if I do, you'll tell me how to help James figure out what happened in the meadow so he can recover and wake up from his coma?"

The voice tittered. The splotch on the screen had faded to that dull yellow again. "Friend. Sure."

"Before I do, I want to know what you mean by 'others.' Are you saying there are other soul walkers that you've conned into doing whatever you want them to?"

"That's such an ugly word, conned."

"Whatever, dude. Answer the question."

"All in good time, my dear. Do I have your promise or not?"

She sighed heavily, uncertain what to do. On the one hand, she wasn't sure exactly what she was promising. She could find herself in some real trouble. But on the other hand, if she refused, James could die.

And on the third hand, there was no way to tell if this disembodied voice, this Marty dude, was telling her the truth or not. Especially since she had no idea who he was.

"Well?"

"Fine."

"Say it. Say you promise."

"I promise. Now tell me what I need to do to save James."

"Soon, Beth. Real soon."

The screen on the laptop flickered and went dark. Panic swirled in Beth's stomach. "Marty?"

Silence.

She gripped it with both hands and leaned forward. "Marty!"

More silence.

She shook it, but the screen remained dark. "Marty!" she screamed. "Come back!"

No response.

Panic and anger filled her. She slammed the laptop shut. "No," she cried. Tears flowed down her cheeks, and she made no attempt to wipe them away.

She had to wonder if Marty was Timmy's "bad man," and if he was, how he was connected to her and James. She suspected he was, somehow, but if so, there wasn't anything she could do about it right now. In order to figure out just what was going on, and more importantly, save James, she would do whatever she had to do.

Hopefully, she wouldn't regret it.

Chapter 32

Sweat beaded up on my forehead as I sat in my car, surrounded by the monstrosities. I felt kind of wonky, and my chest burned a little. I rubbed it, trying to ignore the discomfort, and watched as the creatures raked their claws down the sides of the Le Mans and beat on the hood and trunk. The windows rattled with the force of the blows, and I was afraid that if they didn't stop soon, the windshield would crack. Then I'd really be screwed.

I gripped the steering wheel like I was riding a white-knuckler at Magic Mountain and laid my forehead on my hands. I needed to rest so I would be able to think. If I just closed my eyes for a second…

A solid knock on the window next to my head woke me. I jerked awake. My first thought was that one of those things had gotten inside the car, but when I turned to see who it was, I laughed so hard I nearly peed myself with relief.

"James." The voice was soft and a little on the high side. "James, are you in there?"

That made me stop laughing. Of course, I was in

here. Where else would I be? Couldn't she see me? It was such an odd question.

"James," she called again. "James, it's me—"

"Watts!" we both said at the same time.

Shaniqua's best friend. I was so glad to see her. When I'd first met Watts, she didn't seem like someone I would ever be friends with. Shaniqua always called her a Unique, and with her purple Mohawk, thick black goop on her eyes and penchant for wearing obscure band tee-shirts, oddly-fitting skirts and Doc Martens with everything, she was definitely different. But she was also kind, a great friend to those who took the time to get to know her, and way cool with my being a werewolf.

"Dude, am I glad to see you." I unlocked the door and reached for the handle.

Watts leaned her knee into the door, preventing me from opening it. "Why'd you do it?"

"Do what?"

"I can't believe you'd do something like that."

"What are you talking about?" I pushed against the door, but Watts must have been leaning all her weight on it, because it didn't budge. "Let me out, will ya?" I rattled the handle again and pushed harder.

"What about Shaniqua, James? Did you, for even one minute, think about her?"

"Watts." For the first time since this whole nightmare started, I was pissed. I mean really, really pissed. Not mad because I was scared. Nothing like that. I was really and truly angry. And had just about reached my limit. "What the hell are you talking about? I didn't do anything to Shaniqua. You know I would never hurt her." I rammed the door with my shoulder. "Now let me out of here right this minute."

She backed off the door a little, and I took advantage of it and pushed it open. As I climbed out of the car, I realized Watts was still backing away. The darkness was about to swallow her up.

"Wait!" I was just about to rush after her when I realized where I was.

In the midst of an inky black world determined to do me harm.

There was nothing I could do about Watts, nor did I understand what she'd been talking about. But if Shaniqua was in trouble because of something I'd done, I would just have to redouble my efforts to get to the meadow and take care of whatever it was I was supposed to take care of.

Without warning, monstrosities shot out of the shadows, growling and snarling angrily as they shambled toward me.

"This is a frigging joke," I mumbled as I hopped back in the Le Mans and locked it. "I'm really getting sick of all this *shit*," I yelled the last word as I pounded on the steering wheel in frustration. I closed my eyes and laid my head on my arm, which I'd draped over the wheel. Weariness seeped through my bones, and I wondered if I would ever get out of here, if the merry-go-round would ever stop. If things would ever get back to normal.

My eyes fluttered open, and I gazed into the darkness.

A man, a *human* man, looked back at me. "Hey, James. It's going to be all right. You're going to be okay. Here—" He jiggled the door handle. "—let me help you."

My first thought was to unlock the door and let him in, but at the last second, I hesitated. Something—fear, uncertainty, maybe even a little touch of paranoia—kept me from doing it.

He rattled the handle again. "Hey, come on, now. Let me in."

The rattling got a little harder, a little more insistent.

I swallowed a lump the size of one of those Kia hamster cars and ran my palms across the top of the steering wheel. "Mm, that's okay." I didn't want to look at him. For some reason, I was afraid of what I might see. "I'm good."

"I said…" The man pounded on the window. "Let. Me. In!"

When I glanced at him out of the corner of my eye, a moan started low in my throat and grew until it became an almost frenetic giggle. Struggling to contain my panic, I watched as the man's face lengthened into a hairy muzzle, his teeth becoming razor sharp points that dripped hot saliva that I knew from experience would burn my skin if it dropped onto my arm.

Something, call it intuition or maybe just a hunch, told me that this particular monstrosity wasn't out to get me. Not right now, anyway. It might change at some point in the future, but I was confident I was safe now, at least for the time being. I couldn't say exactly why I knew that, I just did. So I started the car, took a final look at it, and drove off.

Chapter 33

"Is he gone?"

Beth rolled over and blinked at the ceiling over her bed. "What? Is who gone?"

"The bad man," Timmy said. "He was here, wasn't he?"

Beth sat up, pulled her knees to her chest, and dug the sleep out of her eye. "Well, someone was here. He said his name was Marty."

Timmy sat down on the edge of the bed, hugging herself, and looked at Beth. Fear shone out from her dull gray eyes. "I don't know what his name is." She rubbed her arm and looked nervously around the room. "But I can feel that he was here."

"He said that he could help me. I got the feeling that what he wanted to teach me was different than just flipping, like you showed me. I don't know how I know that, but if he can show me something that will help James, then..."

Timmy whipped her head around and stared at her, her eyes wide and panicky. "You're not going to let him, are you? You can't!"

Beth leaned forward, wishing she could reassure her

with a gentle touch on her knee. "It'll be okay. You'll see."

"No, it won't!" Timmy practically leaped off the bed and backed away, her hands waving wildly. "It won't be okay."

Beth got out of bed and tried to calm the little girl down. "It's all right, Timmy. Don't worry."

Tears welled in Timmy's eyes, and a big gray snot bubble hung from her nose. "He's a bad man," she sobbed. "And you'll be sorry."

"Timmy…"

"No! Leave me alone. You're not my friend."

"Yes, I am, Timmy. I am."

"No." She had backed into a corner of the bedroom, still looking about wildly. "He'll get you, Beth. Just like he got me."

"Nothing will happen. I promise." She gestured first at Timmy, then at herself. "And you and I? We'll always be friends."

"No, we won't. He'll get you, and no one will ever see you again. Just wait."

Before Beth could reply, Timmy was gone.

And as hard as she'd tried to reassure her friend, Beth couldn't shake the feeling that she might be right.

Beth just might soon be gone as well.

❧❧❧

Beth was pretty sure she was dreaming. Her room was filled with deep shadows, illuminated only by the flickering light coming from the screen of James's laptop. She watched from her bed as the bouncing splotch inside it spilled out onto the blanket beside her and dripped onto the floor, where it became a huge pulsating oil slick.

"You've had a child in here, haven't you, my

sweet?" Marty's voice was different, somehow. Garbled, like it was coming from underwater somewhere. "A ghost child."

She sat up and swung her legs around, dangling them off the side of the bed. An instant chill went through her legs, and she quickly pulled them up again. "How did you know that?"

"I can just tell." There was a definite edge to his voice. "You want to be careful, Beth. Don't go getting too friendly with a ghost."

"Why not? Aren't we supposed to help them?"

"No, we help spirits cross over to the other side."

"Ghosts, spirits. What's the difference?"

"Spirits are souls whose bodies have just died. When they can't find their way, or are stuck in Shadowland, then we guide them into the Underworld. Ghosts are something entirely different."

"But *how* are they different?"

"For one thing, they're stuck in Shadowland. Not part of the real world, and they can't get to the Underworld. Plus, they're dangerous."

"Dangerous? How? What do they want from us?"

"Just trust me on this. Stay away from ghosts."

"But Ti—" She stopped herself from saying Timmy's name out loud, for fear that if Marty knew it, he might be able to find her. And hurt her.

Or worse.

"What's that, you started to say?"

"She's my friend. The one who was here before."

"She's dangerous!" he shouted. The pool bubbled crazily around the edges, seemingly reaching out to grab her and yank her down into its inky depths. She threw herself back and pushed into the corner in an attempt to get away. A single tendril whipped across her wrist and she cried out in pain and terror.

She wanted to scream. To wake up.

"You stay away from her, or I…"

"Or what? What will happen?"

The pool settled down and seemed to compose itself a little. It ebbed and flowed, occasionally rising up only to crash softly down again, just like the ocean at Newport Beach. It was mesmerizing, and she struggled to tear herself away from it, massaging her reddened wrist.

"Nothing. Just stay away from her."

"Fine." There was no way in hell she was going to abandon Timmy, but this freak didn't have to know that. "Then what do you want, Marty?" In spite of the fact that her legs were now tucked safely underneath her, they still felt like huge blocks of ice, and she rubbed her calf briskly.

"I'm here to help you. Remember?"

"Uh huh." She looked around nervously as a slight breeze ruffled her hair, tickling the back of her neck. The shadows were deepening as they lengthened, giving the room an eerie, off-kilter pitch that reminded her of that old black and white show, *The Twilight Zone*, that they sometimes played on TV.

"I can teach you lots of things."

"You're changing the subject."

"Isn't that why you wanted me to come here? To teach you?"

It was getting colder, and she wrapped her blanket around her shoulders and crossed her arms against the chill. She didn't trust Marty any more than crooks trusted cops, and she wasn't sure she really wanted to know how to deal with being a soul walker, but what choice did she have?

She shrugged. "So teach me already."

⋯⋯

She'd been right. What Marty wanted to show her was better than simply flipping. She'd be able to go into a person's memories. Better than simply appearing in James's subconscious, she hoped to be able to actually see what had happened to him.

But to begin with, she had to have some sort of connection to wherever she wanted to go in the memory. It could be something as insignificant as a place she had always wanted to see. But it was best to start with a place that was special, somewhere she'd had good times with the memory-holder.

As she mulled over where to go, she realized that she'd been right after all. There had to be a connection between her and James and Marty. She'd just have to figure out what it was.

She thought about all the places she and her cousin had gone together over the years: PJ's Diner for hot pastrami sandwiches and chili fries; James's room, where they'd built countless forts and defeated untold numbers of alien invaders; even the playground at the elementary school where she'd once talked him down from the monkey bars and held him while he cried about Riff's death. But eventually, she decided on the last place where they'd had fun. Maybe there'd be some trace of James there, some clue she could use to help him.

"How about Cinemopolis?"

"The three dollar theater?"

"Yeah. That's where I want to go."

"If you say so." The black stain shuddered. Heat rose up from the darkness like the steam from her mother's morning cup of Earl Grey. It began to churn, roiling and boiling, madly bubbling away as it rose up to form shape after shape. Beth watched, wide-eyed, as it eventually took the shape of a man. Before she knew it, the same tendrils that grabbed her before shot out from what appeared to be the shape's wrists and yanked her into the puddle, which had now grown into a small pond. "Keep a picture of the place you want to go in your mind. And hold on tight. Here we go."

She screamed as she was swallowed by the black goo.

Chapter 34

"Y ou need to keep your eyes open, so you can see what to do when you're on your own."

Beth slowly did as she was told. It seemed to take forever and made her dizzy. This wasn't anything like when she went through walls with Timmy. That was something she had a little control over. This was totally different. It felt like she was speeding backward and upside down through a tunnel. She reached out, trying to grab hold of something, anything, to steady herself, but there was nothing there. It was all she could do to keep a picture of the movie theater in her mind.

The darkness filled her, chilling her soul and sending shivers up and down her spine. It carried them along with the swift, unyielding power of an ocean current.

"Stop fighting it," Marty told her. "It'll be much easier on you if you just relax."

"Oh, is that all." But she tried, and before too long, found herself soaring along in more or less a straight line, no longer spiraling out of control.

Then, as suddenly as the journey had begun, things slowed down, and the world finally stopped spinning in tandem with her stomach.

She bent over and rubbed her forehead, taking several deep breaths to steady herself, and looked around. Marty had brought her to the theater, just like he said he would, and they were standing in the street in front of it.

Everything was dark and full of shadows, and she thought maybe she was in a memory. But was it hers, or James's?

"Marty, whose memory is this?"

"Don't you know?"

"Not really."

Marty shrugged but didn't say anything else.

"How did you bring us here?" she asked when she realized he wasn't going to answer her.

No longer dripping black sludge, the tendrils of goo replaced by the shadows of hands, Marty stood next to her as a simple silhouette, like a construction paper cutout. "You just have to focus. On where you want to go, and how you want to get there. For me, it's through the darkness. For you, it might be something else." He had no face, but Beth heard the smirk in his voice. "Probably sunshine," he muttered.

"What?" she asked, knowing full well what he'd said.

"Nothing. Come on." He grasped her hand, but it was rough and heated to the touch, and she snatched it away.

"Where we going?"

The paper cutout turned to look at her. "You wanted to see the theater. So let's go see it."

This time, the doors were unlocked, and they went inside. It smelled like old popcorn. "This is so weird," Beth said. "How come we're in color when everything else looks black and white like an old TV show?" When she'd been here in James's subconscious, everything had been kind of grayish, except the darkness outside. But now, everything was dark and shady.

She looked Marty up and down and smiled. "Well, I am, at least. You're solid black."

"Black's a color."

"Actually, it's the absence of color." She remembered that much from Art class. "What I meant was—"

"I know what you meant."

"So, how come?"

"Because we're not part of Shadowland. Not really part of the regular world, either, but more there than here. Besides—" He turned to Beth again. "—how would we recognize each other, if we were the same as everything else?"

"You've got a point."

They walked through the Lobby and over to the snack bar. What she wouldn't give for some Raisinets right about now.

She leaned against the counter. "Let me see if I have things right. All I have to do to go from reality to…" She gestured around. "…this, is just jump into that black gunk, hold on, and picture myself there?"

"For me, it's the "black gunk,"" he told her, making air quotes. "But, like I said, for you, it'll be something else."

"Hmm." Turning around and pretending to study the candies in the showcase, Beth scrutinized Marty out of the corner of her eye. His shape seemed somehow familiar, but she just couldn't tell for sure who he was. As she studied him, she wondered if she'd be able to travel to some other place without any help. She'd always been a quick study, and if she was lucky, she just might be able to do it.

Images of the blob from the laptop popped into her mind, and how it had turned bright red when Marty had gotten angry. She saw the oil slick bubble, rising up to seize her around the wrist, trying to pull her down into it.

But wasn't he trying to help her? Teach her how to do it on her own? So why would he be angry when she did? She had to risk it. Her mind made up, she focused on James, visualizing his room. The theater shimmered and began to fade away. Dizziness made her stomach lurch, and she was plunged into a blinding white-hot light that seared images of her and James onto the inside of her eyelids.

Hopefully, her leaving so abruptly wouldn't piss Marty off. No telling what he would do then.

☙❧❧

At the last second, she changed her mind and sent herself to the alley behind PJs Diner. She didn't know if this Marty person knew where James lived or not, but in case he didn't, and couldn't find her unless she left a trail from where they'd been to where she went, she didn't want to risk going straight home.

It was a warm evening, but she was still a little cold. Whether from being in her cousin's mind or from actually flipping, she didn't know. Didn't really care. She rubbed her arms briskly and walked quickly down the alley and around the corner of the diner. Peering into the window, she remembered all the times she and James had shared chili fries and Cokes and smiled sadly.

Diane, the main server and owner of the diner since PJ died, looked up from wiping down the counter. When she saw Beth, she smiled and motioned for her to come in.

"Hey, sweetie." Diane came out from behind the counter, threw her arm around Beth, and squeezed her tight. "How are you?"

The thing Beth and James had liked most about Diane was that she always treated them like they were real people, not just annoying kids she couldn't wait to get rid of. Concern etched her face, and Beth could feel Diane's warmth wrap around her like a soft fleece blanket. She leaned into the woman, who smelled faintly of fried doughnuts and chocolate, and let herself enjoy the embrace.

"I've been better."

"Yeah, I'll bet." She steered Beth into a booth and sat down across from her. "How's James? Any better?"

Beth shook her head and was surprised at the tears that welled up. "Not really."

Diane reached across the table and gently patted her hands. Beth wasn't surprised to see tears in Diane's eyes when she looked at her. "I'm so, so sorry, honey. I like James. A lot. He was such a wonderful little boy and turning into a right fine man. I know you miss him terribly."

That was too much. No one had ever acknowledged her feelings in all this, not once. She and James had always been as close as any two people could be, more like brother and sister than cousins, and the thought of losing him, well, she just couldn't bear it. She burst into tears, sobbing and wailing as though the world was ending. If James died, her world *would* end.

And no one even cared.

The diner door slammed open and the bell above it that announced the arrival of a customer tinkled madly.

"Hello, ladies." Sheriff Riggs stood in the doorway, his legs spread apart, hands on his utility belt, a supercilious grin on his face. What Uncle Robbie called his power stance. It made him look even more arrogant than normal.

Beth yanked her hands away from Diane and wiped her eyes. The last thing she wanted was for the sheriff to see her cry. He was nothing more than a skinny little bully who took great delight in tormenting James. And by extension, her. How he'd gotten to be sheriff, she'd never figure out. He was such a doofus. Why couldn't more people see that?

"Well, well, what's going on here?" He strode across the diner to their booth.

"Oh, just a little girl talk." Diane smiled sweetly up at him.

"Well, fine then. That's just fine." He grinned down at them.

Beth rolled her eyes.

"So, Beth. What's new?"

Before she could say anything, Diane rammed her toe into Riggs's shin.

"Ow," he exclaimed. "Dammit, Diane, whaddya do that for?"

Diane tilted her head and rolled her eyes at Beth.

Riggs rubbed his shin and frowned. "What do you mean?"

Diane sighed heavily, nodding at Beth twice this time.

"Huh?" Riggs reached up under his Pharrell hat and scratched his head. He closed one eye and studied Beth. "Oh. You mean that little maggot, James?"

"God, Riggs." Diane got up and pushed him just hard enough to make him take a step back. "Have a little tact for once, will you?"

Riggs watched her as she headed back behind the counter. "Sure, sure." He removed his hat, ran his palm across his well-moused hair, and returned the hat to his head. "So how about some coffee, there, Di?"

Diane held up a pot and swirled the coffee around. "Let me make some fresh. This's been sitting too long."

Riggs nodded as he slid into the booth across from Beth. As he did so, an image of Sheriff Brazelton zoomed into Beth's memory. He'd been a pretty nice guy, never holding the stupid things James had done when he was eleven against him. Unlike Riggs, who had always hated James. Probably why he hadn't bothered to find out who shot him.

"Little lady." Riggs nodded and smiled at her, his eyes sparkling.

"You find out who shot my cousin yet?" A slight noise came from outside, and she glanced at the window. She thought she saw something. It almost looked like someone, some vague shape, was wiping off the window. Could it be?

She shook her head. No way.

"Aren't you the little spitfire?" He made a production of pulling a paper napkin out of the dispenser before spinning the Lazy Susan full of flavored creamers and plucking out three Irish Cream containers.

She turned her attention back to Riggs. "I take it that's a no."

Diane arrived with the coffee, banged a cup down on the table, and filled it. She moved the pot just a little bit before she stopped pouring, and Beth couldn't help but giggle and try to hide it behind her hand when Riggs jumped up and brushed the hot liquid off his pants.

"Hey, watch what you're doing, there, Diane. That's hot!"

"Oh, sorry." She winked at Beth as she turned away, and Beth giggled again, not bothering to hide it this time.

"Sumanabitch," he muttered as he yanked a handful of napkins out of the dispenser and mopped up his lap. When he'd wiped off as much as he could, he tossed the wad on the table and looked at Beth. She'd gotten over her mirth and was now glaring at him. "What?"

"Do you at least have any leads?"

"Leads?"

"On who shot James." Duh.

He waved his index finger at her. "That would be police business, little lady." He smirked. "Not yours."

"Whatever." She slid out of the booth and took a few steps then hesitated. "Even if you're not smart enough to figure it out…" She stepped back and looked Riggs in the eye. "I am. And I will. Little lady."

As she headed for the door, Riggs called after her. "You just better watch it, Beth. Someday, you're going to need me to be your friend. You'll see."

God help her if that day ever came.

Chapter 35

As I drove slowly through the shadows and murk, I realized the darkness was more gray than black, that it had lightened somehow. The outline of the town slowly emerged. I could just make out the Sheriff's office, Anderson's Hardware, and The First Edition bookstore.

And there was PJs. Next to home, my favorite place in the whole world. What I wouldn't give for one of her world-famous pastrami sandwiches and a plate of chili-cheese fries. As long as they didn't taste like sawdust.

A light so dull I wasn't sure what it was at first came on in one of the buildings. I stopped the car and squinted until I could make out the sign above the door the light came out of. The diner!

And were those figures moving around in there?

What did it mean, that there was a light on at the diner when every other building in town was dark and lifeless?

I sat there and watched for a few minutes, hoping to catch sight of…what? People? More particularly, someone I knew? Someone who knew what was going on?

The sound of a small bell tinkling came to me. It sounded just like the one over the door of the diner, the one that let Diane know when she had a customer.

I hadn't seen anyone go in or out, but if the door had been opened, there had to be someone in there, and I needed to see who it was. I climbed out of the car and ran over to the diner, used my sleeve to wipe the window and looked inside. It was so hazy in there that I couldn't see anything. I rubbed the glass again and peered inside, this time wrapping my hands around my eyes to try and see better.

It looked like there were people sitting in a booth, the one that Beth and I always sat in when we were there. We called it our lucky booth, ever since it was the one we'd sat in to eavesdrop on Sheriff Brazelton and Riggs to see if they had any idea that the first serial killer to stalk the town was actually a werewolf.

Of course, they didn't.

Standing outside the diner, I couldn't help but wish I were inside, that Beth and I were sharing a plate of those awesome chili-cheese fries. Even though I wasn't really hungry—why not, I wondered. How long had it been since I'd eaten?—just the thought made me salivate.

Wait. Was that…Beth sitting there, in our booth?

I tapped on the window. "Beth!" I shouted. "Beth, it's me!"

As suddenly as it had appeared, the light went off.

And I was abruptly aware that I was standing in the darkness.

Alone.

With no way to protect myself.

Thursday, April 21, 2016
Day 88

Chapter 36

Exhausted from running through walls with Timmy and flipping in and out of James's mind with Marty, Beth fell into a deep, dreamless sleep and didn't budge for over ten hours. Starving when she woke up, she'd gulped down a couple of James's Pop-Tarts—Breakfast of Champions, he always called them—and fired up his laptop. She was reading an article on the Internet about the latest in a string of rapes and murders of girls in Wolf Creek and the surrounding area when Timmy popped in on her.

"You need to see something," she informed Beth.

Beth didn't even look up from the computer screen. How could it be happening again? First, PJ contracted the werewolf madness known as Moonspell, killing several people. Then Mr. Hansen turned out to be her brother, out to avenge her death by stalking and killing three kids during the full moons and six or seven more at that girl's birthday party before attacking James. Now, this?

"Beth." Timmy stomped her foot and when that got no reaction, kicked the table leg. Beth reluctantly stopped reading and looked at her.

"What?"

"I have to show you something."

Beth turned back to the article. "Later."

"No. Now. Right now."

Beth levelled her gaze at her ghost friend, wishing for once that she'd just go away. "Why? Why does it have to be right this minute?"

"You'll see. But I promise. It's important." She held out her hand, and Beth grudgingly closed the laptop and took Timmy's hand. Instantly, her mouth filled with that metallic taste from before. She had time to think that she must be getting used to it because she was hardly sick to her stomach at all, and then they were gone.

When she opened her eyes seconds later, she was standing on the sidewalk in front of the ghost hospital. Timmy was nowhere to be found.

As she stood there, pondering what that meant, she heard footsteps behind her and whirled around to see who it was.

"Hiya, Beth." Jazz gave her a half-hearted little wave. "How you doin'?"

"Hey, Jazz. You scared me."

Jazz looked over her shoulder. "Yeah, there's a lot of that going on around here."

"What does that mean?"

"Nothing." Jazz took her hand and dragged her down the street. "Come on, I want to show you something."

"What?"

"Just come on."

Beth glanced across the street at the hospital where her cousin was fighting for his life. *I'll be there soon, James. And we'll figure out together how to get you back. I promise.*

As they walked on, she tried to keep track of where they were going, but reading the street signs was almost impossible because everything was gray and misty—the buildings, the streets, signs. The writing on the signs blended into the signs themselves.

"Jazzy, where are we going?"

Jazz didn't seem to hear her.

"Jazz?" Jazz's eyes had glazed over, and she wouldn't look at Beth.

Finally, they turned a corner, and Beth realized they were about three blocks from the center of town. There were alleys behind all the houses here, lined with garbage bins and littered with junk people had discarded, things like couches with ripped upholstery, chairs with busted legs, and an old-fashioned TV with a cracked screen. Shattered glass glinted dully against the grayness.

Weeds trespassed heartily through cracks in the wooden fences separating the alley from the back yards of the houses. Beth followed along behind Jazz, checking both sides of the alley. For what, she didn't know. Jazz simply trod along, looking straight ahead, never at one side or the other. About two-thirds of the way down, they stopped, and Jazzy finally turned to look at a house on their right.

Beth stood quietly next to her, waiting. The house seemed familiar, and it took several moments for her to realize where she'd seen it before. At least, she thought she had, because the last time, it was from the front. She thought it was the house Timmy had taken her to—the house where the bad man lived.

∽∘∾

If she learned anything from her trips out of the real world, it was that she had to stay focused. Otherwise, she might be forever stuck somewhere she didn't want to be. Freaking out would only prevent her from concentrating.

Tamping down her panic, she forced her breathing to return to normal and waited for her pulse to slow, then turned to Jazz.

"Why did you bring me here, Jazzy?"

"Look." Jazz leaned forward, her head disappearing behind the wooden fence.

Beth shrugged and did as she was told, peering into the gloomy half-light. At first, the back yard seemed normal enough with its rusted kettle barbeque lying on its side like road kill, pieces of newspapers and old hamburger wrappers collecting in the corners of the fence and entwined in the long-dead plants along the patio. It was so different from the front, which was nicely manicured with roses lining the driveway and brick walkway that lead up to the house. Almost like whoever lived there was hiding their true self.

A shiny tool shed stood in the corner of the yard furthest away from the house. She could tell it was new by the way it almost shined in the dreariness when everything else was barely more than a murky outline.

"Where are we, Jazz? Is this the bad man's house?"

Jazz pointed at the shed. "Just watch."

The door to the shed opened slowly, and a little girl in a green plaid jumper tiptoed out, followed by one with what looked like what once might have been lustrous auburn hair. Another one, slightly older than the others, with mousy brown hair that hung down in her face, crept out behind them, pulling along a toddler in a party dress.

They filed silently past Beth and Jazz, grim expressions on their faces, and disappeared around the corner of the house. Without even thinking about it, Beth pushed herself the rest of the way through the fence and trotted after them.

"Wait!" Jazzy hissed. "What are you doing?"

"I have to see who lives here. I have to find out

what's going on." Her stomach fluttered nervously, and she wondered why the girls all seemed familiar. She hurried on.

"No! Don't go any closer."

Beth turned to look at her. "Why not?" she demanded. "This *is* where the bad man lives, isn't it?"

Jazz looked at her feet and didn't answer.

Following after the girls, Beth stopped short when she nearly ran into the littlest one, who looked no more than three. All four were standing in a line, facing the side of the house, which reminded her of another side yard from that time almost three years ago when her best friend Lindy had heard strange noises coming from her father's shed. The little girl in the jumper, who seemed to be the leader of the group, pointed at the house. Beth looked to see what she was pointing at, but didn't see anything unusual.

A door slammed, and footsteps clomped toward them. The girls turned as a single unit to look at her. She peeked around the corner and saw a tall figure walking across the patio. If it kept going in the direction it was headed, whoever it was would discover her! Ducking back behind the house, she glanced over at where she and Jazz had first entered the yard, but Jazz was gone. Beth was on her own.

Wanting to tell them to run, she crouched down to make herself as small as possible and turned toward the girls. They were all staring at her.

The girl in the jumper began to scream.

Chapter 37

The other girls joined in and their combined screams bored through Beth's brain like an electric drill. As her hands flew to cover her ears, she flipped without even thinking about it, finding herself back in James's bedroom. She was home. Safe.

"Well, that was weird." Not just the girls screaming at her, but the way she'd flipped back to the real world. Had it happened because she'd been frightened, or was it just getting easier?

It was all too much and gave her a headache.

She went out into the hall. "Uncle Robbie? Aunt Annette? Anyone here?"

Not really expecting a response, she headed for the refrigerator. She needed a soda, hopefully, a Pepsi, but she'd take anything with caffeine. When she passed the kitchen table, she realized that the laptop was still there, and decided to do some research on the dead girls. Try to find out why they seemed so familiar, and what they all had in common.

Other than being murdered, of course.

She rummaged around in the fridge and found a Coke—not a Pepsi, but it was better than nothing—popped the top and took a long swallow. The resulting burp made her giggle. James would have been so proud. She wondered how he was doing, and thought briefly about going to see him but ultimately decided that he would be better served by her staying here and figuring out what was going on, how those little girls fit into the situation, and then bringing that information with her as she helped him.

James. How she missed him.

Refusing to let herself be sidetracked by sadness, she set her soda can down firmly on the table, brought James's printer in from the bedroom, hooked it up to the laptop, and got to work.

Two hours later, the phone rang. She glared at it—why did her aunt and uncle still have a landline, any-way?—but decided it probably wouldn't be a good idea to ignore it. Doing so might get her into trouble. Besides, it could be news about James.

"Hello?"

"Ah, Beth. There you are."

"Hey, Uncle Robbie. How's James?"

"Holding his own. How are you? Your auntie and I were worried about you."

"Me?" The question honestly surprised her. They had more important things to worry about right now.

Uncle Robbie chuckled. "Yeah, you. Or did you think we'd forgotten about you?"

"No, I—"

"I'm sorry we haven't been around much lately."

What, did they think she was five? Too young to un-derstand what was going on? She was almost fourteen. "That's okay, Uncle Robbie. James needs you right now. Besides, that's why I'm here, remember?"

"Yeah. Yeah, I guess it is. I just wanted you to know we're glad you are. Here, I mean."

That made her smile. He'd taken time away from his critically injured son just to let her know that she was important, too. Now wonder she loved him so much. "I know, Uncle." A big lump closed her throat and she cleared it in a vain attempt to get rid of the dumb thing. "I'm glad, too. So how's James doing?"

"Oh, about the same. Your aunt swears he squeezed her hand this morning, but…"

Could this be another sign that he was coming out of the coma? Or did it mean that he was fading and she didn't have much time left? "What did the doctor say?"

"Well, if it really happened, and wasn't just wishful thinking on Annette's part, then it could mean he's waking up."

There was something in the tone of his voice that made Beth sure he wasn't being completely honest with her. "What else?"

"Hmm?"

"There's something you're not telling me, isn't there?"

Uncle Robbie sighed heavily. She pictured him running his hands through his hair before wiping his mouth with the back of his hand—things he always did when nervous. "Dr. Petrelli said that there was a good chance it was nothing more than a reflex. Completely meaningless."

"No, it meant something." She closed her eyes. "It had to."

"Right. We have to stay positive."

Her eyes flew open. "Hey! What about that Scottish coma test thingie they gave him when he first went to the hospital? What about that?"

"You mean the Glascow Coma Scale? He scored something like a ten or eleven, I think."

"Yeah, yeah! And didn't they tell us that that was

good, that it meant that there was a good chance he would wake up?"

"Well, it wasn't as high as they'd like, but yeah, they said there was a fair chance. But he's been asleep for so long, now." Even though he tried to hide it, she could hear his voice catch.

"I know, but that doesn't matter. He'll come out of it soon. I know he will!"

She would make sure of it, even if it was the last thing she ever did.

❧❦❧

"Come on. You can do this." Beth stood in the middle of her bedroom and took several deep breaths. Her hands were curled into loose fists, and with each inhale, she bent her elbows and brought her fists up a few inches, then forced them down again on the exhale. She knew she looked ridiculous—James had told her so many times—but it helped her relax when she was nervous about something. She finished it off by rolling her shoulders and shaking her hands out.

She'd been trying for over an hour, but she just wasn't able to zap herself back into James's subconscious. She didn't understand. It had been so easy the first time. All she'd had to do was just think about him, and poof! She'd flipped right into the theater. So why couldn't she find him this time? Had flipping with Marty done something to her abilities? Made it harder to flip on her own?

Closing her eyes for the bazillionth time, she concentrated on James. "Send me into his mind," she murmured. "Come on. Just take me there already." Frustrated, she shifted her stance a little, splayed her hands as wide as she could to stretch them out, then curled them into tight fists before shaking them out again. "James. James. James."

Nothing. No tingling, no queasiness, no burning energy.

Damn.

She pursed her lips and opened her eyes. The room was filled with shadows that hadn't been there before. "What the hell?"

"I can help you with that."

Beth squinted into the darkness and watched as Marty stepped out of the farthest corner of the room. He was still a silhouette, but there was something a little different about him. He seemed a little less dark. She could almost—but not quite—make out his face.

"Help me with what?"

Marty chuckled. "You can't hide from me for very long, Beth. We're connected."

She tilted her head. "How? How are we connected?"

"Do you want me to help you get into James's mind or not?"

She shrugged. "If you want to."

Although he had no eyes, she could nevertheless feel him staring at her.

"Yes, I want you to help me."

"That's better."

He walked toward her, his cutout arms reaching out, and stopped directly in front of her, his hands on her shoulders. "Okay, now listen. Are you listening?"

"Ye-es," she said, drawing out the word without bothering to hide her annoyance.

"Play nice."

"Sorry."

Marty leaned in, so close that she felt like she might be sucked into his darkness. "Put your hands on my shoulders and look into my eyes."

"Your eyes?" she tittered. How could she look into something he didn't even have?

He took a step back, his arms falling to his side. "Maybe this was a bad idea."

An intense feeling of foreboding surged through her and she grabbed Marty's arms so tightly they seemed to crinkle like tissue paper. She had to get inside James's head. She just had to. "No, I'm sorry. I'm sorry. Just please tell me what to do."

"Well…"

"I'm sorry. Really. I am." She released her grip and smoothed the creases from his paper-like arms and hoped he believed her.

He appeared to search her eyes, although she couldn't really be sure. "Okay." He leaned forward and put his hands on her shoulders again. "Put your hands on my shoulders and your forehead against mine."

She did as he told her, grimacing slightly at the marble-like smoothness of his forehead.

"Close your eyes. Breathe deep and slow."

Seemed easy enough so far.

"Now, you must empty your mind. Don't think about anything. Let everything go."

That was not so easy. Unsure how he could expect her to do that, she nevertheless tried to make her mind blank, but it wasn't working. Every time she felt like she was close, her brain would send her a picture of James, her mother, her father's spirit. Anything that kept her mind from shutting down.

She took a step back, opened her eyes, and shook her head. "It's not working. I can't—"

"You can. You *must!*" he roared at her, causing her to take a couple more quick steps away from him. The silhouette seemed to almost solidify and burn hotly around the edges. She looked around wildly and tried to figure out if she could get past him and out the door to safety. What would happen if she pushed him? He hadn't felt quite solid when she'd put her hands on his shoulders, like grabbing hold of a pile of cupcake crumbs, so maybe he'd just blow away if she drove her shoulder into his stomach and knocked him down.

"I mean, you can do it, Beth." His voice brought her back to the present. "All you have to do is concentrate."

"I just don't know if I can. I keep seeing James, lying in that hospital bed, tubes everywhere." She closed her eyes tightly and shook her head to rid herself of the image.

"Sure you can. Come on." He gestured for her to walk over to him. "Let's keep trying."

"Okay," she said, walking hesitantly back to stand in front of him again. "But I don't think—"

"Shh. Give me your hands."

She did as she was told and he placed them on his shoulders, leaning forward until their foreheads were touching again. Her eyes closed.

"Now breathe deep. Slowly let it out."

They did this several times until her mind actually started to clear. Her arms felt very heavy and it was all she could do to keep them on Marty's shoulders. She shivered, suddenly very cold.

"That's it." Marty's voice was unexpectedly soothing. She was beginning to feel as though she were floating. A dark splotch, that she could only assume was Marty, glided along beside her. "You're almost there."

A picture of James in his hospital bed jumped into her mind. Maybe she could save him, after all.

"Cool, ain't it?"

Before she knew it, they were standing next to James's bed. He looked so small and defenseless. Not like her hero at all. They were running out of time.

Her aunt and uncle were sitting in chairs. The room was dark, shadows lurking in the corners. The machines that monitored her cousin's vital signs beeped softly, their lights glowing green and red in the gloom. Uncle Robbie was dozing, his soft snores a comforting sound. Aunt Annette's head rested on the corner of the bed, a rosary clutched between her hands. They looked utterly defeated.

With her hands on the bedrail, Beth leaned over and kissed her cousin on the cheek. He murmured softly. She stood bolt upright, her eyes wide. Had he just responded to her touch?

"Jamie?" Aunt Annette must have noticed it, too. "Jamie, are you awake?"

Uncle Robbie woke up and rubbed his face with both hands. "Annette? What is it?"

"Did you see that?"

"See what?"

"He said something." She rubbed his leg. "What are you trying to say, honey?"

James remained silent.

"Annette, darling." Uncle Robbie patted her shoulder. "You must have been dreaming."

"No, I wasn't! I was awake." She turned back to her son. "Tell us, Jaime. Tell us what you were trying to say."

"Annette—" Uncle Robbie's forehead crinkled with concern and worry.

"No!" Aunt Annette shrugged his hand away. "I didn't imagine it. I *didn't!*" She began to cry. "I didn't," she sobbed.

Sorrow filled Beth's heart, sending icy chills from her feet through her entire body. Their grief was just too much, and she couldn't take it anymore. "I want to go back," she told Marty. "Take me back!"

There was a slight tug, and she was hurled back through the tunnel quicker than she would have thought possible.

She landed on her feet in James's bedroom but stumbled back and fell on the bed. She lay there, looking at the ceiling, waiting for her pulse to slow and the trembling to stop.

After a few minutes, the bed moved beside her, and she turned her head to see Marty's dark silhouette sitting next to her. "Hey," he said.

She went back to staring at the ceiling. "I thought you said we were going into his mind. But all we did was go to his hospital room."

"We were in his mind. Didn't you see all the shadows? And the mist swirling around your feet?"

She sat up. Now that he mentioned it, her feet had felt like some sort of frozen snake had been coiling around them. And it was dark in there. But was it darker than it should have been? It was nighttime, after all.

"But, everything, every*one*, had looked so…so…"

"So normal?"

"Yeah. So normal."

Marty patted her arm. "Because that's how they look to James. Normal."

"Oh, that makes sense." She chewed on her lip in brooding contemplation. "Will there always be shadows and mist when I go into someone's mind?"

"Probably. But I wouldn't try it too often, or with very many people."

"Why not?"

"Because it can be very dangerous for you. Every time you do it, it will steal some of your essence away."

"My essence?"

"Your life force. Your energy. Your get-up-and-go."

If she could raise a single eyebrow, this is one of

those times she would. "My get-up-and-go?" She giggled. He couldn't be serious. Could he?

"I'm serious, Beth."

Had he just read her mind?

And if he had, what else had he learned that she
wanted to keep secret?

Chapter 38

Backing away from Beth and the diner, I checked nervously around me. There were now shadows within shadows surrounded by darkness, which seems melodramatic but was actually true. The darkness had thickened almost to the consistency of the chocolate syrup Mom used to put in my milk when I was little.

I tried to ignore the quivering in my gut and the twitching of my right eye and hustled over to my car. As I pulled open the door, a chill went through me, and my hands started shaking like Shaniqua's did when she drank too much caffeine. The monstrosities had found me again. There didn't seem to be any escape.

Climbing into my car, I looked over my shoulder and was surprised to see that while there were dozens of those things out there, they weren't trying to attack me. In fact, it was almost like there was some sort of invisible force field or something that was preventing them from getting close. They just seemed to mill about, bumping into each other and snarling, while still keeping an eye on me.

It was obvious that they were being controlled by someone. But why? Always before, they'd attacked and nearly killed me, and I would wind up back in my room. What was so different about this time? Why not just let them pounce and send me back there? Or let them kill me and get it over with?

I was busy trying to figure it out when my cell phone rang, startling me. Swearing softly, I rubbed the spot where I'd banged my head on the window. A small lump was already forming. Keeping one eye on the creatures, I pulled my cell out of my backpack and swept my thumb across it to answer the call.

I should have looked at the caller id.

As I put the phone up to my ear, I heard a deep cackling. A heavy chill surfed across my body, every hair standing at attention, as the force field seemed to have been broken by the ringing of my phone. The monstrosities were now shambling toward me.

"Hello, James."

It was D. R.

"What do you want?"

"Like I told you before, I just want to help you."

"Yeah. Right. That's why you sent more of these…things to get me. 'Cuz you want to help."

"Would you like me to send them away?"

"No, I want them to break in to my car so they can rip me to shreds."

D. R. remained silent.

I rolled my eyes. This guy reminded me of someone, someone in real life, only I couldn't quite figure out who.

"Fine. You win. Yes, I'd like you to send them away. But not like last time. For good this time."

D. R. still didn't say anything.

I was beginning to worry.

"D. R.? You still there?"

"If I send them away for you, what will you do for me?"

I scratched my chest. "What do you want me to do?"

"I want you to get me out of where I am."

"Where are you?"

"In your phone, smart guy."

"But…you've also been in my laptop. So how come you can go from there to my cell but not here, in my car?"

When he didn't answer, I sighed heavily. "Fine. What is it you need me to do?"

"Just close your eyes and wish me out."

"That's all?"

"That's all."

"How will that work?"

"It just will. Now, are you going to help me, or not?"

"Okay, but first things first."

"What?"

I gestured at the monstrosities, one of which was yanking out the antennae.

"Oh, them."

My eyes went wide, and I looked all around. It was as if he'd seen me. But how was that possible? Then again, how was any of this possible?

In the blink of an eye, the monstrosities were gone. Literally. I blinked and they were gone.

"There."

I could almost hear the glee in D. R.'s voice.

"Now, you."

I shifted in my seat and looked around nervously. Those things were gone for now, but would they be back? And if so, would they still be after me, after I set D. R. free? And what would he do when I did?

"Go on," D. R. insisted. "What are you waiting for?"

"So, I just close my eyes and *wish* you out of the phone?"

"Yep."

"Okay," I said, shifting around again. I reluctantly put the phone down on the passenger seat and took a deep breath. "Here goes."

I rubbed my chest trying to get rid of my heartburn, but that did no good. It still hurt like hell.

"I wish D. R. out of the phone and into this…place." I opened one eye and peeked at the phone, still lying on the seat beside me.

Nothing happened.

I cleared my throat and tried again. "I said, I wish D. R. out of the phone and into this place."

Still nothing.

"You can't just say it," D. R. said, a trace of annoyance in his voice. "You have to actually wish for it. Believe in it." His voice got louder, nearly booming out of the cell's speaker. "Make. It. Happen!"

"Right."

Who was he kidding? Just believing it will happen would make it happen? Seriously? It felt silly, like a five-year-old wishing on the candles of his birthday cake and expecting that wish to come true, but since I had no other real choice, I shrugged and took in two huge breaths, letting them out slowly through my mouth. *I believe. I believe. I believe.*

Then I made my wish.

At first, nothing happened. When I opened my eyes, everything looked exactly the same. Then I noticed a wispy ringlet of gray-white smoke coming from my phone. If it was getting ready to burst into flames, I wanted to be able to toss it out the window before it burned up my car. As I reached for it, the smoke darkened until it was black as it thickened until it was nearly solid.

"Dafuq?" I scratched my head, confused.

A thick black tendril shot out from the phone and punctured my chest. It twisted around my heart, somehow squeezing it with red-hot fire and a bitter coldness at the same time. I remember screaming in pain and terror.

Then everything went black.

Friday, April 22, 2016
Day 89

Chapter 39

It had taken some convincing, but she'd finally managed to get Marty to leave, claiming the trip into James's mind had left her exhausted. She had been a bit drained, but she really just wanted to be rid of the guy. He gave her the creeps, and she didn't trust him. Besides, if he could read her mind, it would be a bad thing if he knew that she had no intention of continuing any kind of relationship with him after this was all over, no matter what he'd forced her to promise.

When she'd gone to bed, she'd tossed and turned, disturbing dreams of weird creatures—half werewolf and half zombie, that looked remarkably like the little ghost girls from the bad man's house—chased her, invading her sleep.

Now she was sitting at the kitchen table, a soggy, half-eaten frozen waffle in front of her. If only Lindy were here. She missed her best friend from childhood. After PJ had slaughtered Lindy's father, she'd been shuffled off to one relative after another, and even though they'd promised to stay BFFs forever, eventually, they'd lost touch. Lindy had had a kind of uncomplicated pragmatism about her that Beth had always envied, and she could've used some of that simple wisdom now.

But she couldn't dwell on the past. Right now, she had to figure out how to solve the mystery surrounding the murdered girls and how that fit into what happened to James. She pictured the girls, all in a row, silently staring at the bad man's house. Was he still alive, or had he died and gone…where? The Underworld? If so, he had to be in Hell. But what if he wasn't? What if he was stuck in Shadowland for some reason? Would he still be able to kill?

And what about the girls? She imagined them standing in her front yard, watching and waiting, maybe to hurt her, too, and she shuddered.

"I wouldn't worry about them," Timmy said, emerging from the mist that had begun collecting in a corner of the room without Beth noticing it.

"Oh? And why is that?" Beth wasn't even a little surprised that Timmy had appeared.

"Because they know you want to help them."

"They do?"

Timmy nodded. "And they want to help you, too."

Beth knitted her brow fiercely, smiling to herself as it reminded her of when they were little and James would tease her and call it a unibrow. Thank God she plucked her eyebrows these days or she'd look like a total Neanderthal. "They do? Why?"

"Because the bad man is still alive."

"What? Oh, my God!" Beth looked wildly around the room as if expecting the bad man to appear at any moment. "Do you know who he is? Or *where* he is?"

Timmy shook her head. "Un, un. All I know, all *we* know, is that he's still alive." She paused, picking at an invisible piece of lint on the hem of her tee shirt. "And you're the only one who can help us."

"But why?" Beth pounded her fists on the bed in frustration and fear. "Why am I the only one who can help?"

"Don't know." Timmy shrugged. "You just are."

"I don't even know where to begin. And I have to help James before it's too late. How can I do both?"

Timmy just shrugged again and went back to picking invisible lint.

Beth put her head in her hands and rubbed her temples. She had to do something. But what? The only thing she could think of was to go back into the kitchen and review all her research. Maybe something would occur to her then.

But first, she needed a break. Her head was spinning and her eyes throbbed from looking at the computer screen for so long.

Maybe she should go see how James was doing. And maybe, if she was lucky, he'd be awake. But if not, she was going to make sure he knew she was on her way to help him.

No matter what.

Chapter 40

Sitting at her cousin's hospital bed, Beth took James's hand in hers and squeezed it gently. She leaned forward and brushed his shaggy hair off his forehead, then glanced over her shoulder to make sure no one had seen her. He'd kill her for being so affectionate in public. It always embarrassed him so.

What the hell? No one's around. She kissed his cheek, too, just because she could.

"Hey, 'cuz," she whispered into his ear. "Hold on just a little longer. I'm going to figure out what we need to do, and then I'm coming back to help you."

James moaned way down deep in his throat, so quietly she wasn't even sure she heard it. She pulled away and searched his face for any clue that he was coming out of the coma. "James?"

"What is it? What's wrong?" Aunt Annette swayed in the doorway, her hands covering her mouth. Concern etched her face. She'd aged about ten years since her son was shot.

"Nothing, Auntie." Beth got up and surrendered her seat to her aunt. "Thought I heard him moan, but it was just wishful thinking, I guess. Here." She gestured at the chair. "Have a seat."

Aunt Annette smiled wanly and sat down. Beth leaned over and kissed her on the top of the head. "Think I'll go get a Coke or something," she said. "You want anything?"

"No, thanks, honey. I'm not really very hungry."

Beth patted her on the shoulder. "When was the last time you ate?"

Aunt Annette shrugged. "Oh, I don't know. Breakfast, I guess. Maybe dinner." She waved her hand dismissively. "I don't know. It doesn't matter. I'm not hungry."

"How about I see if I can find a nice blueberry scone or something? Hmm? You like those, right?"

"Sure." Aunt Annette sighed, resuming her usual bedside activity: rubbing James's arm and murmuring to him.

Beth was worried about her. She wasn't eating, hadn't slept in days, and there were dark smudges under her eyes. Beth didn't know what else to do for her. Hopefully, she could help James to do whatever he needed to do to wake up so things could get back to normal. She hated seeing her aunt in so much anguish.

"Okay, well, I'll be back in a little while."

When her aunt made no response, Beth simply shook her head and headed down the hall in search of some small snack she hoped to convince her aunt to eat.

She wasn't surprised that the hospital cafeteria didn't have any scones, but they did have a nice assortment of donuts, and she chose a cake donut with strawberry icing for her aunt, a chocolate buttermilk bar for Uncle Robbie, and poured a fountain Coke for herself.

She was paying for the snacks when Sheriff Riggs sauntered up to the register.

"Hey, little one," he greeted her, a wooden toothpick dangling from the corner of his mouth. He gave her a two-fingered salute off the brim of his hat and smirked.

Beth rolled her eyes and tried her best to ignore him. She took her change from the cashier, dumped it into her pocket, and walked out of the cafeteria, taking a sip of her soda. To her dismay, Riggs trotted after her.

"Whatsa matter, Beth?" he asked. "In too big a hurry to talk?"

"No, I just need to get back and give these to my aunt and uncle." She held up the bag of donuts and was a little grossed out by the grease that had already stained the bag. Even as a little girl, she'd never really liked do-nuts. They always seemed to leave an oily film on her tongue.

"Oh, that's right. He's still in a coma." He clucked his tongue. "Tough break."

Beth stopped and turned to glare at him. "What do you want, Sheriff?"

Riggs seemed taken aback. "Just offering my condo-lences, that's all."

"Right. Great. Thanks. Now, if you'll excuse me…" She turned and headed back down the hall, thankful that Riggs didn't seem inclined to follow her.

"See you around."

"Not if I see you first," she muttered. "What a douchebag."

Chapter 41

JAMES

My head felt fuzzy, as if it was full of thistles that poked into my brain in certain spots while rubbing soft downy fluff in others. Everything looked blurry to me, and I blinked a few times, but when that didn't clear my vision, I rubbed my eyes with my thumb and forefinger.

"That wasn't so bad, now, was it?"

Startled, I whipped my head up and looked at the spot where the voice had come from. Inhabiting the passenger seat was a shimmery black form, which I could see through, a shape that resembled a person, but not.

"Who…Who are you?"

"Who do you think I am?"

It was all starting to come back to me. The monsters, the voice in my cell, the wishing. "D. R.?"

"In the flesh." D. R. chuckled. "So to speak."

"What do you want?"

"The same thing you want. To find the truth."

I scratched my cheek. "The truth?"

"Didn't your little cousin…what's her name again?"

"Beth?"

"Yeah." A flash of a smile seemed to play across D. R.'s lips, but since he was practically see-through, I couldn't be sure. "Beth."

"What about her?"

"Huh?" He seemed distracted, and I wanted to snap my fingers in his face and call him ADD Boy to get his attention. But a ripple of fear washed through me, and I didn't want to antagonize him.

"Beth." I tried to keep the annoyance out of my voice. "You started to say something about Beth."

"Oh, yeah. Beth." D. R. seemed to shift a little in the seat. He was really freaking me out. "She told you that you had to go to the meadow, didn't she?"

Did she? My head was still hazy, and I couldn't exactly remember. I didn't think I should let D. R. know that, though, so I just nodded and waited to see what he would say next.

"So go to the meadow."

"But—"

"No buts, James. Just do it."

I looked through the windshield and peered into the darkness. "What about those things?"

"The monstrosities?"

Still looking for any sign of them, I nodded without taking my eyes off the darkness.

"I told you, they won't hurt you. Not as long as you do what I tell you."

I turned to glare at him. "Yeah, right. That's what you said before, but they attacked me as soon as I left my bedroom."

"That wasn't supposed to happen," D. R. said dismissively. "An anomaly, nothing more."

"Uh, huh." I didn't believe him for a minute. But what he said about needing to go to the meadow rang true, especially since Beth had told me the same thing. "Whatever you say."

He glanced over his shoulder. "You hear that?"

"Hear what?"

"Nothing. I need to go now."

He scowled at me. Even pointed his finger at me, like he was my father and I a little kid who'd done something wrong. I rolled my eyes. Adults.

"Do as I say. Go to the meadow. Now."

And then he vanished.

Chapter 42

After dropping off the donuts and making her aunt promise to eat one, Beth went home and spent several hours poring over her printouts until her eyes went bleary. She pushed her chair away from the table, rubbed her tired eyes, and crossed the kitchen floor, drew another red X on the calendar and chewed on the end of the red marker attached to the calendar by a simple piece of string. Eighty-nine days. That's how long James had been in a coma. Eighty-nine long days. The doctors said he was stable now, but to her, he seemed to be getting weaker. She didn't think he had much longer.

As she sat back down at the table, she thought about what Marty had said about going into someone's memories. Did that mean time could be altered if she was somehow able to change what happened in the memory? Hopefully, it did, but whether it did or not, she knew she would have to act fast and figure out how to stay in his mind long enough to help him find his way. That's what she was meant to do, wasn't it? Why she'd inherited the psychopomp gene in the first place?

There was so much to think about, to deal with. It was mind boggling.

She put her head down on the table and started to drift off. If only…Beth bolted upright, nearly knocking over her chair.

Of course! All she had to do was go back into James's subconscious, root around to find the memory of that night in the meadow, and bazinga—she'd have the answer.

Maybe she didn't even need Timmy or Marty to guide her. Maybe all she had to do was just concentrate. Think about being in her cousin's mind. Think about the particular memory she wanted to find.

Maybe she hadn't believed it enough before, and that's why she couldn't do it without Marty. But now, she *knew* she could do it.

It was worth a try.

She went into James's room, figuring that she needed to be as close to her cousin or his things as she could get, sat on the bed, propped herself up against the headboard, and crossed her ankles. Shifting her body into the covers to make herself as comfortable as possible, she leaned back and closed her eyes.

"Okay, James," she whispered. "What does it look like, inside that big head of yours?"

She squeezed her eyes tight and concentrated. "James's mind. I need to get inside the mind of James. Send me to the night he was shot. The night in the meadow."

Goosebumps prickled her arms. The familiar feeling of motion sickness filled her stomach as the room began to spin. She smiled and gripped the edges of the mattress, even though she knew it wouldn't keep her from feeling as though she were free-falling down a wind tunnel.

When she finally stopped spinning, she opened her

eyes, only mildly surprised to find herself in the picnic area of the Cailleach Canyon park, not too far from the path that led to the meadow where they'd found James. But from that point on, she'd have to rely on her wits. It wasn't like there was a manual to tell her how to do it. Her father sure hadn't been any help. She'd just have to pay attention—not something she was all that good at— and do whatever felt right at the time.

She headed up the trail into the woods, which were illuminated from behind by the bright light of the full moon. There was a kind of ground fog swirling around her feet, except that instead of being misty, it was dark and somewhat thick, as though it was made of shadows.

A slight breeze rustled through what few leaves were left on the branches, and Beth looked up at the trees, realizing that she'd jumped into a memory from sometime in the fall. If it was any more recent, the trees would be either winter bare or spring full and green. It wasn't the memory she'd wanted to find, but hopefully, it was important and not something that meant nothing.

As she continued her trek, she felt like she was being watched, but when she looked around, she didn't see anyone. Then she heard footsteps behind her. A beam of light flashed through the trees. Someone was coming! Darting off the path, she crouched behind a huge oak tree and waited.

A figure wearing a navy pea coat with thick, auburn hair hanging down out of a pink knit cap appeared, walking backward along the trail. She aimed a flashlight back and forth across the footpath and up into the woods. Beth ducked as the light played across the tree she was hiding behind.

A wolf howled in the distance. Frowning, Beth turned toward the call and, without knowing why, thought it sounded familiar. The figure whirled around right in front of her. It was Shaniqua, James's girlfriend, and she was scared. Her eyes were wide, and she was nearly hyperventilating. Beth felt sorry for her.

When the wolf howled again, closer this time, Shaniqua looked like she was rooted to the spot. When it howled a third time, she whimpered. Beth so wanted to help her, but she knew the memory had to play out.

Besides, she didn't even know if anyone besides James would be able to see or hear her anyway.

So she just watched as a shadow, darker than all the rest, slowly moved toward Shaniqua before rising up to a massive eight feet or more.

James! It was James, in his werewolf form. Even though she'd never seen him like that before, Beth knew it was him and marveled at his glowing red eyes. He towered over Shaniqua.

"James?" Shaniqua said. Her terror seemed to be abating as she also realized who this hulking mass of coarse hair and razor-sharp teeth was.

James cocked his head, breathing heavily, as he took a small step toward her.

"James, it's me. Shaniqua." She held out her hand so James could sniff it.

James went back down on all fours and backed slowly away.

Shaniqua took a step toward him, but James growled softly at her. He turned and headed toward the trees, stopping once to look at her again.

Then he lifted his head and howled at the moon, a sound so filled with melancholy and sadness that Beth nearly burst into tears.

She and Shaniqua watched as James trotted slowly away. "Whoa," Shaniqua muttered. "That was awesome." She tilted her head and frowned. "Hope he's okay." She shrugged and turned back toward the picnic grounds.

"And that he doesn't wake up somewhere, naked and confused."

As she left, Beth crawled out from behind the tree. "What a dumb thing to say. This isn't *An American Werewolf in London*, for God's sake."

She continued on down the trail and hoped she could find James.

And that, if he was still in his werewolf form, he would recognize her.

⌘

Beth had no luck finding him. Time was a little different in Shadowland and the Underworld, so she figured it probably was in someone's subconscious, too, but she thought she'd spent about an hour searching for him. It was as if he'd just disappeared.

After another hour of walking along a winding trail, sometimes rocky, sometimes full of tree roots that seemed to reach out and grab her ankles, she found herself in the meadow where James had battled Mr. Hansen before someone shot him. Tall trees and scrub oak surrounded the clearing. It was quite beautiful, even if it was a little creepy in the moonlight. There was a tree stump in the middle of the meadow, and since she was a little tired, she sat on it to rest. Plus, there was that strange shadowy darkness that crept along like some kind of Tim Burton mist that she found herself continually trying to dodge. She was still trying to figure out if that was normal for being in someone else's memories, or if it was a result of the coma, or if there was something else going on.

A delicate breeze stirred her hair. Fallen leaves danced along the ground as the trees above them whistled in the wind. Crickets chirped in that loud, annoying way they have. Bullfrogs—or were they toads? She never could tell the difference—called out to potential mates.

There was something else. Underneath all the normal sounds of the woods. Something that unnerved her.

A spooky kind of silence.

She pressed her lips together tightly and focused on the quiet around her. At first, she couldn't hear anything, except perhaps the strange feeling of the silence, like what she felt when she pressed her ear to a seashell.

Then, just over the silence, she heard them. Muffled at first, but growing in energy.

Whispers. A whole symphony of them.

The whispers continued, muted and unrelenting. She couldn't be sure, but she thought they sounded impatient. Frenzied, almost.

She was frightened.

Then the world around her flickered like the light from a muted television in a dark room. She blinked and looked around, confused. *What just happened?* Things looked just like they had earlier, only now there was a grayness to the meadow and the surrounding woods. A thin mist moved in from among the trees, swirling slowly along the ground as if it were seeking something, wrapping itself sinuously around the bottom of the tree trunks.

"What the hell?" Beth stood, trying to decide if she should run or not. "If I didn't know better, I'd think I just flipped into Shadowland. Wait—what?"

She peered into the gray shadows, unsure about what she was seeing. Several figures gradually took shape across the meadow from her. The mist had moved on from the trees and enfolded the legs of the forms. She watched as seven shapes gelled and became transparent. Each stood silently in front of small mounds of dirt. Curious, Beth left the safety of the stump and slowly approached them.

As she got closer, she pulled up short. "My God,"

she whispered as she realized that the shapes had become the four little girls from the bad man's house. Emma, still clutching her dirty teddy bear, Jazz and Timmy were also there. All seven girls stared straight ahead. Their clothes were disheveled, pieces of leaves and broken twigs stuck out from their hair at odd angles, their faces and bodies filthy. Each one had dried blood on their inner thighs and ugly reddish purple bruises wrapped around their throats.

The eerie silence grew thicker.

"Timmy?" Beth gestured at them. "What is all this? What happened to you guys?"

At first, Timmy didn't respond, didn't move, or even blink.

"Timmy? Timmy!" Beth wished she could shake her to break the little skater girl out of her trance. Finally, though, Timmy blinked slowly, reminding Beth of a lazy cartoon turtle. Her movements were sluggish. Her voice was garbled, as if it came from the depths of an abandoned well.

"This," Timmy said. She pointed across the meadow, toward the woods. "There."

"What?" Beth looked where she was pointing but didn't see anything out of the ordinary. "I don't understand."

"This," Timmy repeated. Her voice was a little clearer but still sounded thick and raspy. "There."

Beth studied the tree line across from her. "Did whatever happened to you happen over there?"

Timmy remained silent, pointing.

"Timmy? Why won't you talk to me?"

Beth pursed her lips. Why wouldn't she answer? Scratching her head, she started across the meadow.

Halfway across, she turned to look back at the girls and wasn't surprised to find that Timmy was right behind her. She seemed to be gaining substance, becoming less transparent, more solid, while the other girls remained almost see-through.

"I'm so sorry for what happened to you." Beth looked over Timmy's shoulders. "For what happened to all of you. It must have been so scary."

Timmy nodded slowly and looked up at the moonlit sky, her gray tongue sticking out of the corner of her mouth. It looked like she was trying to remember something. Maybe who killed her?

When she looked back at Beth, there was a little more color to her, as if she were becoming real. Alive, somehow.

"It was," Timmy said simply.

Not knowing what else to say, Beth continued across the meadow, stopping when she got to the far edge. "Here?"

Timmy nodded.

Beth parted some low-hanging scrub oak branches and stepped into the brush, pausing to hold them so Timmy could follow. It occurred to her that she needn't have bothered, since Timmy was a ghost and could easily pass through things much more solid than a few leaves and tree limbs, but it seemed the right thing to do.

When they came out the other side of the scrub brush, the trees were a little more sparse than they had been, and Beth didn't need to ask Timmy where to go. There was a spot under one of the trees where the dirt was a little darker than the rest of the forest floor, and it was obvious that a hole had been dug there, filled in, and covered up with leaves, twigs, grass, and whatever undergrowth had been nearby.

All the blood drained from Beth's face. Beads of sweat formed on her upper lip, and she had to fight the urge to run away.

She was looking at a grave.

Chapter 43

"Who did this?" Beth asked. "Timmy, who did this to you?"

Timmy's lips quivered, tears filling her eyes. Her voice trembled. "The bad man. The bad man did it to all of us."

Jazz, Emma, and the rest of the girls stepped out of the brush in the same place that Beth and Timmy had come through. Silently, they walked single file around the edge of the small glade, each one stopping about three feet from the girl in front of them, forming a semi-circle around Beth. They turned to look at her in unison, as if joined by some invisible marionette strings, and they were all crying soundlessly.

"Are you—are you all buried here?" Beth asked.

"No," Timmy told her. "But this is where they all died."

"Do any of you know who the bad man is? Or why he did this to you?"

Six of the girls shook their heads. Only Timmy spoke. "No, but you do."

Beth chewed on her lower lip. "I do? What do you mean, I do?"

Timmy opened her mouth to answer her, but then

they all heard a rustling from the other side of the trees and scrub brush they'd tromped though, and almost as one, all seven little ghost girls crumpled to the ground, throwing their arms up to protect themselves from whatever was approaching.

"What is it?" Beth whispered.

"Hide!" Timmy hissed.

Beth did as she was told, crouching behind a large manzanita. She watched, wide-eyed, as a shadowy figure emerged from the bushes. He was lugging something behind him, and Beth, horrified, realized it was one of the little girls. Or rather, her body. The silhouette was dragging her by the arm. One of the shoulder buttons on her jumper was missing, and the straps were in shreds. The rest of the dress was torn and filthy.

Beth watched, helpless to stop him, as he dumped the girl's body into a pre-dug hole. He had obviously planned to bury her here after he killed her. He tossed about a half-dozen shovelfuls of dirt into the hole. A rustling of leaves and thickets came from the same gap in the bushes that they had all come through, and the man stopped what he was doing to listen.

Out of the scrub brush stepped her favorite cousin.

And he was pissed.

જીજીજી

"Hey, what the hell do you think you're doing?" James roared.

For the first time in her life, Beth was afraid of her cousin. Really, truly afraid of him. Even though this was his subconscious, and theoretically nothing could happen to hurt her here, she still feared the rage that washed off him in thick waves.

His eyes glowed crimson, his nostrils flared hugely,

and it was obvious that he was in the throes of transforming. Whether into a werewolf or back to a human, she couldn't be sure.

"Well, well, well." The killer chuckled maliciously. "If it isn't the werewolf of London. Hey, werewolf. No Chinese food here. Although—" He paused, looking down at the body in the hole he'd thrown her into. "—I suppose I could make some beef chow mein, if you'd like."

"Dafuq are you babbling about?" James cocked his head in a truly animalistic way, like a dog listening to his master and trying to understand what he was saying.

"Nothing." The killer leaned on his shovel and sighed. "You're too young to know that song." He gestured at James with his elbow. "I always knew you were a fucking monster."

"Look who's talking. How many little girls have you murdered?"

"Seven. And they were such nice little girls, too. Very tasty."

"You're sick. You need to be put down like a dog."

"Me? What about you? You're practically a canine anyway. So, tell me, dogface. Just how many people have you slaughtered?"

"Only those who deserved it." James took a step toward the killer. Beth watched as his nose elongated into a snout. His teeth lengthened into sharp points and dripped with saliva. Coarse hair stubbled his face and grew down past his shoulders almost faster than she could see. "And, now, I'm going to kill you!"

He charged at the killer. Without warning, there was an incredibly loud bang, and James lurched, stumbled a few steps, and fell to his knees. A dark red blotch stained his chest. He'd been shot. The killer shot him!

Horrified, Beth gasped and immediately covered her mouth, praying that the killer hadn't heard her.

He hadn't. He was too busy laughing.

The killer shoved his gun back in its holster, still cackling like Pennywise from the 1990 mini-series *It*, playing with the noisemaker in the library while balloons float down from the ceiling only to pop and splatter blood all over everyone. As he strode over to where James lay clutching the hole in his chest, the killer stopped and looked over his shoulder. Directly at Beth's hiding place.

Had the bad man heard her, somehow? She shrank back and tried to make herself invisible, or at least as small as possible, while still keeping an eye on him.

As he stood there, scanning the area, Beth peeked carefully around the tree but couldn't get a good look at his face. Even still, he seemed somehow familiar and she couldn't help but wonder if Timmy was right.

Still looking around, probably to make sure he wasn't being watched, even way out here, the killer seemed to pause when he looked in Beth's direction again.

She ducked back behind the tree, breathing hard. Sitting there, leaning against the trunk with her eyes squeezed tight, her knees drawn up to her chest, an image came to her. She was lying in a grave, unable to move while the killer tossed shovelfuls of dirt on her from above, a nasty grin splitting his face.

His face! She'd seen his face. She knew who the killer was.

Chapter 44

She'd always known Riggs hated James. After all, he'd made it totally obvious by the way he was always harassing him. But she never would have guessed that he was also a murderer.

During her research, she'd learned that serial killers usually looked for a certain type of person for their victims. While most of the murdered girls were little, Jazz was Beth's age, so she guessed Riggs's "type" was a girl anywhere from three or four to thirteen or so.

Did the vision she'd had of Riggs dumping her into a grave and throwing shovelfuls of dirt on her mean she was his next victim?

She shuddered at the thought.

But something else lurked deep in her brain, something that nagged at her like her mother did when she wanted Beth to pick up her dirty clothes or clean her room. If Riggs was the killer—and she really believed he was—then who was Marty? And how was he connected to them? What did he have to do with the murdered girls? Or James?

As much as she wanted to figure it all out, it was more important to do something about Riggs. But right now, she had to get out of there. And fast!

She opened her eyes and sprang to her feet, frantically looking for an escape. Instead, she paused a second before starting to giggle. Her glee grew into a chortle, and before she knew it, she was doubled over with laughter.

Without meaning to or even trying, she'd flipped back into the real world and was standing in her cousin's bedroom.

Safe and sound.

No killers lurking nearby.

She was really beginning to like this whole soul walker, flipping-to-the-other-side thing.

And with just a little bit of luck, she'd figure out what to do with the knowledge she'd just gleaned from James's subconscious, and how to help him out of his coma.

୧୨୧୨

She had a lot of ideas about that, like running to the authorities to tell them who the killer of all those little girls was, or letting her aunt and uncle know who'd shot James while saying nothing about the girls, but both of those ideas would mean she'd have to explain how she knew and admit what she was. Not only was she not ready to do that, but who would believe her anyway?

No, the only logical thing to do was to write an anonymous note to Riggs, letting him know that he'd been discovered, that she knew what he was, without giving him a clue as to her identity, and that he needed to turn himself in or she would.

At first, she thought she'd send him an email, and had even gone so far as to search for his email address. But she soon realized that he might be able to trace it, and the last thing she wanted was for a serial killer to know who she was or where she lived. Of course, Riggs already knew where she lived, but that didn't mean he would know she was the one who'd seen him in the meadow. If only she was a computer nerd, she'd know how to send an anonymous email. But since she wasn't, that was out.

"Old school it is," she'd told herself, and hurried to the Circle K down the street from the house for an actual, real-life, honest-to-God newspaper. The dude behind the register had looked at her funny when she'd plunked it down on the counter, along with a bag of Skittles. "School project," she said when she handed him a five dollar bill.

When she left the store, she opened the bag of candy and popped several into her mouth. As she walked home, she noticed a car seemed to be pacing her, and she hurried along, worried it might be Riggs. No matter how fast she walked, the car stayed slightly behind her, just out of her line of sight. Finally, she couldn't stand it any longer. Let whatever was going to happen, happen.

She turned and faced the car head-on.

"Sheriff." She nodded. *Stay calm. You can't let him know that you know.*

Riggs stopped the car and leaned out of the window. "What are you doing out here, Beth? Shouldn't you be at the hospital? With your cousin?"

He smiled at her, and Beth scowled. Something was different about his smile. She shrugged, reminding herself to stay calm. "Uncle Robbie wanted me to go home and get some rest," she told him. "I'll be going back in the morning."

"Then why aren't you?"

"Why aren't I what?" She hoped she looked a lot more nonchalant than she felt. Her heart pumped wildly, and she struggled to keep from panting.

"At home."

"Oh. I'm on my way." She held out the newspaper.

"My uncle asked me to pick up a paper for him." She shrugged and flashed what she hoped was a convincing grin. "He's so old school."

"Uh, huh." He seemed to be scrutinizing her. It made her uncomfortable, and she struggled not give it away by shifting from one foot to the other. After almost a minute, Riggs nodded. "Well, you better get home, then."

"Yeah. Okay." She tucked the paper back under her arm and headed up the hill to the house. Hopefully, there wouldn't be any more interruptions.

Or else she might lose her nerve.

✂✄

It had taken her a lot longer to cut out all the letters she needed than she'd expected. She felt like some kidnapper on one of those old TV shows from the seventies that her uncle watched on the weekends. The letters kept sticking to her fingers, catching on the threads of the gardening gloves she'd slipped on to avoid leaving fingerprints. At least she knew that much after watching all those CSI shows with James and Aunt Annette. But she had a pile of letters ready and thought she could assemble the note as soon as she found the tape.

She rummaged through the kitchen drawers. "Where is it?" she muttered after pulling out a turkey baster, cheese grater, bottle opener, various knives, and other utensils, even a broken chip clip in the shape of an ear of corn. But no tape.

She slammed the last drawer shut, leaned against the counter, and chewed on her thumbnail. "Maybe there's some in James's room."

It was worth a shot, anyway. Heading down the hall, she thought about her next step. It was getting dark out, real dark, not those weird shadows in James's mind, and even though she wasn't afraid of the dark, she didn't want to be out walking around unprotected at night. She didn't think Riggs had seen her out there in the meadow, but he had looked right at the spot where she'd been hiding, and she didn't want to take that chance. Just because he'd driven up beside her on the way home from the store in the daytime without doing anything to her didn't mean he wouldn't do something if he caught her out after dark.

She thought she remembered seeing some tape in James's desk, went straight to the middle drawer, and couldn't help but laugh. There were five rolls in there, all of them half-used. Typical James.

She grabbed one of them, still chuckling, and went back to the kitchen. The laptop screen was flickering, a weird orangey red light that illuminated the room. She stopped in the doorway, unsure what to do. So much had happened, and it was hard to know for sure if Marty was really trying to help her or just leading her on with some ulterior motive underneath it all.

What did she really know about him?

"Oh, Beth," Marty called. "Whatcha doin'?"

She stepped into the kitchen and stared at the laptop screen. The blob was gone, replaced by an indistinct shape that resembled a head but was shadowy in the center and blurry around the edges. It was what was casting the strange glow into the room.

Glancing at the pile of letters she'd cut while simultaneously tucking the roll of tape into the waistband at the back of her jeans, she searched for a logical explanation that would satisfy him without giving away the truth. "Just trying to keep busy," she lied. "Thought I'd make a get well card for James." She gave Marty her most apologetic look, jamming her hands into her back pockets while scraping her toe along the linoleum. "Stupid, I know."

"Not at all," Marty replied. "Kind of sweet, actually."

"Thanks. I just hope he wakes up so he can see it." That part was true enough.

"Well, I guess I'd better let you get back to it. One thing, though."

A sick feeling washed over her, and she closed her eyes and swallowed several times, trying to rid herself of it. "What's that?" she said, attempting to be blasé about it.

A flash of red flared from the laptop and then died almost immediately. But it lingered just long enough to worry her. The last time she saw the red light had been when she'd tried to convince the blob that had eventually turned into Marty that Timmy was just a little girl, and he had gotten mad and grabbed her around the wrist, insisting Timmy was dangerous and demanding Beth stay away from her.

So what was he pissed off about this time?

"I told you before, that little brat you've been hanging around with is dangerous. You must stay away from her. If you don't—"

"If I don't, what? What will happen?"

"If you don't—*you'll be sorry.*"

Beth scowled. Marty frightened her a little bit, but she hated being threatened more than she was scared. "Oh," she said, hitching up her hip and balling her fist and resting it on her waist. "I'll be sorry? Really? That all you got?"

The light flared red again for a brief second before returning to its muted yellow-gray. The silhouette was becoming lighter, clearer, more discernible. She could almost see a face.

Marty chuckled, a grating, malevolent sound that sent ice into her blood. "Don't tempt me, little one. You don't want to see what I got. Just stay away from Timmy."

The light faded and went black.

Marty was gone.

∽∾∽

When she finished taping the letters to a piece of James's printer paper, she sat back, blew the bangs off her forehead, and admired her work.

I know who you are. I know what you did. Turn yourself in, or I will.

"Looks good." She folded it into thirds and shoved it into an envelope. In big block letters, she wrote *RIGGS* on it and then sealed it shut.

Now to decide her next step. Should she flip to Shadowland and slip it into Riggs's mailbox, or just stay in the real world and walk over there tonight? She would risk being seen if she did that, but she figured the risk was small since it was now the middle of the night.

Then again, the last thing she wanted would be to run in to Riggs on one of his nightly cruises through town. Besides, she was so tired. Her eyelids were growing heavier by the minute. Maybe she should get some sleep and flip over in the morning.

Before she could make a conscious decision, she nodded off.

And found herself in a blurry, misty grayness. Indistinct shapes surrounded her, enclosing her in ever-tightening circles. Moaning. Sighing. Whimpering. Reaching out to her. She tried to run but the air felt thick, like cold molasses, and she could do little more than run in place.

Pushing against it, she slowly made her way through the heavy dampness, no known destination in mind, just the need to get away from those…things…whatever they were.

It seemed like a bad dream, but she could tell it was real and was worried about what would happen if they caught her. She remembered all the strange things she'd seen the first time she'd flipped—the colorful animals and birds, the man with the jackal head, even what she now believed was the Grim Reaper—and hoped they weren't what was out there now.

They weren't. As it turned out, what was out there was even worse.

Chapter 45

JAMES

I stared at the passenger seat for maybe a full minute, waiting to see if D. R. was really gone.

When it became obvious that he wasn't coming back, I blew out a puff of air, leaned forward, and started the car. It roared to life, and I paused long enough to check over both shoulders to make sure there was nothing lurking in the darkness, then put the Le Mans in gear and took off.

Could I do this alone? I wasn't sure, especially since I didn't know what I was supposed to do once I got to the meadow. Even though I'd watched Beth's video and now knew that I'd been shot in the chest, what was I supposed to do about that? Was it even possible to prevent it from happening?

I shook my head. "No way," I said. "This isn't one of Beth's *Dr. Who* episodes. I can't go back in time."

Or could I?

After all, who would have thought there were such things as zombie werewolves, nighttime so dark it hid the shadows lurking inside it, or cousins who could appear inside my mind?

Not me, not before this whole thing started, anyway.

A clawed fist shot in through the window, spraying glass slivers into my hair and onto my lap, and grabbed my wrist. The car swerved, and, as I struggled to straighten it out, the monstrosity's long claws dug into my flesh. I tried to pull away and stared, wide-eyed, at its elongated, skull-like face as its jaws snapped and snarled mere inches from me. Its eyes burned with malice and a kind of gleeful eagerness as it pulled me toward it. My heart thundered so hard in my chest that I was afraid it would explode.

The monstrosity held my wrist so tightly it felt like it was wringing my hand off at the bone. I struggled to get away, but it was too strong. The minute it grabbed me and slashed me, the very second I resisted, a sort of swirling darkness, even darker than the one enveloping the town, invaded my mind. I could feel my strength draining away. Every second, I grew weaker and weaker.

My eyes rolled back in my head.

I had no more fight left in me.

I let the darkness take me.

Tuesday, April 26, 2016
Day 93

Chapter 46

"Code Blue," the loudspeaker overhead shrieked. "Code Blue, room 347. Code Blue."

The hallway was flooded with hospital personnel in scrubs and lab coats. Someone pushed a cart full of various hospital implements past Beth, nearly knocking her over.

James was in trouble!

She raced to his room, where Uncle Robbie was holding Aunt Annette just outside the door, preventing her from running back into the room.

"Annette, shh," he said in a vain attempt to soothe her. "Let them do their job."

Aunt Annette sobbed into his shoulder while at the same time reaching out to her son. Her fingers flexed open and shut, open and shut, as if she thought she could make him well if only she could get to him.

Beth peeked around the doorjamb, but all she could see was an over-abundance of doctors and nurses as they worked on her cousin. The machine hooked up to James that automatically recorded his vital signs was screeching.

James was flatlining.

"Uncle Robbie?" Beth turned to her uncle. She couldn't keep the welling tears from flowing down her cheeks. James couldn't be dead! He couldn't be.

Her uncle reached out for her, and she stepped into the comfort of his arms. The three of them huddled together. How she loved these people. They were more her family than her own mother. They seemed to understand her and accept her as she was, without trying to make her into something she not only wasn't but had no desire to be.

And James…well, she was closer to him than she'd ever been to anyone, except maybe her father when she was a little girl.

Beth shook her head and pushed away from her aunt and uncle. "No. No way."

"I'm sorry, Beth," Uncle Robbie said, tears filling his eyes. "I'm afraid he's—"

"No." She backed away from them. She would never accept that James was dead. She couldn't. It just wasn't fair. She hadn't had a chance to help him yet.

"Beth, honey—"

"No!" It couldn't be over. It just couldn't. She raced down the hall and out of the hospital. She needed to flip into James's subconscious—before it really was too late.

⁓⁓⁓

Beth ran and ran until she thought her lungs would explode. She finally stopped when she got to the electrical easement where the town's first serial killer, the Wolf Creek Shredder, had killed Riff.

Beth leaned against the chain link fence cutting off access to the trail and tried to catch her breath. There was a *No Trespassing* sign welded on to the fence with what looked like a bullet hole in the middle, and she wondered who had made the hole and what they'd been shooting at. She hoped it was the sign, and not something else.

A blast of wind hit her in the face, trapping an old candy wrapper in the fence links near her feet. The gust was so intense, it knocked her back a step or two, and she nearly lost her balance. Grabbing hold of the fence, she held on tightly and waited for the wind to subside. When it did, she brushed the hair out of her face and peered up the trail. It seemed narrower than ever, choked with weeds, vines snaking across the path.

"Thank God, I don't have to go up there," she mumbled. "But I do have to find James." She rubbed her lips with a forefinger. "Hopefully, none of those weird things are around him."

Something behind her crackled, and she turned around quickly, peering into the gloom, trying to figure out what it was, but there didn't seem to be anything there. *Must have been my imagination.* She hoped.

"Get a grip," she chastised herself. Her breathing had returned to normal, and it was time to flip into James's subconscious. "Here goes nothing."

She closed her eyes and pictured James, wishing she were with him. Queasiness filled her stomach and seemed to work its way into her arms and legs, which began to tingle.

"Take me to James," she whispered. "Put me in his mind."

At first, nothing happened, but she concentrated even harder, and, before long, the feeling of shooting down a wind tunnel came over her.

She smiled as she started the journey into James's subconscious—and plummeted into a darkness so thick, so complete, so devoid of oxygen, that she couldn't breathe.

⌀⌀

"James!" Beth shook him by the shoulder. It took all her effort since she was still having trouble breathing. "James, wake up!"

She'd struggled through the syrupy darkness until she came across the Le Mans. Inside, she'd found her cousin slumped over the steering wheel. When she pushed him gently back against the seat, there was a giant hole in his chest oozing some gooey black gunk that looked suspiciously like the pool that had become Marty when he'd claimed that Timmy was dangerous.

Shaking James harder, she looked around for help but soon realized that was impossible. They were alone here, in James's subconscious. She had to wake him up. If she didn't...well, she just wasn't ready to face those consequences.

"James!" she screamed, shaking him so violently his neck wobbled like a bobblehead.

She looked around frantically. There just had to be someone, *anyone*, who could help her. But how would she even find someone in all this darkness? She couldn't help herself. She started to cry, silent tears at first, then sniffles that were on the verge of sobs, but there seemed to be something, some sound underneath her weeping, and she struggled to stop so she could hear it. Wiping her nose with the back of her hand, she cocked her head. There it was again!

It was coming from James.

He was stirring slightly and moaned again softly. He was coming around.

"James?" With her hand on his shoulder, she leaned in the car window. "James, you okay?"

He moaned again, loudly this time, and rubbed his forehead. "Wha—what happened?" he asked groggily.

"Don't know." Beth shrugged. "I found you like this."

"Like what?" His hand moved down to his chest and into the black goo.

"Unconscious." She smiled weakly. "I—you scared the shit out of me. I didn't know what to do."

He pulled his hand away from the hole in his chest and rubbed his fingers together. "What is this black stuff?" He looked up at her, his eyes wide. "Am I dead? Is that what this stuff is? My death?"

"No…"

James looked at her in that way that he had. He knew she was hiding something. "What, Beth? What is it?"

"At least, I don't think so."

"Beth…"

"Fine." There was no hiding it from him. She'd have to come clean and hope he could take it. "I came here this time because you were flatlining in the hospital."

"Flatlining?" He struggled to sit up, and she took hold of his arm to help him.

"Dying."

"I know what flatlining means. Geeze."

"Sorry."

"So." He turned to look at her. "I could be dead. Is that what you're saying?"

She shook her head defiantly. "No. No way."

"Yes, way."

"Well, maybe, but I don't think so. I think if you were dead in real life, you'd be dead here, too."

"You think?"

"Yeah, I do."

He opened the door and stepped out, leaning heavily on the door frame, and patted his chest. "What do you think this stuff is, then?"

Sighing sorrowfully, she found she couldn't look him in the eye. Instead, she scraped the toe of her sneaker along the asphalt, but when he reached out and touched her forearm, she looked up at him.

"You know what it is, don't you?"

"Yeah," she mumbled.

"What'd you say?"

She cleared her throat. "Yes, I know what it is."

"You planning on telling me any time soon, or do I have to keep guessing." It wasn't a question.

"What happened right before you passed out? Do you remember?"

"Well, let's see. My phone rang, and it was that weird guy, D. R. He told me he was trying to help me get out of wherever this is, but there was only one way he could do that."

Beth's mind spun. D. R.? Did that stand for Deputy Riggs? She shook her head. There was no time for that now. She turned her attention back to James. "How was that?"

"He wanted me to wish him out of the phone."

It felt like a blow to her stomach so severe it caused internal bleeding. Someone wanted to be wished out of the phone? Could it be—no, that was crazy. No way was it Marty. It simply wasn't possible.

Was it?

"I know, it sounds weird, like a bad dream or something. But I swear, it's the truth."

"I know. Then what happened?"

"It took a couple of tries, but I was finally able to wish him out. Only—"

"Only what?"

"At first, the phone started to smoke, but then it turned into something else."

"What?" She already knew what he was going to say

but felt he needed to say it anyway, just to get it straight in his mind.

James touched his chest again. When he took his hand away, more black goop covered his fingers. "This. It sort of…jumped out of the phone and shot into my chest. I think it's what made the hole."

"Can I see the phone?"

"Sure." James got back into the car and searched the seat and the floorboards, but his smartphone was nowhere to be found. "Where'd that stupid thing go?"

"Let me have a look."

"Fine." He lifted an eyebrow at her in that cocky way he had, and she grinned in spite of herself. He knew how much she hated that. Next thing you knew, he'd be calling her "girlie."

She climbed into the driver's seat and grasped the steering wheel. "Won't be long before I can drive. That'll be so cool."

"Yeah, as long as we get out of here alive."

Beth glared at him. "Bummer man. He delivers."

"Sorry." He said it like he meant it, but she could tell he was hiding a smile. Maybe things would turn out okay, after all.

"Okay, let's see. Were you holding the phone, or was it sitting on the seat when it attacked you?"

"Hmm." He appeared to be thinking it over. "I think…yeah." He nodded vigorously. "Yeah, actually, I was reaching for it. It was on the passenger seat. I went to grab it, and—" He shook his head in defeat. "That's the last thing I remember till you woke me up."

"So it was on the seat. You probably dropped it." She reached down between the seat and the console, her tongue sticking out of the corner of her mouth. When her fingers brushed against something, she smiled, closed her fist around it, and pulled it out. "Here." She held the phone up in triumph, waving it in James's face.

He grabbed it away from her. "Gimme that." The screen was warped and blackened, as if it had been set on fire, and there was a big hole in the middle of it. James tossed it across her onto the passenger seat. "It's useless now." He pursed his lips when she tried to get out of the car, blocking the door with his body.

"What's this all about?" he asked. "You know something, don't you?"

"Yeah, I do." She gripped the door handle and looked at him pointedly. "Let me out, and I'll tell you."

He stepped away. She opened the door and got out. They leaned against the car, both crossing their arms over their chests as if to protect themselves from the inky blackness as she launched into what she was sure was the most bizarre story they would ever be a part of.

Chapter 47

Beth spun a tale of psychopomps, ghosts, and a bad man named Marty who talked to her from inside my laptop and wanted her to be his friend.

That sounded like the dark man who spoke to me.

"Do you think—" I shook my head. "No, never mind."

"What?"

"No, it's just too crazy."

Beth stomped her foot and hitched up her hip in that stance of hers that always cracked me up. "What? Tell me, dammit!"

"The dude who talks to me is called D. R. But he started out talking to me from my laptop, before the phone. The one who talked to you—also from my laptop—is called Marty. They both claim they want to help us figure things out and be our friend. Coincidence?"

"I think not." Beth's eyes were twinkling. "They have to be the same person! But why? What could he want from us? And why use different names?"

"All good questions. Look, I'm pretty sure most of what this D. R./Marty dude says is a lie, but I feel like I still need to go to the meadow. What do you think? You think I should? I mean, he's the one who said I should go in the first place. But if everything he says is a lie…"

"I don't think *everything* that comes out of his mouth is a lie. I think he says whatever he needs to say to get us to do what he wants. But you do have to go to the meadow, James. You just have to. It's the only way."

"The only way? What do you mean, the only way? The only way to what?" She was hiding something. I had no idea what it was, but I could always tell when she wasn't being honest with me.

She took my hand in hers and looked at me with such sincerity that I knew I would do whatever she wanted. "Please?" She sniffed. "Please, James, please just trust me. Okay?"

I drew her to me and put my arm around her shoulders, hugging her tightly. "Okay. I do. You know I do. Right?"

"Right." She wiped her snotty nose on my shirt sleeve and grinned up at me.

"Ew, gross." I grinned back and rubbed my hands together. "Okay, I guess it's off to the meadow we go. Hop in."

She trotted around the front of the car and got in. I started the engine, revved it, flipped on the headlights and headed down the street. I didn't know how long it would take to get there since it was so dark I couldn't go more than about ten miles an hour, but however long it did take, we were on our way.

As long as Beth's bad man or any of his creepy monstrosities didn't show up to stop us.

❧❧❧

"Hey, how come you can enter my dreams when no

one else can?" That was maybe the biggest head scratcher of this whole thing.

"My mom and your mom are sisters, right?"

I nodded. "Yeah. So?"

"So your mom married a werewolf, right?"

"What does that have to do with anything?" God, she could be so exasperating sometimes. "Just spit it out already, will ya?"

"Well, my mom didn't."

"Didn't what?"

"Didn't marry a werewolf."

That stopped me. I always thought Uncle Fred was one of us. Was Beth saying that he wasn't? That he was…what? Some sort of Shaman? Or even…I shook my head. No, it couldn't be.

"Are you saying he was…*human*?"

She squirmed around in her seat and looked at me in that way she had: head turned partly to the side, one eye closed. "Ever hear of a psychopomp?"

"Psycho what?"

"Psychopomp. It's kind of like a cross between a medicine man and a medium."

I shook my head. "Never heard of it."

"Well, basically, when some people die, they either can't or won't cross over. Their souls get stuck here. Usually, because they have leftover baggage they need to fix. Like making sure their family will be taken care of after they die. Or leading the cops to the person who killed them. Things like that. So a psychopomp, or soul walker, as I like to think of them, helps souls figure out how to solve the problem so they can be at peace and head off to the afterlife."

Now I was really confused. "But, you said I wasn't dead."

She shook her head. "No. I guess I'm not explaining it right."

"I guess not."

"See, not only is a psychopomp a kind of spirit guide, but they can also help the subconscious and the conscious talk to each other." She paused and took a big breath. I could almost feel her apprehension. "That's where I come in."

"You?"

"Me."

"But how is that possible? You're a werewolf." I looked at her and frowned. "Aren't you?"

She shrugged. "Not sure, but I don't think so. Remember, I said that your mom married a werewolf?"

I nodded.

"Well, like I said, mine didn't."

"You mean…"

"You got the werewolf gene because both your parents are werewolves. But when only one of them is, there's supposably only a fifty-fifty chance the kid will be one, too."

"Supposedly."

"That's what they say."

"No, it's supposedly. Not supposably."

She rolled her eyes. "Gah. Whatever. You going to give me a grammar lesson now?"

"Sorry."

"Anyway, Dad was a psychopomp. From a long line of psychopomps, apparently." She grinned her lopsided grin. "Awesome, right?"

I shrugged. "I guess."

"What do you mean, you guess? How else am I supposed to get you out of this?"

She had a point. I really did need all the help I could get. Even if it did come from my freaky little cousin.

The psychopomp.

We'd always just assumed she would transform at some point. But now, I guess I'd have to look at her in a new light. I wouldn't be able to help her transition, like Mr. Hansen had me.

Well, not exactly like Mr. Hansen, since I'd eventually had to kill him. But still…

This was going to take some getting used to.

Life was funny that way.

Chapter 48

BETH

Beth debated telling James the truth behind who had shot him but ultimately decided not to. Somehow, she knew that he had to find out for himself what really happened in the meadow. Otherwise, he'd remain flatlined in the real world, and they'd have to say good-bye forever.

She wasn't about to let that happen.

She leaned her head back against the car's headrest and closed her eyes. She was so tired. As she drifted off, she wondered if it was possible for her to dream inside someone else's subconscious.

"What the hell?"

James's muffled voice seemingly came to her from far away, down a long, underground tunnel. She opened her eyes and looked over at him groggily.

"What? What is it?"

"We're here already."

"Where?" Beth rubbed her eyes and tried to wake up.

"Look around. We're at Cailleach Canyon Park." He gestured with his head. "The meadow's just up that trail."

He frowned and pursed his lips as he looked around. "But where the hell's my car?"

"Wait—what?" She looked around sleepily. They were no longer sitting in the car. She hadn't even realized they were standing in a parking lot. "Wow." She ran her fingers through her hair. Apparently, it *was* possible to dream inside someone else's mind. Or at least sleep. She wasn't sure she'd dreamed. "How long was I asleep?"

"That's just it." James looked at her and frowned. "You just closed your eyes like five seconds ago."

"Huh?"

He held up his hand like he was taking an oath in court. "I swear. Five seconds. Maybe less."

"But how is that possible?"

He shrugged. "Beats me." He screwed up his mouth and looked up at the sky. Beth wondered what he was looking for. "But it's kinda creepy, you know?"

"Uh huh," she said absently.

He turned back to her. "What's up with you?"

"I—I think I wished us here."

"What?"

"Yeah. The last thing I remember, right after I closed my eyes, was wondering if I could dream here."

"Here?"

"In your subconscious. And I remember thinking that would be cool. I could dream we were in the meadow."

"And here we are."

"Well, not quite, but close enough for government work." It was a favorite expression of her father's, and she smiled sadly at the thought.

"You okay?" James was looking at her with an odd expression on his face, one that she recognized all too well.

"Oh, no you don't."

"No, I don't what?"

"Don't even think about it."

"I don't know what you're talking about." He headed up the trail toward the woods and the meadow where Beth had watched him get shot.

"You are not going to leave me here."

He turned back to her. "But—"

Shaking both palms at him, she took several large steps toward him. "No. I'm going with you, and that's all there is to it. Period." When he started to say something else, she glared at him. "If you make me stay here, I'll just follow you. You know I will."

He sighed heavily. "Yeah, you would, too. Wouldn't you?"

"Damn straight."

"Fine. You didn't happen to bring a flashlight, did you?"

She patted herself down, wiggling around to check out her back pockets. Empty. "Nope. Sorry."

James was looking up at the sky again, and she followed his line of sight. The world seemed a little less dark out here, which was strange, considering they were in the middle of the woods at night. Even if there was supposed to be a full moon, which seemed to be hidden behind all this black gunk.

When she turned back to mention it to James, he was gone.

Chapter 49

I hated to leave her there, all alone, but I had no choice. I could hear someone—some*thing*—calling me, and I needed to find out who it was. Besides, hadn't she been the one to tell me I needed to come to the meadow so I could remember what had happened to me? That by doing so, I would come out of my coma?

I was really tired of being here, first in the white fluffiness of my room and now in the darkness of…whatever this was, the final showdown?…even if I was reliving it a second time. I'd do whatever it took to get back to normal.

Strange sounds were coming down the trail leading to the meadow, and I'd headed off toward them while Beth was staring up at the moon, almost as though she were in some kind of a trance. At first, I couldn't tell what they were. As I approached the edge of the meadow, they became clearer and clearer until I realized that someone was calling for help.

My instinct was to plunge through the brush and into whatever situation was going on, but I stopped short as I reached the edge of the meadow. Beth said I'd gotten shot here, so I needed to be careful and not lose my head if I wanted to come out of this alive. And *not* in a coma. So instead of barging through, I crouched behind some manzanita and peered through the branches.

Someone had recently dug a hole in the hard ground. From where I was hiding, I couldn't see how deep it was, but it looked big enough to hide a body in because there was a huge mound of dirt next to it.

Movement across the clearing caught my eye at the same time whimpering reached my ears.

"Please, don't hurt me. Please!" A little girl was sitting on the ground, struggling against the ropes that tied her wrists together. "Mommy!" she cried. "I want my mommy!"

"Shut up," her attacker yelled at her as he slapped her across the face.

The little girl bawled.

"Stop crying, you little bitch. Or you'll be sorry." The man's voice sounded so familiar.

The little girl's sobs quieted a little, until he kissed her roughly. She screamed and tried to push him off her, but he was too strong, and she was so little. She couldn't have been more than eight or nine.

"I'm not going to hurt you, little one." The man smiled at her maliciously as he untucked his shirt. "As long as you're a good girl." He unbuttoned the top button of his shirt. The little girl moaned. As he unbuttoned the next button, he cocked his head. "You are a good girl, aren't you?"

The little girl stopped struggling and nodded, her eyes wide, her face tear-stained and full of snot.

"Good." He smiled at her. "That's good. I knew you were a good girl."

The little girl turned her head and saw me.

Terror filled her eyes.

Rage-fueled heat filled my body. I had to do something. I had to save her. It didn't matter that I knew I would get shot and likely die. If I didn't do something, and fast, the little girl would be dead.

I'm not really sure what happened next. When the man saw that the little girl was looking at something, he turned his head to see what had gotten her attention.

That's when I saw who it was.

And he saw me.

Chapter 50

BETH

*D*r. *Petrelli?* Beth's mind screamed. She'd heard the commotion on the other side of the bushes and had crouched down to see what was going on. She almost wished she hadn't.

Dr. Martin Petrelli, the doctor who'd operated on James, was the killer? It wasn't Riggs, after all? She couldn't believe it.

She pushed aside a low branch, squinted and peered into the clearing. "Oh, my God," she whispered. "Is that…Timmy? Is she actually still alive?"

There was a noise like a huge freight train bearing down on some drunk lying across the tracks. Pushing through the brush a little more so she could see where it was coming from, she nearly stumbled out into the clearing as James, in the process of transforming into a werewolf, rushed past her, roaring and snarling with razor sharp teeth that dripped foul-smelling saliva, his elongated muzzle crinkled up in rage. Hair seemed to sprout from every pore.

He charged across the clearing, heading straight for the doctor.

An evil grin cleaved the doctor's face. In his hand was a gun. Not as big as Smitty, Donna Glass's huge Smith and Wesson Magnum .500, but plenty big enough.

"I knew you'd come," Dr. Petrelli said matter-of-factly.

Beth shot out of the bushes toward him, waving her arms like a maniac. "No!" she screamed.

The doctor's eyes flicked toward her. In that split second, James reached him. His teeth latched onto the wrist of the doctor's gun hand and bit it clean off.

Dr. Petrelli screamed, his eyes going wide as he watched his hand fly several feet before bouncing on the ground, gun still clutched in its fingers.

James put his huge paws on the doctor's shoulders, pushed him down, then hovered over him, his massive jaws mere inches from his face. James grinned, savoring the man's screams of pain and terror. Then he bit into his neck, holding on tightly as the body thrashed and flailed around. Blood spurted out of the doctor's jugular, coating James's face and broad chest in thick, red blood.

The Wolf had taken James over completely.

Chapter 51

JAMES

I didn't know how long it had been since I'd been The Wolf, but it felt good. I'd missed it, much more than I ever thought I would.

After killing that douchebag doctor, I'd run off, not wanting the little girl to see more of me than she needed to. She'd be traumatized enough after being kidnapped. She didn't need to worry about being hunted down by a werewolf, or maybe worse, that she was going crazy.

Amazingly enough, I found the Le Mans parked in the park's lot, so after I transformed back from The Wolf, I dug around in the trunk for the spare clothes I'd learned to keep hidden there. As I pulled on an old pair of Dickies and a gray work shirt with a patch on the chest that announced that I was "Billy," I thought about what had just happened. Was everything going to be okay now? Did finding out who the killer of all those little girls was, and that he was the same person who had shot me, mean that I was going to recover?

Had Beth been right?

Not knowing for sure, I cleaned up as best I could with one of the bottles of water I kept in the trunk, grabbed a blanket and a couple more waters and headed back to the clearing. When I got there, Beth was kneeling in front of the little girl, rubbing her arms and trying to soothe her. She'd managed to get her dressed in what remained of her clothes, but the girl was tugging and pulling at them like she couldn't stand wearing them.

"It's going to be okay, Timmy," Beth said.

I stepped through the bushes and scrub brush and approached the girls as quietly as I could, not wanting to scare Timmy any more than she already was. A twig cracked under my foot, and they both whipped their heads around to look at me faster than I would have thought possible.

"Sorry," I said and grinned sheepishly. I rubbed the back of my neck as I walked slowly over to them and handed Beth the blanket and waters. "Here. I thought she might want this."

"Thanks." Beth took them from me and wrapped the blanket around Timmy's shoulders. "Better?" she asked her.

Timmy nodded and looked up at me, her eyes wide. "Is he—he—"

Beth took her face in her hands and turned the little girl's head to look at her, but Timmy's eyes stayed on me. "Timmy," Beth said to get her attention. "Timmy!"

Timmy finally managed to take her eyes off me and look at Beth.

"He's not going to hurt you." She looked at me. "Are you?"

"No, of course not."

Timmy looked skeptical, glancing up at me and back at Beth.

When she looked back at me a third time, I smiled and made an "X" on my chest. "Cross my heart."

That was when I realized that the hole in my chest was gone.

Chapter 52

BETH

James held his hand out to Beth. "Look!" he said.

"What?" She was busy trying to calm Timmy down and didn't have time for his antics. She was so busy trying to get Timmy to drink some water that she almost missed the air fluctuating just a little, like when you went to the eye doctor, and he made you look through two different lenses, asking you to say if number one was better than number two. Then he would click from one lens to the other.

The world around them shifted just like that, and Beth knew it meant they'd somehow gone out of James's memory and were back in the real world. In the present.

"Shh," she said as she turned back to the little girl. She patted Timmy's hair and adjusted the blanket, which had slipped down to her elbow, back up onto her shoulder. "It's over now. The bad man's all gone."

"Beth."

"What?" She glared up at him, impatience marking her features.

He patted his chest, and she finally understood what he was trying to tell her.

"Hey! You did it!" She jumped up and threw her arms around him. "No more hole in your chest!"

"No more hole," he agreed.

His smile was huge. A slight wave of relief went through her when she saw that his teeth had returned to normal. No more sharp wolf-teeth designed to rip human flesh to shreds. Just normal, teenage *human* teeth.

"So does that mean…"

He shrugged. "Don't know." He gestured at Timmy, who was sitting on a large flat rock. Her sobs had quieted down to snuffles, and a huge snot bubble was hanging off her nose. "How's she doing?"

"I think she'll be okay. I can hardly believe she's alive. I thought he'd killed her."

"Can we go now? Please?" Timmy looked up at James pleadingly and wiped the snot away with the edge of the blanket.

"Sure." James took her hands and pulled her up. "Come on."

Beth stood and looked at the ghost girls, who were huddled together watching them.

"Hold on." She walked over to them and smiled. "Thanks for all your help, but I think it's time for you to go now."

"Can you help us cross over?" Jazz asked.

"I think so." Beth knelt and reached out but hesitated before touching the ground. "I'm gonna miss you, Jazzy."

Jazz smiled sadly. "I know. Me, too."

"I hope this works," Beth whispered as she touched the ground with her index finger. She had no idea if her natural psychopomp instinct would kick in and call spirit guides to come and help Jazz and the other girls cross over.

When the same shiny, Nutella-like darkness spread out from her finger just like it did when Timmy first showed her how to do it, Beth couldn't help but giggle.

Two dogs, a horse, an owl that looked suspiciously like it had come from Hogwarts, an orange tabby cat, and a little white mouse stepped out of the dark pool and headed directly for the girls, who seemed happy to see them. The girls waved at Beth as they slowly dissipated until there was nothing left. Beth stood and brushed her hands together, pleased and amazed that it had actually worked.

Maybe being a psychopomp wasn't such a bad thing, after all.

"Um, what just happened?" James asked from beside her.

"Huh?" Beth couldn't resist flashing him a big smile. "Oh, that? That's just something I learned recently. Now come on. Let's go."

A twig snapped somewhere, and Timmy cried out.

"No, shh," James told her soothingly. "It's okay. It's only an animal. A furry little woodland creature. Like that little fox, Judy something or other, from *Zootopia*. What's her name?"

"Hopps. Judy Hopps." Timmy giggled. "And she's a bunny, not a fox, silly."

James grinned his famous sloppy grin, and Beth watched as Timmy visibly relaxed. Timmy took James by the hand and let him lead her from the clearing.

When they'd made it through the scrub brush and were walking down the trail toward the car, Beth trotted up next to James and elbowed him gently in the side. "Hey," she whispered. "Since when do you watch movies with furry little woodland creatures?"

He shrugged. "I don't," he whispered out of the corner of his mouth. "But her socks have the word "Zootopia" on them. And sometimes, I watch movie trailers on YouTube."

Beth nodded knowingly, not believing a word of it. "Uh huh."

"Seriously."

She looked up at him. "Sure, okay." She turned away and chuckled under her breath. "I believe you."

"Beth…" James warned.

"What?" she replied, all innocent.

James glared at her for about half a second before he chuckled, too. "Yeah."

When they reached the car, Beth climbed into the passenger seat, and James helped Timmy lay down in the back. While he tucked the blanket in around her, he glanced over his shoulder at Beth, then leaned down and kissed Timmy gently on the forehead.

"Try and get some rest," he told her. "We'll take you home now."

He gently closed the door and climbed into the front seat. Beth's heart was full of love and gratitude for her cousin. Although he'd tried to hide it from her, she'd seen him kiss the little girl and was thankful that even though he was a werewolf, his true nature was that of a sweet, loving guy who would never willingly hurt someone. She couldn't help smiling at him as he reached into his pocket for his keys.

He frowned over at her. "What?"

"Oh, nothing." She continued to smile at him.

"Well, cut it out. You're giving me the creeps."

"Let's go home," she said, still smiling, and turned to look out the window as James started the car and drove out of the lot.

Chapter 53

JAMES

We dropped Timmy off at her parents' house. They were so happy to see her, I thought they were going to explode. Her mother screamed with joy and relief, wrapping her arms around her and holding her tightly, and I was afraid she might smother the poor kid. Her dad kept patting me on the shoulder, over and over again. Pretty sure it was going to leave a mark.

They invited us in for milk and cookies, I guess thinking we were five instead of teenagers. Hell, I'm a man, and Beth, well, she's…Beth. But I guess they didn't realize that, and we agreed to come in. I loved milk, especially when it was icy cold, and drank a full glass, but Beth hated the stuff and claimed she was lactose intolerant.

But neither one of us realized just how hungry we were until Timmy's mom set a plate of homemade oatmeal pecan cookies down on the table in front of us, and we devoured them, secretly thankful they didn't taste like sawdust.

The whole time we ate, she kept wiping Timmy's

face and hands with a washcloth and picking pieces of leaves and grass out of her hair.

The look on Timmy's face was hilarious. Even after suffering such a huge trauma, you could tell she just wanted her mom to stop fussing over her. She looked at me and Beth and rolled her eyes.

It was all we could do not to crack up and avoided looking at each other for fear we might do just that, spraying them with milk and cookie crumbs in the process.

After the cookies, we explained where we had found Timmy, avoiding how we happened to be there in the first place.

"And he was—" Her dad's face was flushed. I hadn't seen anyone look that pissed off since Mary Fitzpatrick's mother yelled at Sheriff Brazelton that day at the town meeting after Mary had been torn to pieces in their own home.

"Yeah." I couldn't look him in the eye and picked at a hangnail instead.

He got up from the table so hard his chair toppled over. Timmy jumped, scared by the sudden loud noise. She'd probably jump at loud noises for a while.

He paced back and forth, running his fingers through what little hair he had left. "Where's my gun?"

"Alex, please," his wife said. When he looked over at his wife and daughter, who was trembling visibly and looked like she was trying to hide inside her mother's sweater, Timmy's mom shook her head and frowned. "We should just be glad our baby's back home, safe and sound." She wiped Timmy's damp bangs gently off her forehead. "She was gone for so long."

"Sorry." He righted the chair and sat back down. "I just—" He looked at me pleadingly. "—feel so helpless."

"I know. I wish there was something I could do."

"Young man," Timmy's mom said stridently. "You've done so much to help us already." She looked over at Beth while she continued to stroke her daughter's head. "You both have."

Beth smiled at her and stood. "Thanks. I think we'd better go now."

"Yes, all right."

Beth walked over to Timmy and touched her cheek. "You call me if you need me, okay, Timmy?"

Timmy looked up at her with tears welling in her eyes and nodded.

I walked over to her and put my hand on her shoulder. She stiffened for just a second, and I pulled my hand away as if I'd been burned. She looked up at me, smiled, and then launched herself into my arms with so much force I had to take a step backward so I wouldn't fall flat on my butt.

"Oh, well," I said, looking at her mother as I hugged her back. "Okay, then."

She stood on tippy toes and kissed my cheek. "I'll never tell," she whispered in my ear. "Not ever."

"Thanks," I whispered back. She went back to sit with her mother. I turned to Beth. "We better go."

It was time to figure out our next move.

♥♥♥

We'd barely gotten back into the car when Beth started up with the questions.

"Do you think it's all over? That everything's fine again? And what about that doctor? Is he—"

"Wait a sec, will ya?" I shook my head. "Just hold on." I started up the car and backed out of the driveway, paused for one last look at Timmy's house, and drove off. I cleared my throat. "Okay, now. Let's see if we can figure this out. You asked if I thought it was all over." I shrugged. "I can only hope so. It seems like it should be. Petrelli is dead, Timmy is back with her parents, and—" I pulled the collar of my tee shirt out and looked down the neck hole. "—no more hole in my chest."

"So," Beth said. "Does that mean you're okay? That you never got shot? That Timmy was never killed?"

"Don't know. Maybe."

"Hey!" Beth exclaimed and made me jump a little. "Hey, stop the car!"

I turned to look at her. "What?"

"Just stop the car!"

"Okay, okay." I pulled the car over to the curb and idled the engine. "What is it? What's wrong?"

She was staring out the window at a bright yellow, two-story house. There was a large oak tree that shaded the front door and a rose garden that bordered the drive-way.

"That's the house where Timmy took me. Where all the little ghost girls—I guess they were the doctor's victims. Where they showed me where the bad man lived."

I pointed to the mailbox, a standard black thing with a red flag and little gold squares with the individual letters of the owner's last name on them. P-E-T-R-E-L-L-I. "Look."

"What? Where?"

"At the mailbox."

"What about it?" She looked, and her face paled. "Oh."

"Didn't you see that when you were here as a…whatever it is you are?"

"Soul walker. And no, I didn't see it. It wasn't even there before."

"It wasn't?"

She shook her head and looked at me. "No. I think he must have hidden it from me, somehow."

"Could be." I nodded. "Stranger things have happened."

She grinned. "Smart ass."

"Yeah!" I put the Le Mans back in gear and headed off down the road. We were both quiet for a few minutes, each thinking our own thoughts. It wasn't long before Beth broke the silence.

"James?" Her voice was soft and sounded kind of weird. I turned and looked at her, keeping one eye on the road.

"Hmm?"

"Does it look…lighter…to you?"

"Lighter?" I looked through first the windshield, then the side windows, and finally into the rear view.

"Like the shadows are retreating or something."

"Yeah, I think you're right. Instead of how they slowly disappear when the sun comes up, they're just kind of receding, fading away."

"It's exactly like that. It's almost like water at the bottom of the sink, how it just gradually goes down the drain after you pull the plug. You don't even notice it is until it's gone."

And before we knew it, the darkness was gone, and the sun was shining brightly.

Chapter 54

Where should we go? Home, or the hospital?" I asked.

"What do you think will happen if you show up at the hospital, all in one piece, and your body is still lying there in a coma? Will it mess up the space-time continuum or something?"

I couldn't help but laugh. "You watch too much *Dr. Who*."

"But something bad *could* happen, couldn't it?" There was so much wide-eyed innocence in her look that I felt bad for teasing her. Besides, neither one of us really knew what would happen, did we?

"Yeah. You're probably right. Maybe we should just head home."

"But if nothing's changed, and by some slight chance your parents are home, then won't they freak out if they see you?"

I scratched behind my ear absently. It was a head-stumper, that was for sure. "Why don't we go home and you go inside first? If anyone is home, you can feel them out and see if it's safe for me to be out and around."

"Guess that's about all we can do. So why do you think the doctor did all this, anyway?"

"Because he's a sick, child-killing perv."

"No, I know that. Hopefully, it won't be too hard to prove. What I mean is, why did he send those zombie werewolf things after you? And how did he learn to go into the laptop? What was up with that?"

"I have no idea. It's so freaky, his being able to turn himself into that black, inky junk and talk to us that way. I mean, why would he even want to?"

"Maybe he's a psychopomp, too, and just wanted to screw with you. Remember that time when Sheriff Brazelton said Donna broke up with Mr. Anderson to start hanging out with Martin Petrelli when they were in high school? The doctor must have been that Martin. Maybe he was still in love with her, and when she died, maybe he blamed you. Maybe."

"Maybe," I agreed.

"And maybe when you didn't die when he shot you, it was the only way he could get to you. If he'd tried to kill you in the hospital—you know, smother you or inject an air bubble into your brain or something—he might get caught."

"Yeah, that's true." I shook my head. "I still don't get it. Did he just one day wake up and decide to kill him some little girls?"

Beth shrugged. "Who knows?"

"You think maybe Donna found out what he was really like and that's why she broke up with him?"

"Could be."

"And when did he find out he was a…what did you call it? Psychopomp?"

"Uh huh, but I like soul walker better."

"Whatever."

"Maybe he's always known and has just been biding his time until he thought he could get away with it. As a respected doctor, who would ever suspect he was really evil?" She chewed on a strand of hair for a second. "You know, Dad told me that sometimes, all it takes is a severe shock or some sort of trauma for some people to be able to tap into hidden talents. Maybe his talent let him use that blobby thing in the laptop for something bad."

"Could be. But what would his trauma have been?"

She shrugged. "Who knows? I mean, what do we really know about him, anyway? Other than he was a psychopath. Obviously."

I glanced at her, a snicker escaping my mouth. "And that he's a douche?"

She giggled in response.

"You know," she said a few minutes later.

"What?" I glanced at her and almost burst out laughing. Her unibrow was back. But she looked so serious, I stopped myself. Barely.

"I really thought it was Riggs who shot you."

"You did?"

She nodded. "Uh huh."

"How come?" I knew he hated me, but would he really try to kill me? Was his hatred that great?

"Because I went into your subconscious once without you."

I gripped the steering wheel tightly. The thought of someone prowling around in my mind without me knowing about it—even Beth, even if she had been trying to help me—freaked me out. "You *what*?"

"Sorry, but it was the only way I could think of to help you." She fiddled with her seatbelt and couldn't look at me.

I felt sorry for her, and relaxed my grip. "It's okay, I guess. So why did you think it was Riggs?"

"Because when I saw the killer's face." She shook her head and shrugged. "I honestly thought it was him. They are both kind of built the same way. Tall and skinny." She turned to look at me. "And when you said your blob was called D. R., I thought it stood for Deputy Riggs. D. R."

"That makes sense. I hadn't thought of that." I grinned at her. "Pretty smart."

"Except it was wrong. I almost accused the wrong person."

I giggled and looked at her from the corner of my eye. "Wouldn't be the first time."

She giggled, too.

"Maybe it stood for doctor," I said. "You know, D. R. Doctor."

"Guess so. It's as good a theory as anything else, I suppose."

"You know, once D. R. told me that we don't always get the answers we seek." I shrugged. "Guess he was right."

A few minutes later, I slowed the car down, edging it over to the curb, and put it in Park. My house was across the street, and I sighed heavily. "Here we are."

We sat there, staring at the house. The lawn was brown and scraggly from the drought. The paint was beginning to chip and peel, and I vowed right then and there to paint the house this summer.

Maybe Mom would like something bright like Sunshine Yellow. Or Neon Green.

"Well," Beth said as she slowly opened the door and stuck one leg out. "Here I go."

"Good luck."

"Yeah, thanks." She stepped out of the car and closed the door.

"Hey, Beth?" I called to her. She leaned down and looked at me through the open passenger window.

"Yeah?"

"It'll be okay."

She grinned, tapped twice on top of the car, and headed up the walk.

I only hoped I was right.

Chapter 55

I watched as Beth paused at the front door, her hand on the doorknob. As she stepped inside, she turned and shot me a look that I didn't understand.

It worried me.

Anxiety made me restless. Unable to sit still, I got out of the car and walked around to the front, leaning against the hood with my ankles crossed. But that didn't help me settle down, and my foot tapped like rapid-fire gunshots. I crossed and uncrossed my arms. I paced around the Le Mans.

After several turns, I settled back against the hood, and the whole thing started all over again: crossing and uncrossing my ankles and arms, tapping my foot. Plus, I'd started to sweat.

"This is ridiculous," I muttered. "You should just go check for yourself, see what's going on."

I'd just started creeping up to take a peek in the window when my father burst out of the front door.

"There you are!" he cried joyfully.

I ran gratefully into his arms. "Dad!"

"Hey, now, what's this all about?"

I bear-hugged him and tried not to laugh at the puzzled expression on his face. Finally, I pulled back, laughing, and wiped the tears out of my eyes. "Nothing. I'm just glad to see you."

"Well," he said, putting his arm around my shoulders as we headed back up the walk. "Good to see you, too. We thought you'd gotten lost!"

"Lost?"

Dad opened the door, and we stepped inside. The living room was no longer shrouded in darkness. Instead, it was decorated with crepe paper and balloons. A Happy Birthday banner was strung over the entryway to the kitchen. Fall Out Boys' "The Phoenix" blared out of a brand new iPod docked in a nice speaker setup. It even had a big red bow wrapped around it.

Everyone was there: Mom, Aunt Judy, Shaniqua, Watts, Diane, even Beth's friend Lindy. They were laughing and joking with each other. A table was set up along the wall, filled with deli trays holding more of PJ's pastrami sandwiches than I could eat in a week, a crockpot full of what I could only hope was her chili for the foil-wrapped container of the fries I was smelling, a punchbowl filled with the nasty pistachio punch Beth loved, and tons of presents wrapped in brightly colored paper.

Beth ran up to me and leaped into my arms, wrapping her legs around my waist and hugging my neck so tight I couldn't breathe for a second. She was laughing so hard I almost dropped her.

"Did you know?" she squealed. "It's my birthday. Isn't that awesome?"

"Your—birthday?"

Her eyes twinkled mischievously, and she was grinning like a goon. Leaping off me, she grabbed my hand and pulled me into the living room. She spun us around like a mad teacup, laughing and chortling like a hyena. When she finally let go, we both went flying, me into the

couch and Beth into the food table. Luckily, it only wobbled a little bit.

"That means…"

"Yep," she said as she steadied the table. "It's my
birthday. April twenty-sixth. I'm fourteen!" She pointed
at me. "And you're—"

"Me." I laughed and patted my chest. "I'm me. And
I'm all right."

About the Author

After sixteen years as a paralegal, Lisanne Harrington staged a coup and left the straight-laced corporate world behind forever. Now she panders to her muse, a sarcastic little so-and-so who delights in getting the voices in her head to either all speak at once in a cacophony of noise or to remain completely silent. Only copious hamburgers and Diet Cherry Dr. Peppers will ensure their complicity in filling her head with stories of serial killers, werewolves, and the things that live under your bed.

When not writing, she watches reruns of Gilmore Girls, horror movies like Sharknado and Fido, and Investigation Discovery crime shows. She likes scary clowns, coffee with flavored creamer, and French fries. Lots and lots of French fries. She lives in SoCal, in the small town she fashioned Moonspell's Wolf Creek after, with her beloved husband and persistently rowdy but sweet miniature pinscher, Fiona.